PRAISE FO

# THE YELLOW

'An astounding debut.' —*Brisbane News*

'Creepy and atmospheric . . . It's a measure of the skill of the writing that this uncomfortable, often ugly tale is such an immersive and evocative story, with a sense of horror that is never far from the surface.' —*Herald*

'A tautly written thriller.' —*The Big Issue*

'An intriguing look at human nature and how assumptions about family and who you are related to can colour what people think of you—and what happens when these secrets come out—and how far some people are willing to go to hurt people and cover it up.' —*The Book Muse*

'O'Grady is a talented storyteller; it's her narrative skills that make this grim tome so compelling.' —*Australian Book Review*

'*The Yellow House* is highly accessible literary fiction . . . Emily O'Grady has such a talent for clearly conveying the unstated, and the visual imagery that she injects into her writing just leaps from the page. I'm still thinking about this novel and expect to be for some time.' —*Theresa Smith Writes*

'Compelling and accomplished . . . a powerful novel about the legacies of a notorious, violent crime in a family and in a small rural community where everyone knows everyone else's business. Through Cub's delightfully natural and chatty account, we see how her strong personality and down-to-earth assessment of the people around her help her come to terms with her discoveries and with the ways in which her family is still affected by them.' —*Eclectica Magazine*

'It's not an easy thing to nail the voice of a child in a way that's both authentic and alluring, but O'Grady does just that from the get-go.' —*Debbish*

Emily O'Grady is a writer from Brisbane. Her debut novel, *The Yellow House* won *The Australian*/Vogel's Award in 2018 and was shortlisted for the 2019 Ned Kelly Award for Best First Fiction. *Feast* is her second novel.

# FEAST

EMILY
O'GRADY

This is a work of fiction. Names, characters, places and incidents are products of the author's imagination or are used fictitiously. Any resemblance to actual events, locales or persons, living or dead, is entirely coincidental.

First published in 2023

This project has been assisted by the Australian Government through the Australia Council, its arts funding and advisory board.

This project has been assisted by a Queensland Writers Fellowship. The Queensland Writers Fellowships are supported by the Queensland Government through Arts Queensland and State Library of Queensland. Queensland Writers Fellowships are administered by Queensland Writers Centre.

Allen & Unwin
Cammeraygal Country
83 Alexander Street
Crows Nest NSW 2065
Australia
Phone: (61 2) 8425 0100
Email: info@allenandunwin.com
Web: www.allenandunwin.com

*Allen & Unwin acknowledges the Traditional Owners of the Country on which we live and work. We pay our respects to all Aboriginal and Torres Strait Islander Elders, past and present.*

A catalogue record for this book is available from the National Library of Australia

ISBN 978 1 76106 711 2

Typeset in 12.8/19.4 pt Adobe Garamond Pro by Bookhouse, Sydney
Printed and bound in Australia by the Opus Group

10 9 8 7 6 5 4 3 2 1

The paper in this book is FSC® certified. FSC® promotes environmentally responsible, socially beneficial and economically viable management of the world's forests.

FOR MY MOTHER

# ALISON

ALISON KNEELS BESIDE THE RABBIT. Its right hind leg is clamped into the trap and it takes quick, shallow breaths, heart pumping, lungs expanding and contracting. The surrounding field is thick with pale tussocks and crispy heather, the neighbour's cottage and the road to the village just beyond the hill. It is early still and Alison is out here in the cold because last night she dreamt of her mother, who served her three chanterelles on a dinner plate. In her dream, the mushrooms glowed, and when her mother—looming like a cast-iron statue in the centre of a colonised city—opened her lips to speak, the grotto of her mouth glowed also, her tongue orange and bulbous and radiating light. When Alison woke at dawn, she rose and went out to search the woods. She found no mushrooms, but she did find this, the rabbit. She applies pressure to the levers of the trap until the steel jaws open and the rabbit's mangled leg is freed. A hissing sound escapes its mouth as she presses her palm to its throat. She does not speak to it or soothe it with soft, maternal clucks. It stares up at her, eyes pink as tourmaline, but doesn't struggle until she presses down with the same swift motion she uses when cracking Patrick's back on the bedroom floor when he comes to her, weary and tense after a long day hunched over piano keys.

She gathers the rabbit by its back legs and rises. The joints in her own legs are stiff and she rolls each ankle. Usually, it feels good to walk, early and in the spring, when it's no longer cold enough to preserve a corpse, but she is too warm in Patrick's shearling coat and sweat dampens her chest. Though home is only a short walk past the woods and the stables, she's hit with the inexplicable fear she has strayed too far and won't be able to find her way back again. The illogical ache of homesickness, of feeling far from where she is safe. She closes her eyes and imagines herself suspended in a bubble of liquid, gummy and unthinking as a jellyfish. She tries to leave her body and hover above the feeling world, but her brain is hot and swollen, its weight gluing her to the earth. When she opens her eyes to find she's still earth-bound, a gush of vinegar surges up her throat and she leans over to be sick. She hasn't eaten breakfast and a viscous puddle coats the rocks at her feet. Forty-eight years old and pregnant for the first time. For her entire life she's been nothing but careless and until last week, when the test she ordered arrived in the post, assumed she'd been blessed with sterility. The baby is a girl, she can feel it. Not that it matters. She's not going to keep it.

Alison brushes hair from her eyes. With the rabbit knocking against her calf she tramps through the brambles, the wild thistle, the velvet grass towards home, where Patrick will be waking up, wondering where she's gone.

They live outside a small village north of Edinburgh, Patrick and Alison and, as of two months ago, Patrick's daughter, Neve, who is on a gap year after graduating high school last November. Alison bought the house for her mother, Frances, almost ten years ago now. It is solid, grey stone, three storeys high and severe. Even with the heating on, it's always cold inside; the geriatric parts rubbing up against each other sound like the breathing of something ancient. Yet for all that, it's not so grim. In the summer, raspberries burst from ragged bushes in the garden, dense and sweet. The landscape is lush and crisscrossed with trails. (Sometimes, a pair of enthusiastic walkers will wander off path, trudge down the hill with their hiking poles and ergonomically designed backpacks. Alison does not enjoy small talk with strangers—or with anyone, really—but if Patrick is around he greets them warmly and nudges them in the right direction, recommends the better pub in the village while waving off occasional looks of recognition.) They own a very impressive car but only Patrick drives it. Both their appetites are enormous and they eat and drink constantly and with gusto. Because he is the better chef, Patrick does most of the cooking, but once a week or so he'll go into town and return with a parcel of fish and chips and a tray of oysters. If they don't keep track of the days he'll go on a Monday by mistake and return with a curry because the chippery is closed, which is fine, Alison thinks, but not as nice. Her irritation is as gentle as a gland swelling, retreating. She hasn't felt real anger in years.

After crossing the driveway lined with pines, she cuts through the garden. The grass is getting long and scratches at her ankles. She makes a mental note to remind Patrick to call the gardener. Patrick is a useful person and takes care of all things practical, almost like a housekeeper, but one she is extremely attached to and does not pay a wage. She descends the steep set of steps, enters the house through the side entrance that opens to the kitchen. She scrapes the peat from her boots on the doormat and forces the stiff door shut behind her. The sky is breaking, dusty light filtering through the higher windows and spotlighting the table. Patrick and Neve sit at opposite ends. Patrick is slathering blue jam on toast, and there's a plate of scrambled eggs in front of Neve. They wear the matching tartan dressing-gowns Patrick bought Neve as a welcome gift when she arrived from Sydney at the beginning of February. They are hideous and Alison has been meaning to steal both from the laundry and set them alight.

She strides towards the deep copper sink. The mammal smell of musk and urine is beginning to ripen, but now that she's home her stomach has settled. She slaps the carcass down on the benchtop and turns to Neve. 'Does your mother like rabbit?'

Neve looks up from her eggs. An ellipsis of pimples dot the crease in her chin and the colourless tangle of hair is bird-nested atop her head. Like her father, she is tall. With her dressing-gown and bad posture she gives off an air of malnourishment and resembles a shrivelling pensioner, like Patrick perhaps will in twenty years. 'Did you kill that?' she asks. Her expression is characteristically inscrutable and Alison can't tell if she's revolted by the rabbit or deeply uninterested.

'No,' she replies. 'It was caught in one of Gareth's fox traps. Already dead.' She flips over its body and stretches out its limbs. 'Patrick can make a stew for tomorrow night, when your mother arrives. Something nice and stodgy.'

'Mum doesn't eat meat,' Neve says. She fiddles with her phone, places it screen down on the table. The case has rubbery cat ears protruding from the top and its bulging, panicked eyes watch Alison from across the room.

Patrick snorts. 'Since when?'

'Since forever.'

Alison watches Neve take in the rabbit. According to Patrick she's a genius, but Alison is yet to see any evidence of that. Twice a week she cycles to her part-time job at Gareth's cafe in the village, returns with stale bread and pastries. She constantly burns coffee grounds and sheds her hair throughout the house like a husky. As a teenager herself, Alison had no interest in teenage girls. She still has no interest in teenage girls, but that cannot be helped.

'I can take you hunting, if you like?' Alison says to Neve, because yesterday Patrick had again reminded her to make an effort to bond.

Neve shakes her head. 'I could never kill an animal.'

Alison shrugs out of Patrick's coat and slings it over the back of a chair. 'But you eat meat?'

'Eating an animal is different from killing it.'

Patrick interrupts. 'Neve's a Buddhist.'

Neve sighs. 'I'm not a Buddhist,' she says. 'I'm not anything.'

'If you insist.'

'I'm not.'

'Did you know Alison's a pagan?' he asks Neve. 'She descended from druids. That's why she's so . . .' He magics his fingers in the air, trying to snatch up the right word. 'Esoteric.'

'I'm not a pagan,' Alison says, opening the refrigerator. 'And I descended from gamblers and drunks.' She picks through the top shelf: thick wheels of soft, pungent cheeses, a container of shaved ham, a depressed loaf of brown bread. Craving something sweet, she takes out the rhubarb she stewed last week.

'Remind me to go shopping on the way back from the airport tomorrow, both of you,' Patrick says. 'The menu's confirmed with the caterers for the party, but we'll want champagne as well as wine, obviously. A proper feast.'

'We can just go out to eat or something,' Neve says. 'It doesn't have to be a big deal.'

'It's already planned, Neve,' Alison says, opening the container and spooning up a mouthful. 'Your mother is expecting a party. And Gareth's boy. What's he calling himself now? Estrogen? Epigraph?'

'Elixir.'

'It's your eighteenth birthday,' Patrick adds, clinking his mug of green tea against Neve's coffee. 'We want to celebrate properly, your mother and I. And Alison.' He glances her way, raises his eyebrows. 'Think of it as your official welcome party.'

'Five people isn't a party,' Neve says.

'An intimate soiree then. Much more sophisticated.'

Neve picks up a crust. 'I just don't want you to go to any trouble.'

'It's not about you,' Patrick teases. 'We haven't let loose in ages.'

Alison picks up Patrick's coat from the back of the chair, bats off the grass and rabbit fur. 'You're right, Patrick. I've never understood why we insist on making birthdays all about the child.' She gives the coat a final shake and hooks it to the back of the door. 'The mother is the one who goes through the agony of childbirth, yet it's she who has to buy the gifts and organise the celebration and bake a cake. We should be throwing Shannon a party.'

Neve slumps further in her chair. The sleeves of her dressing-gown are long and she flaps them in front of her face in exasperation. 'You don't have to bake me a cake.'

'Of course there'll be cake,' Alison says.

'Just as long as there's drink and dancing,' says Patrick, draining the dregs of his tea.

'No dancing,' Neve says.

'If there's Shannon, there'll be dancing.'

'I don't even know why Mum's bothering,' Neve says. 'It's only been a couple of months.'

'She's your mother, Neve,' says Patrick. 'She misses you.'

Neve shrugs. There's a scatter of crumbs on the table and she gathers them into a small, neat pile with her fingertip. As Alison spoons rhubarb onto Patrick's plate, Neve points to her hand and grimaces. 'You're bleeding.'

There's a red smear across two of Alison's knuckles, puffy with arthritis. She glances back at the rabbit lumped on the bench. Other than a broken neck and leg, its body is plump and immaculate. As Alison moves towards the sink, she is aware of Neve watching her. There's something penetrating about her gaze, as though she's lapping Alison up. Alison hasn't told Patrick how uncomfortable Neve makes her feel, always watching, staring; that it's not been easy to have her here, and she is self-conscious now of the way her body smells after the strenuous walk, the faint smell of rancid food scum wafting up from deep in the sink. They used to have a cleaner come once a week, a pretty girl Patrick found from the village, but she fell ill and they haven't got around to replacing her. Alison looks towards the window. The top of the earth is level with her eye line. Though the ceiling is high and the furniture spare, it feels cramped with too many morning bodies, unwashed, cruddy with sleep. Patrick's cough is hacking, like a crotchety old man, though he is younger than Alison. She turns on the tap to wash her hands. The plumbing is ancient and the pipes inhale. The water is ice. It is a peculiar sort of agony when her hands go cold and then numb.

After breakfast, Alison goes upstairs to their room. The best bedroom is up on the top floor, with a view of the woods and the hills when it's clear. Patrick suggested emptying it of Frances's things, giving it to Neve for her stay, and Alison was relieved when Neve chose instead to sleep in a small nook beside the kitchen, musty and cramped, with no natural light. When Alison bought the house for Frances it was full of inherited oddities, Neve's room home to the two life-size lion statues that guarded the driveway when the property housed a zoo in a past life. But Neve insisted on it. When she claimed the space, Patrick borrowed Gareth and his wheelbarrow and together they carted the statues into the woods, discarded them among the moss and pines, where they now squat like incompetent gargoyles, flecked white and teal with bird shit and mould.

Alison sifts through the cast-off clothes on her bedroom floor—the vintage French-linen nightgowns she compulsively orders online, the woollen coats that belonged to her father—and changes out of her trousers and shirt, climbs back into bed. Patrick is in the shower. The water shudders off and soon he comes to join her, slings his wet towel over a chair and climbs in between the sheets.

She uncaps a pen and puts on her glasses, begins to leaf through the script she received in the post last week. It will be her first job in six years. When her mother's health declined, she pulled out of a film days before start of production and moved from London to Scotland to care for her, Patrick following soon after, though they'd only been together a few months at that point. There were plenty of work offers during the months Frances was in the process of dying—some of which Alison would have killed for when she was younger—but when the time came to return to the life she'd carved out with precision, she found she didn't miss any of it. She didn't miss being hungry. She didn't miss the constant waiting around, the boredom. She didn't miss the regular implication that she is too old or too fat or too strange-looking. And so, once Frances died, instead of putting the house on the market and returning to London like she'd planned, she decided to stay. A few times a year Patrick travels to Berlin or New York for a recording session, to Sydney to visit Neve. After a while, he stopped asking Alison to join him, and she had no reason to leave the house until last week, when the pregnancy test arrived in the post and, in some sort of insane hormonal fit, she agreed to do the film.

When Patrick stirs, Alison glances down to see if he's awake. He's never been handsome, not even in photographs from when he was in his prime, long before they met, but his face is especially ugly when he sleeps: his lips slack, jowls flabby. A slit of white visible behind his right eyelid. Alison prefers to avoid looking at him until he is fully awake and animated. Asleep, he could be anyone.

Patrick nuzzles his face into her side and inhales. His hair is wet from the shower and she feels a slick of it on her arm. 'You're still tired,' she says, stroking his forehead.

'You kept me up,' he says. 'Clattering around all night.'

'I wasn't clattering.'

'You were,' he says. 'You were up and down, opening windows, closing windows. Dressing and undressing.'

'I don't remember that.'

'Sleepwalking.'

'I don't sleepwalk.'

'Possessed then.'

'I'm not possessed.'

He props himself up on an elbow to peer at the script over her shoulder. Under his breath he mouths a few lines, vulgar in his broad accent. He trails off and Alison continues reading, scribbles some marginalia, and then pulls the hair band from around her wrist and ties her hair back into a nub at the base of her neck. She's kept it short for years but Neil, the director, asked her to grow it for the role. The longer style makes her and Patrick look incestuous, both with dark hair skimming their shoulders: hers flecked with wiry silver; his satiny and opaque from the packet dye he has Alison apply monthly.

'When will you be away?' Patrick asks.

She turns a page. 'Not for another six months.'

'You don't have to do it, you know.'

'I have to eat, don't I?'

Patrick scoffs. 'We don't need the money.'

'Why do you still work then?'

'I never retired,' he counters. After Patrick met Alison and followed her to Scotland, the band he'd started with his best friend, Nick, when they were teenagers unofficially disbanded. Rather than taking a moment to breathe, he began scoring films full time, something he'd sporadically dabbled in for years.

'People come out of retirement all the time,' Alison says, though she wasn't aware her break from acting constituted a retirement.

'We're happy how we are, aren't we? You a lady of leisure, me slowly rotting away.'

'I told Neil I'd do it.'

'It's not too late to pull out. You don't owe him anything.'

'I want to do it.'

'It's a lot to take on,' he says. 'Are you sure you can manage it?'

'Of course I can,' she replies. 'I'm not an invalid.'

Outside, a black bird scratches against the window. They watch it chisel at the sill paint with its dainty yellow beak. The window is slightly ajar, and when Patrick whistles, the bird looks up at them through the glass before swooping away.

'I'm going to London next week to meet with Neil.'

He looks confused. 'For how long?'

'A few nights. I'll stay with him and Essie. God, she's so smug—I don't know how Neil puts up with her.'

'When did you decide on this?'

'Yesterday,' she says. 'Neil phoned when you were at the cinema with Neve.'

'So, it's settled then,' he says. 'You're going to do it.'

'I already told you I was.'

'Yes, but I mean, you've signed the contract? Has Marie looked over it?'

'That's why I'm going to London.'

'Can't Neil just email it?'

'Yes, I suppose he could.'

She turns back to the page. She'd like him to be quiet and let her concentrate but knows he isn't done prodding. Last week, when she told Patrick that Neil had been in touch, he'd actually laughed out loud. They were on the patio, late afternoon, and halfway through a game of cards. He wasn't being cruel; he seemed taken aback, at first, and then incredulous. 'But you don't travel,' he said.

'What do you mean I don't travel?'

'When was the last time you went anywhere?'

'What an insane thing to ask,' she said, and left him with his losing hand, the sky clear and royal before the night came quickly.

She knows how it could seem: Patrick wanting a kept woman, fearful that she'll meet someone else once she's back out in the wild. Concerned, perhaps, that she'll get a fresh taste of fame and never come back. But it's not like that. Patrick loves their life. He loves her, truly loves her, and Alison knows he only wants her to be happy and well.

She expects him to continue needling her, but instead he turns his face up to her like a pet dog would, open and simple. 'Do you want me to come then?'

'What, next week?'

'Later in the year. For filming. Belfast, you said?'

'I assumed you would. You'd go mad with longing otherwise.'

'What about Neve?'

'Who knows what her plans are for the rest of the year? I assume she'll be sick of us by then.'

'I suppose she can stay here by herself.'

Alison takes a sip of stale water from beside the bed. She's not yet used to factoring Neve into her plans. Sometimes, when she comes across her taking in sun in the garden or playing guitar badly in the library, she feels a jolt of surprise. If she's not right in front of her, Neve ceases to exist, and it's as if she and Patrick are here alone, perfectly content, the way things have been, the way it will return to once Neve goes back home. Except that now, right at this moment, Alison can conjure Neve with startling precision: the look she gave Alison in the kitchen earlier, as though she were trying to catch her out. She imagines Neve with the run of the house, upstairs in the master bedroom, lounging on Frances's bed and pawing through her collection of spy novels, Alison's father's journals. Stroking the silky flap of seal skin he gave Frances when he uprooted her to Scotland: a memento, a token of luck. Neve holding it to her cheek then discarding it like a cheap souvenir.

'She can't stay here without us,' Alison says.

'Why not?' Patrick asks. 'She won't burn the place down.'

'She'll be bored to death.'

'She's not bored now.'

Alison pauses and pretends to consider it, circles a line on the page. 'You should both come, then,' she says. 'Neve will like Belfast.'

'Maybe.' He reaches for her pen and she lets him take it. She puts the script down. Patrick tucks the pen behind his ear and places a hand on the dent of Alison's hip. 'Do you think she's happy here?'

Alison remembers how sullen Neve was when she first arrived. Patrick brought her home from the airport in her beanie and skinny jeans, her scrappy backpack covered in key chains. It was clear the house wasn't what Neve expected; so monstrous, so remote. 'I think she's more comfortable.'

'But do you think she's happy? Do you think she wants to stay here?'

How could Alison possibly tell? Neve is too quiet, too bland to truly grasp. 'No,' she says firmly, as though it's something she's considered deeply before. 'I don't think she's happy. I don't think she's a happy person.'

Patrick frowns. 'But it was her idea to come here,' he says. 'Surely she'll want to stay.'

'What does her mother think?'

'Shannon wants her to go back to Sydney, of course. But it's up to Neve.' Patrick lies back down, closes his eyes and presses his palms to the sockets. 'We can talk about what to do with Neve this weekend. All of us together.'

Alison sighs. 'Don't turn it into a mediation. I don't want any conflict in this house. No hostile energy, please.'

'There won't be.'

Alison plucks the pen from Patrick's ear, picks up the script and resumes reading.

'Have you thought about where we're going to put Shannon?' he asks.

'I don't know. Wherever she likes.'

'We'll have to make up a bed.'

'What about the room at the end of the hall? The yellow one with the twin beds.'

'What about giving her Frances's room?'

Alison shakes her head. 'It's not ready.'

'I can sort it. I'll take the afternoon off.'

'No,' she says. 'It's too big a job. There's no time.'

'It's one room.'

'She'll think we're trying to hide her away. It'll be easier if she takes one of the rooms down here. We'll be close by if anything happens.'

'What would happen?'

'Nothing,' she says. 'But just in case.'

'Alright,' he says, throwing back the sheets and climbing out of bed. 'The yellow room then.'

Patrick opens the chest of drawers and pulls on underwear, a pair of navy trousers. Alison watches him stride to the wardrobe. His fingers are long and delicate and, bird-like, he pecks them through the coathangers, deciding on a crisp white shirt, red and gold applique around the collar. He buttons swiftly, puts on a jacket, a belt, before assessing his body in the full-length mirror by the window. Black spots mushroom in the corners, and there's something off about the way it echoes; wavering and incomplete, as though a slice of the reflection is lost in transmission, something essential snatched away. Patrick steps towards the mirror and inspects his face close up, stretches down the loose skin under his eyes, smooths back his hair with his fingers.

When he finally leaves, Alison returns to the script. For the first half of her career she was typecast as a gasping, ditzy idiot destined to die loud, gratuitous deaths over and over. It wasn't until Neil showed an interest and cast her in his debut that she began to be taken seriously. In the final film they did together, she played a vengeful banshee wreaking havoc on a family of Irish immigrants to colonial Australia. She spent months on her Irish accent, lost ten kilograms, learnt to ride a horse and shoot a gun. The script she's reading now is a sequel of sorts and takes place ten years later, the family having been slaughtered for their various transgressions. Alison's character has returned to Ireland, where she has had a child and is leading a small, quiet life. It is good, Alison thinks, as she arrives at the third act; even better than the first. She'll have the entire script memorised by the end of the weekend.

Finishing the final scene, she sets the pages down on the bedside table along with her glasses. There's a thrill inside her, certain lines already imprinted on her brain. She tries to hold on to the feeling, but knows there is a very good chance that come Tuesday morning, right at the moment the plane is taking off, she'll email Neil from bed and tell him she's no longer available, block his number, delete his emails. The script will go in the bin. In the afternoon, she'll emerge from bed and ask Patrick to drive into town for fish and chips. He will do as she asks. He will be kind enough to say nothing about it. As Patrick reminded her, it's been so long since she's been anywhere. The outside world has become scary and unfamiliar and she's not interested in any of it. If she were never to leave the house again, she'd be a very happy woman.

She is falling asleep when the dream comes back to her, intrusive as a vision—Frances, the chanterelles, her orange mouth. Alison gets out of bed and goes over to her mother's jewellery box on the bureau. The box is a tacky, lacquered wood, the jewellery tangled to a shining clump: a string of purple and green glass beads; an assortment of glittering brooches Alison played with like pets when she was a girl; a fine silver chain studded with knots. None of it is valuable except for the sapphire pendant Alison bought Frances one Christmas, the diamond earrings gifted on a birthday. She never saw her mother wear either. Alison rifles through the lurid cocktail rings Frances hoarded from charity shops, the nasty metal greened, until she finds her mother's engagement ring. Simple and elegant, but likely chosen as the cheapest her father could find. She's surprised he never pawned it.

Alison's mother was perfect. She knows most children feel that way about their mothers, but it's true. When she was small, Alison thought she couldn't live if her mother died. For her seventh birthday, Frances gave Alison a soft cloth doll with red hair made of wool. Her name was Patti and she came dressed in a spotty pinafore, her hands and feet round and smooth and fingerless, toeless. Each evening before bed, Alison would press Patti's face to her lips and whisper a wish for her and her mother to die at the same time. A road accident or a house fire. It didn't matter, just as long as she wasn't left alone. Before Frances became ill, when Alison imagined her mother's death, there was a quickness to it, a cleanness. Living and not living. Here and then there. There was no dying involved, no fugue state of soiled sheets and temper tantrums, no slipping in and out of focus. No mourning for a half-life that continued to go on, limping. When it happened, it was excruciatingly slow.

Alison had long banished Patrick to the lower levels of the house by the time Frances died. She'd let the carer go by that point as well; though fussy and cheerful, she had a blankness behind her eyes Alison did not trust. Frances had lived in the village until Alison started making proper money and bought her the house. It came with all the furniture: dark, polished oak, oversized and decadent. Deep red carpet, now threadbare and tongue pink. Alison had wanted to have it redecorated, modernised, but Frances adored it and insisted it remain unchanged. Her mother had seen inside the house just once, years before Alison made the purchase. For a few months in her forties she worked on the grounds caring for the zoo animals and Mr Ross had thrown a holiday party for the staff. Frances wore her wedding dress and bought a new pair of low-heeled cream pumps from the shoe shop in the village. All night, Alison lay awake in bed waiting for her mother to return home. She pressed her hot-water bottle to her feet, and as the rubber burnt a pea-sized blister into her ankle, she imagined her mother ramming into a tree and immolating into flames; a head-on collision, her body crushed and flattened. When she heard the familiar choke of the engine, heels clattering up the path, clear to her even through the din of the pub next door, she felt her body relax, the tension release. She was asleep before the key was even turning in the lock. Over breakfast the following morning, Frances told

Alison every last detail of the party in the big house by the zoo outside the village. Even towards the end of her life, when her mind was all but gone, she would talk about how they served crème de menthe, describe the dancing in the drawing room.

❧

At the kitchen table Alison sets down a cutting board and lays the rabbit on its side. This part she remembers clearly: her mother in her lemon-yellow apron, making a cut on the rabbit's back, feet burrowed in socks and sandals on the cold floor, hooking her fingers under the skin and ripping it apart. Alison does the same. The skin peels away from the muscle easily, and when she reaches resistance she picks at the sinewy flesh with the knife blade. She grabs the carcass by its back legs and tugs and twists until the fur gathers at the rabbit's feet and around its broken neck. In one final tug, the hide comes off and she sets the blanket of crumpled fur to the side, the carcass fetal and slick.

Wiping her hairline with her forearm, she looks up to see Neve standing in the doorway. 'Hello there,' Alison calls out. She has no idea how long the girl's been watching. 'Do you want to help?'

Neve doesn't reply, but she steps into the kitchen and pulls out a stool from under the table. The smell of tea-tree trails her, her bigger blemishes shiny. She pokes the pelt with her finger and then strokes gently along its length, as though caressing a pet. 'Where'd you learn to do this?' she asks.

'My mother showed me.'

'Did she kill them too?'

Alison shakes her head. 'My father was the hunter.'

Neve's mouth twists. 'Just rabbits?'

'Rabbits, pheasants, ducks. A red stag once.'

'What about lions?'

Alison peers at her. She told Neve about the zoo the day she arrived and cannot tell if she's being daft or sarcastic. 'The lions were in cages.'

'Oh,' she says. 'Yeah.'

'And he didn't hunt around here, anyway. My mother only started working here once my father was gone.'

'What did she do?'

'Mucked out stalls, fed the animals, that sort of thing.'

Flipping over the rabbit, Alison tries to remember what comes next. She considers fetching the laptop, searching for a dumbed-down video tutorial, but her hands are mucky and she knows if she takes a break she won't bother to come back to it. She can sense Neve watching and glances up. The afternoon light streams through the window, clearer now, making Neve's eyes look exceptionally green. She's pretty in a doughy, basic way. She looks like her mother. Alison has only seen pictures of Shannon—a few of Patrick's photographs, plus what she found online: Shannon on a rooftop, by the harbour dressed in white, always with a cocktail or glass of pink fizzy wine in hand.

Alison feels a pang inside her brain. She closes her eyes as her head spins, quickly settles. There's a smudge of coppery blood on her shirt. She spits on it, dabs at the spot with a tea towel.

'Are you sick?' Neve asks.

'No,' says Alison.

'You look sick.'

She smiles. 'I'm fine.'

Neve pauses. 'I heard you throwing up the other morning,' she says.

Alison has been using the bathroom downstairs so she doesn't wake Patrick with the morning sickness. She didn't even think of Neve down here, listening. 'Just a stomach bug. The ham had turned.'

'When Mum was pregnant she used to vomit like that. Not just in the morning, though. It was all the time.'

The admission takes her by surprise. Alison has seen a photograph of the stillborn, just the once, around the time she and Patrick first became involved. Neve beside the baby, her maroon school uniform. They haven't talked about it in years, not properly, and she is ashamed to admit she'd practically forgotten Patrick had ever told her.

Eager to steer the conversation away from her own body, Alison asks the first thing that comes to mind. 'Has your mother ever wanted any more children?'

Neve shrugs. 'Don't think so.'

'I'd suppose not.'

Neve does not respond, continues to look intently at the rabbit. Her hands are close enough to touch its slimy little body and she flexes her fingers as though daring herself to do it. It would be too strange to bring it up with Patrick again after all this time, Alison thinks. If she were to ask Patrick about it, he'd be suspicious. He'd think she was trying to tell him something. She asks, 'Do you think about her often?'

'Who?'

'Anya.'

Neve doesn't look up, and for a moment Alison is mortified, thinking she's got the name wrong. Anna? Annie?

'Not really,' Neve says eventually.

Relieved, Alison continues: 'What about your mother?'

'I don't know,' Neve says. 'It was ages ago.'

'I imagine it's not something you would ever really get over. If you wanted it in the first place, that is.'

Neve looks uncertain. 'I don't think Mum would want me talking about this.'

Undeterred and still wanting to shift the conversation even further from her morning sickness, Alison says, 'It's important to talk through grief, otherwise it builds up and festers inside you like poison.'

'I know, but I don't think she'd want me talking about this with *you*.'

Alison is not used to being rejected. She wipes her hands on the tea towel and throws it onto the bench, tries to repress the sting. 'Well, lucky for me I'm too old to have to worry about any of that.' It's not a lie—she *is* too old to be pregnant, without science intervening at least—but still, it feels serpentine coming from her mouth, smooth and toxic.

'It probably wouldn't even make it past the first trimester,' Neve says. 'And if you did have a baby it would probably have Down's or something. By the time it was my age, you'd be nearly seventy.'

Neve has come out with these tactless jabs before, and as her gaze strays to the window again, Alison's hand becomes unsteady, the heat returns to her head. She's already decided to book an appointment when she's in London next week. Maybe her old assistant Martine can organise it for her, drive her to the clinic. She swallows and focuses on the rabbit, tries to forget about the clot of cells sucking away at her from the inside, the inconvenience of it, but she's forgotten what she's supposed to be doing. The steps have become a blur again, the iron smell of blood turning to taste in her mouth. She places her hands on the rabbit and like osmosis remembers what comes next. She cracks the ankles one by one, angles a foot on the board and begins hacking through the muscles and tendons. She's on a roll now. Snaps the neck, twists it free, slices off the tail and pulls it away along with a string of intestine sliming from the anus. Everything severed, she gathers the offcuts and dumps them in the sink. With the knife, she makes an incision in the rabbit's belly. The blade is dull and again she has to hack through the skin and muscle to get to the organ cavity. A prickle of shame rises at the butchery of it. What was she thinking? She doesn't even like rabbit. She has a pressing, petulant urge to be done with this, and as the innards reveal themselves, smooth and grey, wishes she'd left it to suffer and die in the trap.

She is about to scoop out its entrails when the door thuds shut, startling her. Neve is gone. A rank smell wafts and she looks down into the rabbit's insides. The knife has nicked the intestine; stomach juices leaking, the meat spoilt.

Alison washes her hands and heads upstairs. In the bathroom, she opens the toiletries cabinet and picks through Patrick's shelf—razor blades, moisturiser, goat milk soap, vitamin gummies, laxatives, lubricant—until she finds a packet of painkillers. She considers crushing and snorting one for the warm rush, but instead pops two tablets from the seal, swallows them down with water. Finding the laptop on Patrick's bedside table, she sinks into the chaise by the window in the bedroom and enters the password. She types her name into the search engine, clicks on an image of herself and follows the link to a collage of pictures from when she was young and thin and utterly luminous. There are a few of them together: a photo taken at Brighton Pier, another from the London premiere of the first film Patrick scored, a cluttered Gothic mess about depressed cowboys she could barely sit through. Patrick is dirty and dishevelled, entirely underdressed, Alison in a tiered floral gown, hair long and shiny. She looks like another person, or a genetically linked version of herself—a sister, perhaps, or a cousin.

Alison closes the site and opens a fresh page. She looks up the news, Patrick, the correct way to skin a rabbit. When she checks her email there is a new notification. It has no subject line and the contents of the message is formatted in one dense, angry paragraph. From the syntax of the first sentence she can tell who it's from. She hasn't received an email from him in weeks. The last one was fairly benign, if intense, but today he's in a particularly vulgar mood and proceeds to outline exactly what he plans to do with her body once he has slaughtered her. Alison reads it again then drops it into the folder labelled 'Fan Mail'. The first one arrived about a year ago, and she's been receiving them consistently ever since.

She doesn't show them to Patrick anymore. After the second or third, he kicked up a fuss and had an elaborate system of security cameras installed. After a few weeks they glitched, and they never bothered to get them repaired. Only in the few hours following an email does Alison feel on edge. Then the specific fear fades, becoming an abstract threat she doubts will ever manifest. She's come to view him as a reliable pest. She'll probably feel slighted if he starts to leave her be.

Alison logs out of her email and moves to the window. It's begun to rain. Patrick is in his studio; her nerves are prickling and she wants to be near him. She taps a finger to the glass and thinks: *Look up.* And he does! He disappears from view, and then appears outside the studio on the grass. She waits for him to turn towards the house, to come inside and come to her, but he faces the woods, arms akimbo, and a moment later

Neve emerges from the direction of the stables. She stops when she reaches her father, who places his hand on her shoulder and pulls her in for a hug. They separate, continue to talk, though the rain grows heavier. Neve looks up and raises a palm to the sky.

Alison closes the laptop, goes downstairs. As she passes through the kitchen, she is assailed by a foul smell and remembers the rabbit. It's lumped in the sink still: the pelt and the innards and the disembowelled carcass, a sloppy mess of slick fur and gamy flesh; the nubby, talismanic feet, cute as baby bootees. The scope of the task feels extraordinary but the smell is nauseating, so she finds a bucket and scoops out the muck with her fingers. She rinses her hands, takes the bucket and steps towards the door. As she reaches for the knob it turns from the other side and Patrick appears before her.

They look at each other. Alison sets the bucket down and dries her hands on her trousers. Patrick's hair is flat from the rain, his nipples stiff through his shirt.

'I thought you were working?'

'I was,' he says. 'What happened?'

'I eviscerated the rabbit.'

'No,' he says, wiping the rain from his face with his shoulder. He shakes his hair out like a dog. 'What happened with Neve?'

'Nothing happened.'

'She was crying.'

Alison is taken aback and flicks through their conversation in her head. If anyone should be crying, it's Alison. 'No, she wasn't.'

'I just saw her skulking around in the grounds. Crying.'

'What did she say I said?'

'I couldn't get it out of her.'

She wouldn't have told him if he hadn't asked directly. 'Well, we talked about my mother, and about rabbits, and then we talked about Anya.'

'Why were you talking about Anya?'

'It just came up.'

Patrick stares down at the bucket, taps at it with the toe of his loafer. He puts his hands on his hips and looks up at her quizzically. 'Why the interest all of a sudden?'

She removes a wet leaf from Patrick's collar, lets it fall into the bucket. This is exactly what she'd been hoping to avoid: everyone reading into things. Creating tension where there is none. 'I've always been interested.'

'Don't bring it up with her again, please.'

'Why?'

'It obviously upset her.'

'Neve's hormonal,' Alison says, picking up the bucket. 'That's all.'

She takes a step towards the door, but Patrick shifts to the side, blocking her path. The rain is coming in and his shoulders are growing damp. He exhales through his nose, lowers his voice. 'She's a child, Alison.'

'You're always going on about how brilliant she is. You shouldn't mollycoddle her.'

'She's smart, not an adult.'

'Don't you want me to bond with her?'

'Take her shooting. Paint her bloody fingernails. I don't know.'

'She doesn't want to go shooting,' she says. 'She's a Buddhist, remember?'

'Please, Alison.'

'I was only making conversation,' she says. 'I'm very sorry for doing exactly what you told me to do.' She is embarrassed, and to stop the blood from prickling in her cheeks, she reaches into the bucket, picks up the rabbit head and holds it close to Patrick's face. 'Should I perform a pagan ritual to redeem myself? You'd like that, wouldn't you? Filthy thing.'

Patrick grimaces, pushes her arm down at the elbow. Alison relents and drops the head back into the bucket. It lands moistly. She looks down at the rabbit head, swimming among its own intestinal muck. Its glazed eye glowing blue and planetary from the hue of the plastic.

Patrick lets go of her arm. She looks up and watches his face closely, willing some feeling to radiate from him, for him to give her what she needs to feel better. It used to be telekinetic between them. They used to be obsessed with each other.

'Be sweet to her,' he says.

She can see he's exhausted, feels a rush of tenderness. Touching a hand to his breastbone, she says, 'I'm not a monster, darling,' and waits until he places his hand on top of hers.

It's raining lightly as she crosses the grounds. When she reaches the stables she stops and sets down the bucket. The wooden cages inside the stalls have been dismantled but the foundations of the stables have remained sturdy despite years of neglect. They surround a courtyard, a smoothed slab of hard grey dirt. Tangles of weeds snake along the earth and up the wooden posts. A rustling nest of finches is perched in the corner of the rafters of the first stall, underneath which is a rack of gardening equipment. She finds a shovel. The handle is stripped of its paint, rust peppering the head. It scrapes against the stony ground and the sensation makes her shudder.

She takes the bucket and shovel and walks to a nearby field. After Alison bought the house for her mother, whenever she'd come up for visits—every few months or so—the two of them would take walks to where Frances claimed she and the other workers carted the bodies to be buried after they'd slipped into death or been shot out of kindness. The smaller animals—exotic birds, reptiles, chimpanzees—they'd take whole, Frances said; the larger ones—lions, panthers, bears, an Indian elephant named Big Pinky—were dismembered into portable chunks at the stables. Though Frances couldn't remember whether she'd eaten breakfast, how many glasses of sherry she'd had before dinner, she could rattle off the names of animals she'd supposedly hacked up and buried. She'd take Alison by the elbow and guide her through the grounds, pointing out each nondescript grave site covered with thick grass, berry bushes. Sebastian (llama), she'd say, drifting past the wooden gate. Mallory (chimp), closer to the edge of the woods. Archie (tiger), by the stream.

Alison wasn't convinced but always indulged her. Frances had never mentioned the dismemberment, the disposal, until she became unwell. One evening, right after Alison moved in, Frances—despite her frailness—managed to get herself down two flights of stairs and find her way out here. In the morning, when Alison went to bring her tea, she discovered her mother's bed empty. She searched the house, expecting to find her crumpled body at the bottom of a staircase or snapped and stiffened on the gravel below the window. But this was where she had come. Alison spotted her from a distance, but it wasn't until she got close that Frances turned to face her, filthy with mud, dirt piled around her. She was leaning against a tree, panting softly, sitting placidly, as though waiting to be retrieved. From the ground she'd dug up a curved yellow stick that very well could have been a rib and presented it to Alison like a gift. She was wearing only her nightgown but didn't appear to be cold. Her bare arms were brittle and scabbed, thin strands of stark white hair wisping out from her armpits. She'd finally gone feral, Alison thought. Her brain well on its way to rotting, no more cognisant than an animal.

The earth is soft and Alison pushes the shovel into the soil. It takes no time to dig a modest hole, a foot deep. Though the rain is only misting down lightly she is again damp beneath her clothes. She ploughs the shovel into the grass so that it stands vertical, picks up the bucket, tilts it so that the remains of the rabbit slump into the hole. The blood has continued to drain from its body, mixing with the rain to make a shallow pool in the bottom of the bucket. She keeps it tipped as the liquid runs out, pooling in the hole before being absorbed into the earth.

Back in the yard, Alison hoses out the bucket. Patrick hasn't returned to his studio. She wonders if he's called the masseuse to work out his knots and they're set up for a session in the library, but Magda's hatchback isn't parked in the driveway. Alison faces the house's facade. She has the sensation she is being watched. She looks up and finds Frances's room on the top floor. The curtain is still, but as she stares, she's sure she can see a flicker of something solid behind the pane. She presses the heels of her palms to her eyes then looks again. She doesn't have the imagination to entertain the idea of ghosts, but there is a blur of static, something abnormal at the window. Her eyes begin to burn, and when she blinks the static is gone.

Back in the kitchen, she scrubs the dried blood from the creases in her hands with a wad of steel wool, writes a list of groceries on the back of an envelope and sticks it to the fridge with a magnet. She speaks Patrick's name out loud in the hope that he is close by and will appear.

She calls again, a little louder, and waits a moment before heading up upstairs.

It's Neve, not Patrick, who she finds standing outside their bedroom door. She has a box in her hands and is studying the back of it. It's a packet of Patrick's hair dye. He buys them in bulk from the pharmacy and keeps them in the cupboard under the bathroom sink. The woman on the front of the box has very white teeth. Her skin looks like it's made of plastic, hair belonging on a doll or a horse.

Neve doesn't seem to be upset, not in the way Patrick described, and thrusts the box towards Alison.

Alison doesn't feel particularly bad about having made Neve cry, but she agrees to help her anyway. Neve waits by the bathtub while Alison finds the stash of pale blue towels streaked dark as if stained with oxidised blood from the last time she did Patrick's hair. Though Alison pretends it's a burden, she quite enjoys the process. He becomes feeble as she colours his hair, while Alison transforms into someone who is matronly and fussy, feminine and nurturing.

'Take off your top then,' Alison says, and lays one of the towels on the tiles in front of the mirror. 'You'll ruin it otherwise.'

Neve turns her back to Alison, peels off her hoodie and then her t-shirt, tugs up her leggings so they sit higher on her waist and conceal her bellybutton, as though that is the most private part of her body. Alison arranges the other towel around Neve's neck, pulls out the stool from under the window and nods at Neve to sit down. It has a slight wobble and clicks against the tiles. Alison opens the window and the cold air stings.

Neve has already taken her hair from its elastic and it hangs around her shoulders. Alison runs her hands through Neve's hair to untangle the knots. It's dry at the ends but the scalp is oily and she can smell the unwashed musk of it. She smells like Patrick.

Under her fingers Alison can feel a cluster of pea-sized bumps on the scalp. 'You should get these looked at,' she says.

'What?'

'Your father had a melanoma cut out, just last year.' Alison works her fingers through Neve's hair; the girl winces when she hits a snag. 'Have you heard of phrenology?'

'What's that?'

'It's being able to tell what someone's like by the shape of their skull.'

'Sounds fake,' Neve says sceptically.

'My mother could do it. She told me I was going to be spectacular.'

Neve continues to watch Alison warily in the mirror.

'Do you want me to do yours?' Alison asks, holding her hands over Neve's scalp like she's reading a crystal ball. 'I can do it right now.'

Neve looks horrified, shakes her head vigorously so that the towel loosens and reveals the thick beige strap of her bra.

Though perplexed by the overreaction, Alison pretends she hasn't noticed her distress and picks up the hairbrush by the sink. 'It's nonsense anyway,' she says as Neve readjusts the towel. 'Pseudoscience disproved centuries ago.' She hands the brush to Neve, who forces it through her hair. The girl treats her body like a piece of drying clay, beating it into submission.

Alison puts on the plastic gloves and prepares the kit, squirting the dye into the developing solution. When she's ready, Neve straightens her back. Her hair is frizzy with static. She catches Alison's eye in the mirror, and then looks away, settles her gaze on the small still life on the wall over her shoulder.

Alison squeezes a strip of the dye onto Neve's scalp and massages it in with her fingertips. She moves across the right side of the girl's head, squirts the nozzle around her ears, which are tiny, perfect shells. 'You have very small ears,' she observes.

Neve reaches up to touch them before remembering the dye, letting her hand hover and then placing it back in her lap.

'Don't be embarrassed,' Alison says. 'They're lovely. I had enormous ears when I was a child. Great flapping things.'

'They don't look that big.'

'I got them pinned when I started working. I used to be a very vain person, believe it or not.' She tilts Neve's head forward, squirts the dye into the hairline. 'You don't have your ears pierced,' Alison notes.

Neve doesn't answer. *Be sweet to her*, Patrick had urged, but the effort to continue the conversation is exhausting. 'I can take you to get them done, if you like? It can be your birthday gift.'

'Maybe,' she says.

Alison straightens Neve's head, continues massaging the dye into her scalp.

The girl's arms are hugged around her stomach, and when a breeze rasps through she shivers. 'Can we close the window?' Neve asks.

The fumes lodge in Alison's throat. 'We'll suffocate.'

'Yeah,' Neve says. 'Sorry.'

'You apologise too much,' says Alison. 'And we're nearly done anyway.' She continues to work through Neve's hair, heavy and tar-like, slick as liquorice. 'What are your afternoon plans, then?' she asks after a long silence.

'I'm hanging out with Elixir.' Neve hesitates, swallows. 'Actually,' she says, 'I was going to ask if he wanted to stay over here, come to the airport with me and Dad in the morning to pick up Mum. Dad said we could go early and have a look around Edinburgh.'

A swell of nausea passes through Alison's body. She turns her face towards the window, sucks in air. 'Where will he sleep?'

'On the sofa in the library? He won't care.'

Alison gives Neve's head one final going-over before twisting her hair into a knot and pulling off the gloves. He's just a boy, she tells herself. Harmless.

While Neve rinses out her hair, Alison returns to the kitchen. Patrick is there, waiting for the kettle to boil. She wants to go to him, to touch him, but cannot tell if he's cross with her. 'There you are,' she calls across the room.

He glances over his shoulder. 'What's wrong?'

'Nothing,' she replies. 'I've been looking for you.'

'I've been here,' he says.

'Hiding from me.'

'I haven't been hiding.'

'Where did you go?'

'I didn't go anywhere. I've been here.'

'Were you in my mother's room?'

'No,' he says. 'Why would I be?'

'You tell me.'

'Well, I wasn't.'

'I saw something by the window. A figure. There was someone in there.'

He doesn't respond. The kettle begins to scream. Patrick turns off the gas and pours water into the teapot.

They move into the library. Patrick looks out the window and blows on his tea. Alison searches for signs of Neve in his face but the layout of the girl's features has already slipped from her mind, unable to be conjured easily. She wonders which of them the baby would take after, were it to be born, would be curious to dip into an alternative future to see its face aged five, fifteen, forty. Just to see.

'You're staring at me,' Patrick says, without turning his head.

'I'm admiring. Not staring.'

'Do you want something?'

'I don't want anything. I'm looking at how lovely you are.'

'Well, thank you,' he says. 'You're lovely too.'

Somewhere, a door closes, and moments later Neve appears in the library entrance, her hair rinsed and damp and hanging loose. Patrick whistles. 'Look at you.'

'Do you like it?' She reaches for a clump of black hair, raises it in front of her eyes. It looks like a garish Halloween wig.

'It's terribly chic, Neve.'

'Alison did it.'

'Did she just?' Patrick replies, glancing at Alison, eyebrows raised.

Neve remains awkwardly in the doorway. She looks wan and sickly. The colour doesn't suit her at all.

Patrick claps his hands together. 'How about a picture, then? I'll grab the camera.'

Neve steps out of his way then drifts to the window. The rain has eased again, the sun breaking through the clouds. Soft light streaks into the library. It makes the sun-faded, silk wallpaper look even more worn, the olive-green background murky, red thistles bloodless, the swirls of leaves more yellow now than gold. The sun is warm. Alison turns to face the window and feels it on her face and arms. She imagines the fetus as a seedling photosynthesising, then turns her back to the light.

Patrick returns with his camera case and tripod, begins to rearrange the armchair by the window. 'Perfect,' he mutters. He removes the camera from its case, changes lens before securing it on the tripod. 'Here,' he says, pointing to the chair. 'Alison, you sit down here. Neve, you on the arm.'

Patrick continues to fiddle with the camera, peering through the lens. He nods contentedly then straightens, takes a comb from his breast pocket. He rakes it through his hair, peering into the glossy piano surface to assess his reflection. 'Ready?' he asks, setting the timer. He strides over to the chair, adjusts his jacket and drops down on one knee, leaning into Alison, placing a hand on her thigh. He glances over at Neve and smiles, a smile that will appear genuine and radiant next to Neve's grimace, Alison's steely lack of expression. When Alison smiles for photographs she looks deranged, and so she doesn't.

The camera flashes and clicks, momentarily blinding her. When Patrick sends the roll to get developed her eyes will be closed but she doesn't tell him to take another.

Later, on the patio: falcons flying overhead, the smell of wet earth. It's getting cold but Patrick pours Alison another glass of wine. He has recorded what he worked on that day and she is listening through headphones. It's melodic, delicate. When it's over she takes off the headphones and hands him back his phone. 'Remind me what the film's about?'

'Climate catastrophe. Apocalypse preppers.'

'It's quite elegant, isn't it? A little too romantic for a film about destruction.'

'It's still rough,' he says. He looks hurt, as he always does when Alison's feedback isn't effusive.

'I know that.'

Patrick places his palms on the table, stretches out his fingers. He readjusts the leather band of his wristwatch, though the battery went flat months ago. 'It was nice of you to do Neve's hair.'

'It looks awful, doesn't it? The black with her complexion.'

Patrick snorts. 'Shannon will have a heart attack. She'll think we're corrupting her. Converting her to Satanism.'

'She's still strange around me,' Alison says. 'It's been months now. I'm not that awful to be around, am I?'

'She'll get used to you.' He takes a sip of wine. 'I caught her googling you this afternoon. We read your Wikipedia page together.'

'Odd thing to do.'

'I told her about the film, about Belfast in October,' he says. 'She finds you very interesting.'

'Does she?'

'Apparently you've made a resurgence on the internet.'

'I hope not.'

'Neve said something about an insufferable social media brat mentioning you in a video. The young people are very intrigued by you.'

'The young people?' she repeats.

'Maybe that's why Neil is so eager to have you.'

Alison leans back in the chair, readjusts the cushion at her lower back, crosses and uncrosses her legs. 'What else have you told Neve about me?'

'Lots,' he says. 'Everything.'

She's not happy, but knows she can't be upset about the two of them having a conversation about her. Instead, she turns the wine bottle to read the back of the label. It's Spanish and contains notes of blackberry and walnut. Patrick spends a small fortune getting crates delivered from McLaren Vale, the Cape Winelands, Hawke's Bay, but it all tastes much the same to her. An ex once told her she has the palate of a bulldog, which is a mostly fair assessment, though she's become good at faking it.

After a minute, Patrick squints into the distance. 'Look who it is.' Coming through the field towards them are Neve and Elixir. Neve is a head taller than Elixir, but he bounces enthusiastically as he walks, which largely makes up the difference.

'He's staying the night,' Alison says, draining her glass of wine.

'Since when?'

'Neve asked me this afternoon.'

'And you said it was okay?' He pours her another glass, tops his up as well.

'Why wouldn't it be?'

'Well, it took a lot of convincing before you were okay with Neve living here.'

Alison trails her finger through a splash of spilt wine. If she had her way, Neve wouldn't be here at all. 'He's not living here, though, is he? It's just for a night.'

Patrick raises his eyebrows. 'You've changed your tune.'

'He'll sleep downstairs—I'll barely see him,' she says, trying to sound relaxed to hide how annoyed she is that he won't let it go.

'Do you reckon they're fucking?' Patrick asks.

'That's not really our business, is it?'

'Should I be worried? Is this a thing to be worried about?'

'I don't know,' she says. 'You're the parent.'

They watch them approach. There's a gap between them, an absence of intimacy, and it's unclear if Neve and Elixir are actually fond of each other or friends of convenience. Though Alison has known Elixir for more than half his life, their paths rarely cross anymore and she hasn't had a conversation with him in years. When Frances moved in, Gareth made himself known early on, always nagging her mother to watch the boy on weekends when the creche was closed and he had to run the cafe. Whenever Alison came to visit, Elixir would always be over. He even had a bed made up in one of the spare rooms, a box of toys he kept here. Gareth too seemed to come and go as he pleased. More often than not, it would be Gareth, rather than Frances, who would greet her in the driveway, ask her how the flight was.

Alison sees him sometimes from a distance, when she's out for a walk and he's pottering in his garden or washing his car. They've not properly spoken in years either.

Elixir waves high over his head as they pass the studio. 'Hiya,' he calls out.

They slow as they reach the patio.

'Hey, mate,' Patrick says, leaning over the table to shake Elixir's hand.

He's wearing a teal jumper, tight maroon jeans, grass-stained white sneakers. His septum is pierced, his haircut neat and sensible, like a cadet. 'Da told me to give you this,' he says, handing Alison a box of chocolate mints, a silver ribbon tied in a bow at the top. 'Thanks for having me.'

'Last time you were here, you were running around in the nude,' Alison says, setting down the mints. 'You used to strip off and streak around the garden. Tell me, are you still an exhibitionist?'

'Ah,' he says. 'My streaking days are behind me, sorry to say.'

'We're going to put his stuff away,' Neve says.

'I brought a sleeping bag,' Elixir says, cocking his head towards the duffel bag slung over his shoulder.

'We'll put you on the sofa,' Patrick says. 'Downstairs with Neve.'

Elixir nods, glances at Neve.

Alison watches Patrick assess them, as though he is trying to get a sense of whether or not they've seen each other naked. 'Are you two hungry, then?' he asks.

'I had an early tea, cheers, Pat.'

'Let's go inside,' Neve says, taking Elixir by the sleeve.

Elixir waves again, grins. 'Ciao.'

They pass the table, go down the stairs and into the kitchen. Once the door closes Patrick turns to Alison. 'Funny little fellow.'

'He is strange, isn't he?'

'Is that true about the streaking? Gareth seems far too strict to let that fly.'

'He was a child.'

'Neve never did that.'

'It's a male thing. Obsessed with presenting their manhood to the world. Swinging it around like a lasso.'

It grows dark, and Alison calculates how long it will be until he goes home.

---

They are going upstairs to bed when they find Elixir in the library staring at a wall. His sneakers are off, white socks kneading the carpet. In the corner of the room is his duffel bag, a water bottle on the side table, stainless steel with a camouflage pattern. A pair of enormous headphones, an energy bar. He's looking at a painting hanging beside the fireplace. Patrick had given it to Alison for her forty-fifth birthday. It's drawn from a photograph, the pair of them sitting outside on a bench, sweet, skinny Susie between them. Her paw is resting on Alison's lap and Patrick's back is turned. There was a cracking sound right as the photo was taken; that's why he turned away, to see the tree falling. Omitted from the painting is the blur of oak plummeting to the ground.

Elixir turns and grins at them, then returns his gaze to the painting. 'Hope you don't mind me having a gander.'

'Gander away,' says Patrick.

'It's a great painting,' he says. 'Really captures your personalities. Creative, like.'

'It does, doesn't it?'

'I've become a bit of a fan of yours, believe it or not.'

Patrick smiles. 'Your old man's never mentioned. We can listen to some old demos, if you like. Neve's not all that interested.'

'Oh,' Elixir says, turning to face them again. 'I meant of Alison. I mean, I like your music too . . .'

Embarrassment blooms across Patrick's face. 'Right,' he says, with excessive cheer. 'I'm a pretty big fan of her myself.'

Alison places a hand on Patrick's shoulder. 'That's very kind of you, Elixir.'

'I didn't actually know what you really did until recently, but I've watched a bunch of your films now. All of them, probably. The one where you're decapitated by the dentist is brilliant!'

'I'm glad you enjoyed it.'

'I always just thought it was Patrick who was the big deal. I didn't think you did anything, really.'

Alison squeezes Patrick's shoulder and tries not to laugh. Elixir reminds her of a brain-damaged ferret. Hyperactive and stupid, just as she remembers him.

'Neve said you're going to be in a new film soon.'

'That's right.'

'I want to be in the industry. Directing, producing, something like that.' He pans his gaze across the room, taking everything in. 'Actually, Alison . . .' He snaps back to focus.

'I'm wondering, would it be possible, if I could maybe interview you?' He takes his phone from his pocket and holds it up beside his face.

'Interview me about what?'

'I'm making a documentary for my film school application. It's going to be about, you know, the creative process of artists and creative types.'

'I'm sure Patrick would be happy to help.'

'Oh,' Elixir says, narrowing his eyes. 'It's just that, the thing is, I really want the female perspective. No one values the opinions of old white men anymore. No offence, Pat.'

Patrick shrugs. 'None taken.'

'I have nothing to say about any of that,' Alison says.

'Go on, Ali.' Patrick nudges her in the side. 'She'll be happy to do it.'

Irritation rolls through her. 'I'm sure you'll find someone else.'

'Yeah,' Elixir says, shoving his phone back into his pocket. 'Yeah, that's alright.' He stretches his arms over his head, tousles his hair. 'Anyway,' he says, 'I'm going to see what Neve's up to.'

Patrick puts his hand around Alison's waist, gently steers her towards the door. 'We'll leave you to it then.'

Elixir picks up his water bottle, rocks back and forward on his toes. 'You've got a really nice house,' he says.

'Thank you.'

'Just as big as I remember it.' He glances up at the ceiling, back down again. 'You know, when I'd hang out with Franny. Thanks again for having me over.'

'You're welcome anytime,' Patrick says.

Elixir opens his mouth as if to say more, then appears to reconsider. When he turns and exits it's as though the energy of a small, raucous toddler has swept through the room, and only once they are alone can Alison catch her breath.

Upstairs, Alison plugs the bath, turn on the taps. The water gushes, cold and then warm and then close to boiling. She readjusts the temperature, opens the window a fraction, goes back over to the sink.

'You have an admirer,' Patrick says, smearing toothpaste on the head of his toothbrush and then Alison's.

'Rubbish,' she says. 'He was trying to butter me up. He's probably after money.'

'Not a chance,' Patrick says. 'Gareth wouldn't have raised a shitbag.'

'You hardly know Gareth. All you do is get drunk together.'

He scoffs. 'I know him far better than you do,' he says. 'And I know you have an admirer.'

'I've lived next door to him for years. If he was such an admirer, wouldn't I have found him peeping through the windows and stealing my knickers from the line?'

'Maybe he's discreet.'

'Why did you have to tell him he could come over whenever he likes?'

'He's Neve's friend.'

'Yes, but it's my home. I don't want people swanning around unannounced.'

'I live here too, Alison. And Neve.'

'I didn't mean it like that.'

He wets the head of Alison's toothbrush and hands it to her. 'What harm would there be in helping the kid out? Give him an interview.'

'I have nothing to say.'

'No one'll see it except a couple of crusty uni professors.'

'I'm not going to have my privacy exploited by a smug teenager.'

'Bit of an exaggeration,' Patrick says. 'And he's hardly smug.'

'If he's truly talented he'll have a long and prosperous career without my help.'

'Come on, Ali,' he says. 'He's had a tough go of it. He's probably looking for a bit of maternal guidance.'

'It's not my fault his mother had sepsis.'

'Fuck's sake, Ali,' he says. 'Do you have to be so brutal all the time?'

They watch each other in the mirror, toothbrushes vibrating in their mouths. Alison turns away as Patrick flosses, flicks particles into the sink, scrapes the white film from his tongue. As he swishes with Listerine, gargles, spits into the sink, Alison undresses. She takes a tin of bath salt and sprinkles it into the water, watches the granules sink and dissolve and turn the water cloudy. When the bath is full she turns off the taps, tests the temperature with her big toe. The water burns her feet and ankles and shins, and she waits a moment to acclimatise to the heat before sitting. She holds her knees to her chest, sinks down until her shoulders, then neck, then head are submerged. Her stomach, bloated from alcohol and carbs, islands above the surface, the forest of dark pubic hair flat beneath the water.

When she cannot hold her breath any longer she rises. Patrick has placed the stool to the side of the bathtub. He rolls up his sleeves to his elbows and takes off his wristwatch. His fingertips trail in the water. He reaches for the shampoo bottle on the caddy, uncaps the lid and empties a lug into his palm. Alison turns away from him, her hair seaweed around her shoulders. He rubs his hands together before pressing the flats of his palms onto her head.

As Patrick kneads at her scalp, foam flirting down her temples, she brushes her hand against her belly. There's a skeleton inside me, she thinks, and imagines the steaming water absorbing through her skin, cooking it from raw.

# NEVE

NEVE WAITS ON HER BED for Elixir to return. She can hear him talking to Patrick and Alison somewhere down the hall—about what, she has no idea. The two of them had spent an hour watching videos on the internet until Elixir shot up and announced he was going to the bathroom. He's been gone for twelve minutes now, but it feels like much longer. Since arriving in February, Neve has discovered that time moves exceptionally slowly here. Or, rather, time is a completely unnecessary construct for people like Alison and Patrick. Other than phones and laptops, there are no working clocks in the house. They don't even have a microwave. In her first few days here, she'd ask Patrick what time dinner would be ready. *Dinnertime*, he'd say absently, or, when pressed, *Eight*, and at eight she'd come into the kitchen, which would be empty, and he and Alison would still be outside on the patio, in the freezing dark, or upstairs napping—again, somehow, as though they are a pair grizzly babies who can only function for short bursts before needing to recharge—and they wouldn't eat until ten, eleven. Now, she doesn't bother asking and has learnt to have a big lunch.

She stares at her phone, itching to rescue Elixir, but she's spoken to Patrick and Alison more today than she has for the last week and the thought of more of it is tiring. She touches her small ears, feels around for suspicious lumps on her scalp. She leans back on the pillow of her narrow bed. When she arrived, she unpacked the best she could: clothes neatly folded in a cardboard box, shoes lined along the wall: hiking boots, a pair of sneakers, black ballet flats. A set of paperbacks is stacked beside her bed: *Pride and Prejudice*, *Anna Karenina*, *The Turn of the Screw*. Displayed on the side table Patrick dragged down from somewhere along with the mattress and rickety bedframe is a tin of Rescue Remedy pastilles, antihistamines, a three-pack of Australiana-themed tea towels patterned with banksia and gumnuts and wattle sprigs. She bought them from a tourist shop at Circular Quay the day before she flew out of Sydney, with the idea to gift them to her friends here, if she made any. Looking at them now, the likeliness of Elixir finding them entirely dorky seems certain and she gets up to shove them under the bed, hoping he hasn't already seen them.

When she hears Patrick and Alison at last head upstairs, she goes into the library and finds Elixir beside the sofa, watching something on his phone, the screen light contouring his face. Neve switches on a lamp and warm light floods the room. She throws a pillow and blanket onto the sofa.

Elixir puts his phone down and lurches over to her. 'Ready for a sleepover, Nevey?' Wrapping her into a bear hug, he traps her arms by her sides, does a little wriggle so they both rock back and forth in awkward unison.

Once released from his grip, she asks if he wants to watch something.

'Yeah, in a minute,' he replies. 'Let me settle.'

He unzips his duffel, takes out his sleeping bag, undoes the drawstring and pulls it from its pouch. With a flourish he rolls it out and spreads it onto the sofa. It's khaki, made of thick canvas smelling faintly of wet dog and mud, as though it spent a period of time in a trench. He positions the pillow at the top end of the couch, the folded blanket at the other end.

That afternoon, Neve had made the ten-minute walk over to Elixir's. She'd already sent him a message asking if he wanted to sleep over and come to Edinburgh the following morning, but found herself trudging through the woods and, without planning to, came to the field overlooking his house. Down the hill, she could see Gareth on a bench by the front door of their small, squat cottage, the blue door open. A colourful bed of flowers under the window, and their scruffy mutt lying at his feet, eyeing the sandwich on Gareth's plate without much enthusiasm.

Closer to the house, Gareth spotted her. 'Happy birthday, birthday girl,' he called out. He was in a flannel shirt, his salt-and-pepper hair loose and out of its usual ponytail. A single gold hoop in his ear. Smudge of a tattoo on his neck.

'Not till Saturday.'

'Good of you to invite James to your party,' he said. 'I've told him to be on his best behaviour.'

She shrugged. 'It's not much of a party.' Immediately, Neve had a vision of Gareth sitting out there alone in the dark on Saturday night, egg sandwich for dinner, longneck of stout decanted into a glass. Before she had the chance to chicken out, she said, 'You can come as well.'

When he smiled, Neve could see the pity on his face. 'That's sweet, pet, but I'm due in town to see the lads, I'm afraid.' The rejection gouged deep and she wished she could take it back. He was kind enough to change the subject quickly, which made Neve even more embarrassed. 'And off to Edinburgh tomorrow?' he said. 'That'll be lovely.'

'Yeah,' Neve said. 'To pick up Mum.'

They went inside, where Gareth offered her tea, handed her the steaming mug, a gentle squeeze on the shoulder. Neve liked going over to Elixir's. Their home was small and shabby, but it was always cosy, a fire crackling, Chet Baker on the record player, always cake or scones on offer. As he turned to go back outside to finish his lunch, Gareth called out for Elixir, who shuffled from the hall in his bathrobe and slippers, just out of the shower.

'You're eager,' Elixir said, and, after becoming more alert, 'Look at your hair!' He yelped, putting his hands on it, running his fingers through the shiny black strands.

After Elixir had dressed and packed his things, they said goodbye to Gareth, who was washing his plate and both their mugs in the sink. There was a small box of chocolates on the table now, a ribbon tied around the top. Neve assumed it was for her, a gift for her birthday, and she felt a flush of warmth, but Gareth picked it up and handed it to Elixir.

'Give this to Alison; a thank you for having you over.' He grabbed his battered leather wallet from the bench, pulled out a twenty-pound note and crushed it into Elixir's palm. 'For your feed tomorrow.'

'Bless you, old man,' Elixir said. He gave Gareth a one-armed hug and a peck on his scraggly cheek.

They said goodbye and set out over the hill. The sky was a metallic shade of steel, the sun glowing silver behind the thin wash of clouds. Elixir tossed the chocolates into the air, caught them. 'You know, your stepmam's always been a real dickwig to Da.'

'Alison's not my stepmother.'

'Whatever,' he said, waving away the correction. 'There's something kind of arousing about a woman who thinks you're scum.'

'That's disgusting.'

'Does she ever talk about Da? Or about Franny?'

'Who's that?'

'Alison's mam. She used to take care of me when I was a wee lad.'

Neve remembered Patrick telling her about Alison's mother, who had dementia and died at home soon after Patrick moved in. She thought about it constantly when she first arrived, and was furious that Patrick had offered her Frances's room, knowing full well that she'd be sleeping in a bed where someone had died. 'No, not really.'

He furrowed his brow, went quiet for a moment. 'She probably thinks Da's too common for her, or whatever.'

'Your dad's great.'

'Yeah,' Elixir said. The end of the ribbon curled against his wrist, sparkled like treasure. 'He is.'

They walked in silence towards the house. The afternoon was cool, the air crackling with light and shadows. When she snuck a glance at Elixir he was looking at the sky, his face turned to it like a sunflower, blissful and serene.

The sofa made up, Neve picks up Elixir's phone which had fallen beneath a pillow. 'You're not still going to make this weird movie, are you?'

'It's a documentary,' Elixir says, taking the phone from her. 'Maybe a podcast as well. I'm going to sell it to a production company. It'll be my big break.'

'Who'd want to watch a documentary about some random woman?'

'Are you having a laugh?'

'She's not even famous anymore.'

'That's the point,' he says. 'She completely disappeared. It's totally weird.'

'She's pretty private,' Neve says. 'I don't think she'll say yes.'

'That doesn't matter,' he says. 'She won't know. I'm going to be really discreet about it. I'm going to get footage from around the house, at your birthday party. Catch her off guard. *Au naturel.*'

She'd tried to talk him out of it but it was her idea in the first place. A joke, more than anything, when he told her he wanted to go viral but needed the right subject. She had seen the seed sprout, the flash of acquisition, and regretted it immediately. 'Do what you want,' Neve says. 'But she's not all that interesting.'

'I bet she's mental,' he says. 'I bet she's really kinky.'

'She can be a bit of a bitch,' Neve says. 'But not on purpose, I don't think. It's just because she's rich and everyone's always told her how great she is, swooning over her and that.'

'I'm going to find out all her secrets,' he says. 'I asked her for an interview just now—I told her it was for a uni application.

I think she believed me but she said no anyway. Doesn't matter, though; I've already got some footage.'

Elixir angles the screen towards Neve and presses play. The video was taken from outside, through the kitchen window, the glass covered by a dusty film. You can see the side of Alison's face and body, but it's shot upwards so that her calf is engorged, her proportions all wrong. Movement flares across the screen—Patrick's hands, wildly gesticulating. The video is silent except for Elixir's breathing, his wet mouth sounds.

'Wow,' Neve says, rolling her eyes. 'So thrilling.'

'Don't be a little cow. It's just preliminary shots. Set the mood and all that.'

In her gut, Neve is alarmed but can't tell if she's overreacting.

Elixir distracted by the video, Neve goes into the kitchen. After Alison started asking weird questions about her mother, about Anya, she cycled into town and bought a bag of junk food: salt and vinegar crisps, chocolate biscuits, sour worms. She still isn't used to someone wanting to spend so much time with her and, in an anxious panic, went overboard with the snacks, spent almost half her last pay. Back in the library, she arranges the food onto the ottoman, sits on Elixir's sleeping bag and begins to scroll through films on her laptop. As she searches for something she thinks Elixir will like, he wanders around the room, asking her questions about Alison, about how much money Alison has, about whether Neve thinks the house is haunted, none of which she knows the answer to.

He turns around, watches her as he licks the back of a biscuit, puts half into his mouth. 'Let me get a video of you,' he says eventually.

'What for?'

He contemplates for a moment. 'You'll add a bit of light and shade to the film. It's all about dynamics, you see.'

Neve doesn't see, but lets him take her by the elbow and position her in front of the enormous portrait of Patrick and Alison mounted on the wall. He sits her down so that the top of her head skims the bottom of the painting.

'Okay,' he says, pressing record. 'Go.'

'Go where?' she asks.

'Don't go anywhere,' he says. 'Say something.'

'What do you want me to say?'

'Something about Alison. I don't know—whatever you can think of.'

She's always been awkward in front of the camera and can feel her face heating up. Patrick used to try to photograph her when she was a child: right after a bath when her hair was still wet, or when she'd just woken up and was hazy in the face, white cotton underwear, singlet straining over her pot belly. He positioned her limbs where he wanted them, tilted her head up and down, towards the light, away from it. He'd grow frustrated by her stiffness, and once he accepted she was no model he gave up and the developed photos never materialised. Months later, a large Bill Henson appeared in Patrick's music room, of a young, slight child, sharp angles, lush blue light. Neve felt bad in her ungainly body, not good enough for a stripped-back version of herself to be hung on a wall. But the photograph was beautiful and she could not look away. She wanted to bottle the heavenly blue that bathed the child in light and drink it up.

'You're not very good at this, are you?' Elixir asks.

'You put me on the spot.'

'We can try again later.' He lowers his phone, looks towards the stairs. 'Can we go up there?'

'I thought we were going to watch a movie.'

'We can watch after.'

'There's nothing to see. It's just a bunch of empty bedrooms.'

He raises his eyebrows. 'So why are you sleeping in a cardboard box?'

'It's not that small.'

'It's the size of a fingernail, Neve,' he says. 'Even my room is bigger.'

'We'll wake up Dad and Alison,' Neve says. 'They'll get annoyed. They get shitty when I bother them.' This isn't true at all. They've been nothing but kind, even Alison, in her own, indifferent way.

'Fine,' he says. 'There anything to drink?'

In the kitchen she finds a half-bottle of chardonnay and two cleanish glasses, which Elixir pours full. As they clink their glasses together Elixir pouts and, after taking a sip, says, 'You're the first friend I've ever had who doesn't make me play football or drink nasty rum and colas, and after a year you're just going to leave me again.'

Neve eats a chip, the vinegar stinging the cold sore on the corner of her lip. Though she made the decision long ago, she's never said it out loud. 'I'm not going to go back, actually.'

'What?' he asks. 'Since when?'

Neve shrugs. 'I don't know. Just then.'

Elixir knocks their glasses together again, leans into the sofa while Neve presses play on the movie. Before she left home, she told her parents she'd deferred her degree for a year, but in fact she hadn't even accepted her university offer. She always aced her exams but only got top marks because she has a good memory and finds that, contradictorily, studying helps switch her brain off, like running or meditation. Also, she considers herself to be a not-very-good person, something that, she feels, is antithetical to studying medicine.

Neve takes another sip of wine, feels it spread to her head. Already she can feel a loss of her inhibitions, and when she goes to take another, she only wets her lips with the wine. When Elixir goes to the bathroom, she pours a bit into his glass, a bit back into the bottle.

They fall asleep on the sofa and sometime after midnight Neve jerks awake. Quickly, things piece back together: the sliver of yellow light wavering from the kitchen, the crinkled spread of food packets, crumbs down her front, fingers licked clean, her laptop splayed open and hibernating on the ottoman. Beside her, Elixir is curled into a sphere at the end of the sofa, hugging his pillow, his mouth gaping open. Neve's own mouth tastes stale, her face feels oily and unwashed. Out the window, she can see the glow of the moon behind the trees.

She closes the laptop, gathers up the packets and takes them into the kitchen. Patrick and Alison have left dirty dishes and cutlery and chopping boards in a teetering, haphazard pile beside the sink. The dinner hasn't been put away and she opens the lid of the casserole dish on the stove, spoons up a tomatoey mouthful of soft zucchini, and then another. When she closes the lid she loses her grip and drops it; a chip of ceramic breaks off and falls into the ratatouille. Fishing it out, she rinses it in the sink, dries it on her leggings and rifles through a drawer looking for superglue. When she can't find any among the clutter of oddities—ornamental teaspoons, Christmas bonbons, a curved yellow stick—she licks the rough edge of the ceramic in the hope that her saliva will gum it back into place, but when she lets it go it falls back into the dish. She opens the window, stands on her tiptoes and flicks it into the grass.

She turns off the kitchen light. She wants to shower off the grease of the day but the sound of it will wake the house. Instead, she goes back to the sofa and, knowing it's creepy and shameful, watches Elixir sleep for a few moments: his steady breath, his peaceful, uncomplicated face. Without waking him, she heads to the stairs. She'd spent hours pacing the corridors that first week, trying to memorise every corner of the house, to speed up the process of it becoming familiar, becoming home. She disliked it right away, as soon as Patrick pulled into the driveway, Alison not appearing until late in the afternoon, weary and distracted as though she'd forgotten Neve was coming. This was where her father had been holed up these past few years, Neve had thought. No wonder he'd never invited her to stay. Despite her efforts to acclimatise, there still remains a molecular unease Neve feels whenever she goes upstairs, all of those depressing, fully-furnished rooms. It's as though the house was once home to a large, happy family that mysteriously vanished, their rooms now enshrined and the house in perpetual mourning.

Reaching the first floor, Neve can see Patrick and Alison's door is open, so she holds her breath and continues up the next set of stairs to the top level of the house. Her body tenses and it feels dangerous, though really the stakes are low. She lives here; she's not doing anything wrong. Neve only ever used to snoop through her mother's things when she was home alone and, like now, she was never looking for anything specific. She once found a letter from her father tucked under the jumble of Shannon's bedside table. It was written in the awful months after Anya was born—or unborn, really, though Neve is still unsure of the specific terminology—and she skimmed it quickly, the words and her head swimming, before returning the letter to the drawer and backing out of the room. She never went through her mother's things again.

The top level has just one room: the master bedroom, the one Patrick said Neve could have if she wanted. It has a view and an ensuite; she'd have her privacy. *If it's so great, why don't you and Alison sleep there?* she'd wondered but did not say. *Why don't you sleep in the corpse bed?*

She goes for the doorknob, turns it. Locked. She jiggles it a bit, takes a step back, then tries again with more force. She feels a surge of annoyance at being denied, then is immediately embarrassed by her childishness.

Deflated, she turns to go back downstairs. When she reaches the top step, she hears noise down below. Someone is up, meaning she won't be able to go down the stairs without being seen. She takes a step back up to the landing, hovers by the banister to wait. The noises continue: a door opening, loud footsteps. After a moment Alison appears in the hall. She's completely naked and Neve's face grows warm. She expected an obvious bump and is surprised to see her body is large and soft and nothing remarkable.

Other than her mother and a few friends of her parents, the only pregnant person Neve has known is Eugenie Conway from school in the grade below; pretty and petite, large-breasted, a spray of freckles along her nose and cheeks. When she disappeared a month before Christmas holidays, there was a solid week of gossip at the lunch table in the courtyard, gumnuts dropping, frill-necked lizards darting from the undergrowth, making the girls jump and shriek as performance. The conversation was feverish, but concurrently lazy and abstract and easily derailed before eventually circling back to the main event. They discussed what they'd do if it happened to them, as if there were a possibility they might find themselves pregnant despite the glaring fact that none were having sex. Dominica said she would be stuck working as a check-out chick for the rest of her life, as if that was the very worst thing. It was illegal to get rid of it, it was a sin and Eugenie's life was ruined; she wouldn't be allowed back after the holidays, not to a Catholic school, not with a baby. Thuy suggested throwing herself down the stairs or being punched hard in the stomach. Kirby said there were all sorts of herbs you could take, like medicines that would poison it right out of you; her older sister—who reeked of sandalwood and had a Frankensteinian bolt pierced into the nape of her neck—told her so.

Neve had tried not to pay attention. Whenever the topic of doomed Eugenie and her doomed baby came up she'd pull out a textbook and pretend she hadn't finished her chemistry homework for next period, or go to the canteen for a Pepsi Max, or to the bathroom, where she'd sit on the closed toilet lid with a terrible feeling in the pit of her stomach.

But still, memories of those conversations had made their way through and are burnt into her synapses, a fundamental part of her knowledge now. As Neve watches Alison enter the bathroom, switch the light on, shut the door, the various toxins flicker through her mind as a mantra: mugwort, pennyroyal, black cohosh, parsley, aloe. Her pulse ticks in unusual places: behind her ear, inside her cheek. The light under the door radiates a bar of gold and Neve has a stark vision of the future, where there is a baby, in the yellow room down the hall maybe, or in a cot beside Alison and Patrick's bed. The baby is a girl, or so Neve assumes, for no reason other than the fact that she, Neve, is a girl and Anya was a girl, leading her to the random, but possibly scientific, conclusion that her father's sperm is only capable of producing female offspring. In this vision, Alison is waking to feed the baby, who has been crying, crying, crying all night. She is holding it to her chest and walking it up and down the corridor for hours on end, the baby clinging to her breast, sucking, sucking, sucking . . .

There is a creaking from the bottom of the stairs, a shadow figure in her peripheral vision. Alison is still in the bathroom and Neve grabs hold of the banister. She calls Elixir's name softly. No response. When she goes back downstairs, she finds Elixir where she left him on the sofa. His chest is rising, falling, deep in sleep. The air feels unsettled, as though a ball of energy had ripped through moments earlier. When Elixir stirs and turns onto his side, she is sure she can see the whites of his eyes glowing, but when she looks closer, they are shut tight.

It's past seven when Neve wakes. She has told everyone they will need to leave by eight, but of course this means nothing to Patrick. After showering and dressing, she tidies her bathroom, removes the dark hairs coiled to the bathroom wall like cracks, tries in vain to scrub off the bruisy flecks of dye from the shower curtain from when she rinsed her hair. She picks the hardened toothpaste from the cap, puts the empty box of tampons into the bin, beginning to smell faintly of rot, and leaves the rubbish bag by the back door. She makes a pot of coffee, green tea for Patrick, and leaves a mug beside Elixir, who is still asleep, a small patch of drool on the pillow beside his open mouth. At some point after she'd gone to bed he'd stripped off his jeans and shirt down to his underwear. The space below his rib cage is concave, and she has an urge to put something in there, a trinket or small gift for him to wake up and discover. She picks up his phone and unlocks it, having seen him type in his passcode many times before. She mutes the volume and watches the video he filmed of her below the portrait the night before. With her dark hair she looks more like Alison's child now than Shannon's. It is as if Patrick and Alison are her real parents and she is finally where she belongs.

She locks the phone and goes upstairs to make sure Patrick is awake, the mugs warm in her hands. She's sure she burnt the coffee but it's too hot yet to taste. Their bedroom door is open and she peers in through the gap. No Alison. Her father is still asleep, flat on his back, arms folded across his chest. As she goes to nudge the door further open with her knee, she loses balance and drops one of the mugs, coffee splashing her shin, puddling onto the carpet.

'Ali?' Patrick groans.

Neve enters the room and moves towards her father. The four-poster bed gives him the air of a delicate, sickly princess.

'Where's Alison?' she asks.

'Ah . . .' Patrick says, turning to look at the empty space beside him. 'Somewhere, I'm sure.'

Neve sets down the tea beside a vape pen, the room smelling faintly of artificial grape. She recalls him pouring Alison wine the night before, and realises now that he does not know she is pregnant. Alison must know that Patrick doesn't want another baby, not after Anya. Probably, she is biding her time, trying to come up with some insidious way to convince him it's a good idea.

He's pulled back the blankets and is sitting cross-legged now in a pair of silky pyjamas, navy blue with white piping. She is relieved he does not also sleep naked and is surprised by how craggy he looks, his eyes sunken in, heavy lines around his mouth, like a puppet. She's embarrassed by it, by him, feels she's imposing on this adult, intimate space: a pile of Alison's clothes lumped on the floor, a scrap of underwear inside out, a scrunched tissue beside the bed. Beneath the smell of grape is musky skin, body parts.

'We need to leave soon,' Neve says.

'What time is it?'

'Nearly eight.'

'Christ,' Patrick says, running his hands through his hair. 'I thought she doesn't land till later, though.'

'You said we'd go have a look around the city first. Have lunch.'

'Did I?'

'Yes.'

'When did I say that?'

'Last week. That's why Elixir stayed over. He's coming with us.'

'Right,' Patrick says, picking up his cup and blowing on the tea. 'Well, I'd better get up then.'

Neve waits a moment, but he doesn't make any move to rise.

'Are you looking forward to seeing your mother?'

'Not really.'

He puts the mug down without taking a sip. 'I'll get cracking and we can hit the road. Maybe then you'll be in less of a crabby mood.'

'I'm not crabby.'

'Come here,' he says. He takes her hand, pulls her onto the bed and hugs her, kisses the top of her head. 'Are you happy here, Neve-bean?'

'Yeah.'

He pauses. 'We're glad you're here,' he says. 'Alison and I.'

'Thanks,' she says. Her voice is a squeak. She feels like a baby, being coddled. Patrick is prone to these outbursts, sudden, excessive declarations of his affection, and she tries to initiate her escape with a subtle squirm so as not to hurt his feelings.

'Do we need to pick up Elixir?' Patrick asks, freeing her. 'Maybe Gareth could come for the drive.'

'Elixir stayed the night. He's already here. He's downstairs.'

To hide her exasperation she gets off the bed, goes to the door. She sees the wet puddle of coffee steeping into the carpet, the mug turned on its side, and is filled with a swift and dramatic feeling of dread. She wants the weekend to be over already. Wants her mother to have been and gone. If Neve were at home in Sydney she would have got a sponge and bucket of water, scrubbed out the coffee immediately so it did not stain. She kicks the mug with her toe and it skids across the hall.

They spend the morning in Edinburgh, walking slowly through the New Town with takeaway coffees. When they pass a two-storey sweat-shop conglomerate, Patrick offers to buy Neve a new dress to wear for her birthday. Instead, Neve finds a charity shop close by and, after sifting through the jammed, musty racks, discovers a dress she doesn't hate; cornflower blue, long sleeves, a wrap waist. They have burgers and pints at a pub, go into a shop selling magic wands made of plastic and stuffed owls wearing scarves. They walk up the Royal Mile to the castle but Patrick is put off by the crowds and they do not go in. Standing outside St Giles', Patrick is recognised, and he stops for a photo with a tourist and his selfie stick. The man isn't much older than Neve; mid-twenties, maybe. He has a German accent, is wearing hiking boots and a backpack, thick-framed glasses, a navy puffer jacket. Patrick puts his arm around the man's shoulders but does not smile for the photo.

'I thought Alison would be coming,' Elixir says as they watch the interaction from a distance. 'Why didn't she?'

Neve shrugs. 'Don't know.' She hates when he gets like this, obsessing over Alison. She's not an idiot; she knows that part of her appeal is access to Alison, his weird little crush or whatever it is.

'I wanted to get some footage of her out in the wild.'

'She's not an animal.'

The German man tries to continue talking to Patrick, who is nodding while backing away. He eventually raises his hand into a wave and cuts the man off mid-sentence. 'Take care then,' Patrick says briskly and turns back to Neve and Elixir. He rolls his eyes, glances around as though to check whether anyone else has spotted him. The surrounding crowds are none the wiser and he slips on the sunglasses perched atop his head.

'Do you get recognised often?' Elixir asks.

'Less and less,' Patrick says. 'People think I'm dead. They're not expecting me.'

At the airport, they buy smoothies from a kiosk and wait in arrivals for Shannon. The plane is delayed and Patrick wanders off to make a phone call while Elixir and Neve sit on the hard-backed chairs and slurp their drinks.

'I've never been on a plane,' Elixir says wistfully.

'What?' Neve replies. 'Never?'

'Nope.'

'Why not?'

'My da runs a tea shop, Neve. We can't all be swanning across the world just because we want to.'

'I'm not swanning,' she says.

Elixir sighs. 'I didn't mean you,' he says, taking out his phone. 'Just, in general.'

She hates how he always brings up that sort of stuff, tries to hold it over her, make her feel guilty. She knows how it looks: Shannon's monthly, eight-hundred-dollar hair appointments; Patrick spending two grand on a single pen; the first-class air travel, the slew of investment properties, the artwork, the cars. She is well aware her parents are obscenely rich. She also knows they haven't always been rich and, using that logic, tries to justify their extravagance—to others, but mostly to herself. She is staunch in her distaste of people being paid grotesque amounts for doing very little, knowing that she, by default, will always be a rich person who did nothing to deserve it.

'Franny and me used to talk about going on a plane somewhere together. Just the two of us, maybe Da as well. It was all talk though, I suppose.'

'Where was Alison?'

'She didn't live here then. It was just Franny for ages, until your da and Alison showed up.'

A crowd surges from the arrivals gate and as Neve scans for her mother, she thinks of Frances, upstairs in the master suite. 'Did you know she died in the house?'

She thinks this will shock him but he rolls his eyes. 'Duh,' he says. 'Of course I knew.'

'Don't you think it's creepy?'

'Why would it be creepy?'

'I don't know,' she says. 'Old people should die in hospitals, in nursing homes.'

'She wasn't that old.'

'I hate living where someone has died.'

When he goes quiet, she knows she's said the wrong thing. Playfully, she pinches his arm. 'What was she like then?'

'The best,' he says. 'She looked after me. Da too.' He turns to her. 'But you shouldn't talk about her like that. Like she was nothing.'

She doesn't apologise, but makes a mental note not to bring up Frances again.

They are throwing their finished smoothies into the rubbish when Shannon finally appears, looking stylish and refreshed in black leggings, white sneakers, blonde hair pulled into a bun. She lets go of her large suitcase to hug Neve, who then gestures towards Elixir and mumbles an introduction. 'This your boyfriend then?'

'God, Mum. No.'

Patrick strides over, still on a call. He smiles at Shannon, holds up a finger. When he hangs up they embrace, and the four of them head out to the car park, Patrick wheeling Shannon's suitcase for her.

In the car, Elixir sits up front with Patrick, the city a haze of grey out the window. Though she'd been dreading her mother's visit, Neve is, in fact, happy to see her, and listens to her talk about the flight, what she ate on the plane, what films she watched, without interrupting. After a few minutes of inane chatter, Shannon turns her attention squarely on Neve, tucks the dark strands of hair behind her ears. 'This is different.'

Neve asks, 'Do you like it?'

'You look frightening. I don't recognise you.'

Neve takes it as a compliment. When she glimpses her reflection in the rear-view mirror her expression is smug. She doesn't recognise herself. She presses her palm against her mouth and rests her head against the window.

There is no sign of Alison when the three of them get home; they'd dropped Elixir at the bottom of the hill. In the kitchen, Patrick puts on the kettle. Her parents talk for a while about the film score Patrick is working on, and Shannon tells Patrick about one of his old schoolfriends from Wantarra—the unremarkable rural town in Queensland they both grew up in—who's just been charged with an array of offences: child trafficking in Thailand, some online stuff too. He wasn't the mastermind or anything; just one small cog in the machine.

Patrick doesn't seem surprised. 'We used to skip maths and look at dirty magazines together by the bike rack behind the hall.'

''Course you did.'

'He was an alright bloke, wasn't he? Wonder what happened.'

Patrick makes Shannon a coffee. He does most of the talking, repeats himself, pours boiling water on his hand and swears loudly. Neve sits there quietly, watching it all. She has nothing to add. They're not talking to her.

'I've got a bit of work to do,' Patrick says, handing Shannon the mug. 'I'll see you a bit later, then? Make yourself at home.'

While Shannon goes for a shower, taking her coffee with her, Neve stays in the kitchen. She picks at a scab on her wrist, rubs at a blackberry dye stain on her forearm. When the taps are turned on the house begins to groan and she thinks of Patrick's friend in Thailand, wonders how much time he'll spend in prison. She thinks of her father, who's been to prison once—before Neve was born and not for long. As they always do eventually, her thoughts turn to Alison and the baby, parsley, mugwort, aloe, and she finds herself rifling through the disorganisation of canned goods and dried beans until she locates the dried herbs stashed in a basket on the lower shelf. They are all in packets, most opened and unsecured so that a beach of soft powder sands the bottom of the basket, the smell of it gingery, bitter, brown. She picks through them: cumin, coriander, peppercorns, turmeric, smoked paprika. When she finds the parsley, she pockets it impulsively right as Shannon comes downstairs, her hair wet and combed. She's changed into another pair of leggings, an oat-coloured, slouchy jumper. She goes to the sink, pours a glass of water and sighs dramatically. 'I'm so dehydrated,' she says. 'I hate flying.'

'Sorry,' Neve says from the stool.

'Not your fault, baby doll.' She takes a small sip, tips the near-full glass back into the sink. 'So, this is it then?' Shannon asks, looking up to the ceiling.

'Yep.'

'It's big.'

Neve can tell she's not impressed. Her mother likes clean, modern things, glass and chrome, empty, airy spaces. Neutral colours. Subtle pops of pastel. Neve knew Shannon didn't understand why she wanted to come here, what she'd planned to do here for an entire year. She told her to go to New York or London—somewhere fun and cosmopolitan—instead of idling her life away in the middle of nowhere. Her mother didn't understand that it wasn't about fun. She wasn't looking for a holiday. At the time, Neve couldn't even articulate to herself what it was about, but it certainly wasn't that. Shannon tried to sway her, but Neve had already spoken with Patrick when she told her mother she was deferring her degree. She always felt grubby asking her parents for money and had worked casual shifts in the delicatessen of a bougie supermarket since she was fourteen, always smelling of fatty chicken thighs, thawing tiger prawns, gelatinous salmon. Patrick offered to pay for her flight but she'd already bought the ticket outright.

He transferred her the money anyway and didn't notice when she transferred it back.

'I'm going to have a lie-down,' Shannon says. 'Where am I staying?'

'You'll have to ask Alison,' Neve replies, and wonders if they'll try to force her into Frances's room.

'I'll sleep in your bed for now. Upstairs?'

'No,' Neve says. 'I'm down here.'

'Down here?' Her eyebrows rise. 'Where?'

Neve gets up, walks over to the archway leading out of the kitchen and stands in the doorway of her bedroom. Neve can see the room through Shannon's eyes, how cramped and bleak it is, squid ink mould blotching from the corners, the wallpaper yellowing in streaks where the damp has seeped through like sweat stains. Back in Sydney, her bedroom faced east, and in the morning the sun sparkled onto her bedspread in a kaleidoscope of light. Squawky flocks of sulphur-crested cockatoos and rainbow lorikeets nested in the plane trees lining the footpath outside the terrace, and before school they would eat pumpkin seeds and stale heels of sourdough straight from her palm.

'My God,' Shannon says. 'Are they keeping you as a slave?'

'No,' Neve says.

'They live in a bloody castle and you've been shoved down into the dungeon.'

'I like this room. I chose it. I feel safe.' She regrets the word choice the instant it's uttered.

'Why wouldn't you feel safe?'

'I just mean it's cosy.'

'Is your father feeding you?'

'Of course he's feeding me,' she snaps, though she is annoyed with herself, not her mother. She's always made an effort to choose Shannon over Patrick and is only now realising that, by coming here, she's done the exact opposite. She vows to be kinder to her mother, to try to turn her affection outwards.

❧

By the time Alison appears, the afternoon is deepening. The air is clear and crisp now; no rain, fogless. Neve has been waiting in the kitchen for her mother to wake. She sat at the table and scrolled the internet. In the fridge she found some cheese and bread, a single pickled onion she rolled about her mouth like a cold marble. Restless, she opened her journal, jotted down the date, drew a daisy in the corner of the page, a snail wearing roller skates, a demonic clown. She is unable to write without the fear that, at some point, someone will get their hands on the journal and shame her for its contents, and so she keeps things light: her impending birthday, how one might feel about turning eighteen and how the course of her life will dramatically shift once this milestone is reached. She writes about Gareth, how he is good-looking in an unobvious, rugged way and how strange it is that Alison doesn't like him. Maybe she propositioned him and he turned her down, her disdain a consequence of humiliation. Physically, Gareth reminds her of a teacher from her high school all the girls seemed to have an unfathomable crush on. He was acerbic and cruel, face like a crumpled paper bag. He taught ancient history and Mandarin and was at least sixty. She writes about him too. She writes about her new dress, and the movie she and Elixir fell asleep watching the night before. She writes about Elixir in his underpants, the dip between his ribs she wanted to put things into.

When Alison sweeps into the kitchen, Neve closes her journal, hides it under a newspaper.

'Where is she then?' Alison demands.

'Asleep.'

'Asleep where?'

'In my room. I didn't know where else to put her.'

Alison fills a glass with water and turns to the table. There's a light sheen of sweat along her hairline, a gold band on her ring finger. Alison notices Neve looking and glances at the ring, twists it around so that the smooth, garnet teardrop is on display. 'My mother's,' she says, though Neve didn't ask and does not particularly care. She holds her hand out for Neve to inspect.

Neve peers across the table, pretends to admire the ring. 'It's pretty.'

'It is, isn't it?'

The knives Alison used to dismember the rabbit are still in the sink, the blades crusted brown with blood. She turns to the sink, picks one up and begins to scrub. 'I decided against rabbit,' she says over her shoulder.

Hunched over the sink like that, sleeves rolled to her elbows, Alison looks like some sort of medieval peasant. It's impossible to imagine her on a red carpet, being photographed for a magazine. As Alison places a knife in the drying rack and picks up another, Neve puts her hands in her pockets and feels the parsley. The packet has been warmed by her body heat and she rubs it against her thumb. The fact that she'd taken it makes her feel appalling, but not bad enough to put it back.

'You can take me hunting if you're still offering.'

Alison continues cleaning. 'I thought you were a pacifist.'

Neve scrambles for a lie. 'I've been thinking about what you said. If I'm happy to eat meat, I should be able to kill it myself.'

Alison places the knife in the rack and turns to Neve, her hands dripping suds onto the floor before she dries them on her shirt. She looks pleased, smug almost, as though she's just won a game Neve didn't know they were playing.

Neve is surprised when Alison appears in the kitchen the following morning; she'd assumed she'd forget or would simply not be bothered. She looks tired, but there's a wiry intensity to her accentuated by the gun slung over her shoulder. Neve has never seen the gun in the house and is surprised by how large it is, how comical-looking. It looks like the type of unwieldy weapon you'd see at battle re-enactments; an heirloom, an antique.

Neve has dressed for the occasion: thermals, a parka, her grotty little beanie. In her backpack is a water bottle, insect repellent, a thermos of tea, and she feels like a boy scout as they traipse across the gravel oval, along the grounds and towards the woods. At first the canopy is thick and there's an eerie, green tinge to the air before they step into a patch of light. There's something about the unfamiliarity of the early morning, the quiet cold, that makes Neve keenly aware of how anxious it makes her to be out here alone with Alison. She realises the tea was a stupid, childish idea. She woke early to prepare it, steeped the parsley in hot water, added green tea leaves to mask the flavour. It seemed logical, brilliant even, yesterday, but now she wonders how much herb-infused tea you'd need to drink to induce a miscarriage. Litres probably, and even then it would likely just cause some sort of undetectable birth defect.

But she's here now, and may as well make the most of it. Alison doesn't tell Neve what her role is, what she's supposed to be doing, so she watches the ground for movement while Alison goes on ahead. Neve can smell the brine of the stream, the damp air. She is unsure if they are headed to any particular spot, or whether the plan is to plod on until they stumble across something that looks old or slow enough to take out. When Alison eventually spies something in the distance she motions for Neve to be still, but before she can do whatever it is she needs to do with the gun, the rabbit springs up on its haunches, its neck tall, face alert. Neve can't imagine Alison walking quietly, doing anything quietly; getting close enough to an animal without it hearing the bigness of her. The rabbit bounds away a moment later and Alison continues on without a word.

Scanning the ground, Neve spots a cluster of mushrooms. She crouches among a sludge of slick leaves. They are nestled in the soil, small and brown and meaty. They remind her of child thumbs, and Neve takes one by the stem, plucks it from the dirt and holds it to her nose. It smells like soil, ripe and musty. When she looks up Alison is completely obscured by the dense trees and Neve scrambles to her feet. She spots her a few yards away and jogs over, her backpack thumping against her lower back. 'Look,' Neve says, holding out the mushroom.

Alison is unimpressed. 'My mother used to forage for mushrooms,' she says. 'We'd eat them on toast for breakfast, cooked in gravy powder and tomato paste. She drew them as well, these magnificent, scientific drawings. She really was quite talented.'

Neve rolls the mushroom between her fingers. 'Can you eat this?'

Alison takes the mushroom and examines the underside of the cap. 'You shouldn't,' she says. 'But it won't kill you.'

'How can you tell?'

Alison hands it back before replying. 'There was a family in the highlands,' she says, 'who went foraging one afternoon, a year or so ago, cooked up the mushrooms for their tea and fell ill that night, all of them hospitalised with organ failure.'

'Did they die?'

'No,' she says. 'But they're all on dialysis still.'

'At least they didn't die.'

'They all blamed each other and now everyone is suing everyone.'

'Would be easy to make a mistake, right?' Neve considers the mushroom still in her hand. It looks utterly ordinary.

'No doubt it was intentional,' Alison says. 'A love triangle, perhaps. A rift over an inheritance.'

'Then the person who did it wouldn't be sick.'

'All part of the plan,' she says. 'That's what I would do anyway.'

They continue to tramp through the woods. As Neve passes a towering pine, she touches her hand to the trunk, which is covered with moss, the colour of it radioactive. The moss is wet and soft and pillowy. She cannot remember the last time she drank a full glass of water and has an urge to press her lips to the green and suck.

The further they walk, the more Neve is convinced Alison doesn't know what she is doing. She hasn't shown Neve how to use the gun and it remains strapped to her back like a prop. They spot a deer in the distance, and while Alison is distracted, Neve takes a bite of the mushroom she has held on to. A nibble really, just to taste, though she doesn't mind the idea of falling violently ill and having to miss her birthday entirely. The muscular flesh squeaks between her teeth, the taste of it peppery, foul. She can't stomach it. It sits in her mouth, slimy and masticated, and she spits it into the foliage before Alison notices.

Neve wants to ask Alison more about the mushrooms. She was expecting the Scottish landscape to be wild and threatening, but until now everything has seemed inoffensive and benign. A thought crosses her mind to somehow feed the mushrooms to Alison, send her body into complete shock so that nothing inside her can keep on living, but the prospect of it going wrong makes her shiver and she tries to quell the thought. She doesn't want Alison to get hurt. Her dad loves her. Neve is happy he is happy.

She wants to go back now. She wants for this strange little outing to be over, and is about to tell Alison she is feeling unwell when Alison again raises her hand to silence her. Neve looks around for the target as Alison clamps the same hand to her mouth. She lurches a few steps forward and vomits into the moss. Neve watches the back of Alison's bobbing head as she retches once, twice, three times. She's known Alison is pregnant for a week or so, found the test in the rubbish bin in her bathroom last week. She hadn't gone looking for it; Alison hadn't even tried to hide it. Still, Neve has always felt she is particularly receptive to secrets. It's not that people ever confided in her—she was never close enough to anyone to be trusted in that way—but she has an uncanny ability to disappear into a background, appearing so unassuming that people never bother withholding in her presence. At school, she kept a notebook in which she listed interesting or scandalous tidbits she overheard: whose nudes were in circulation at the brother school; who tried to overdose on paracetamol and Robitussin over the weekend. She had vague and malicious ideas to extort someone with what she uncovered, but there was no one she disliked enough to want to humiliate, nothing she could think to ask for.

Neve takes the thermos out of her bag and waits until Alison stands upright, wipes her mouth with the back of her hand. 'Here,' Neve says, passing her the thermos.

Alison unscrews the lid and takes a sip of Neve's tea. 'That's vile,' she says, grimacing.

'It's herbal,' Neve tells her. 'It's good for nausea.'

'It's revolting,' Alison says, handing back the thermos.

'The ham again?'

'Hmm?' Alison runs her hands over her forehead, through her hair, presses her palms to her eyes and exhales deeply through her mouth.

'Food poisoning. Did you keep eating the ham?'

'Mmm,' she says. 'I must have.'

Neve holds out the thermos again, wills her to take it. Alison holds up her hand to reject the offer, and when she meets Neve's eye there is something in her gaze that nearly knocks Neve over. Neve's face starts to hurt. Her ears are ringing. Alison's face goes fuzzy, and when it comes back into focus she is looking at Neve with alarm. 'What's the matter with you?'

It's Neve's hands that are trembling now as a deranged thought descends: there is a glitch in the universe and the barrier between her physical and internal self is being torn down. She is sure that Alison has seen into her mind, can see her thoughts and knows exactly what she knows, exactly what she is trying to do by forcing the tea onto her. Neve tries to make her mind blank. If her mind is empty, Alison won't be able to see into her, won't be able to get inside her head and read her thoughts and realise what a foul person she is. She is imagining her mind as a clear, glass bowl, unable to be penetrated, when something even stranger happens: her hand rises from her side as though levitating. Her fingers spread and her hand reaches, palm out, towards Alison's stomach. The moment it connects, Alison flinches backwards, out of Neve's reach.

'What are you doing?'

Neve's hand drops to her side. She is dizzy and can smell the vomit on Alison's breath. 'Why haven't you told Dad?'

She didn't mean to ask. Like her hand rising, the question came out of her as a compulsion.

Surprise flickers across Alison's face before her expression grows cool. 'What are you talking about?'

Neve tries to swallow. Her mouth is dry and she can feel her throat constricting. 'I'm not stupid,' Neve says. 'A baby. I know you're having one.'

'Don't be ridiculous.'

'I'm not being ridiculous.'

Alison wipes soil from her palms onto her trousers. She considers Neve for a moment, eyes narrowed, before she says, 'This is pointless. It's like speaking to a child.'

'I am a child.'

'No, you're not,' she says. 'You're an adult, Neve.'

Neve looks down at her hands, which have stopped shaking but are blueish from the cold. 'Dad doesn't want another baby,' she says, knowing how desperate she sounds, how tragic.

'Do you think I don't know that?'

Alison turns and walks back in the direction from which they came. Reluctantly, Neve follows, iron pulsing through her, a pure bolt of contempt for Alison, for the baby. She's tried manifesting it gone for the past week: channelling her thoughts towards Alison, the whole of her body's feminine, intuitive energy fixated on flushing out her womb, having it absorb back into her cells. She can't be that far along, not far enough for its absence to be a real source of suffering, not like how it was with Anya. It's probably the size of a macadamia, the size of a marble, a nothing glob of tissue still. It's not even real yet. It doesn't even exist.

Beneath her feet, twigs crack. She hurries to keep up so as not to get lost. She doesn't want to be near Alison, doesn't want to trail her pathetically, but continues forward, the idiocy of what she's revealed now clear. Why doesn't she have self-control like everyone else? Why can't she be a normal girl with normal thoughts?

As they near the house, Alison walks around the back of the stables while Neve heads down the drive. She is hoping to slip inside and go back to bed without anyone noticing she's been up, but she spots her parents on the patio. Her head is throbbing and she wants to be unconscious, considers sneaking around and entering through the front door, but she is spotted before she has the chance.

'Morning, darling,' Shannon calls. She is smoking a cigarette, and when Neve arrives at the table her mother reaches over the steaming ceramic mugs and squeezes her hand. 'What are you doing up?'

Neve shrugs. 'Went for a walk.'

Shannon looks concerned and peers towards the woods. 'Is it safe?'

''Course it's safe, you daft bitch,' Patrick interrupts.

Neve remembers this strange form of affection from when she was small, the casually cruel way they sometimes spoke to each other. He's never talked to Alison like that.

'I saw a deer,' Neve says, as Shannon takes a drag of the cigarette. She stares at her mother with a look of repulsion, trying to make her feel bad. 'You shouldn't be smoking.'

'Exactly what I said,' Patrick says. 'Utterly putrid.'

Shannon taps ash into the grass.

'Doesn't smoking age you?' Patrick continues. 'What's the point of pumping your face full of chemicals—on my dime, might I add—if you're just going to put that shit in your body?'

Something flashes behind Shannon's eyes but she masks it well. Neve has always been impressed by her mother's ability to keep her cool and maintain the peace. Neve doesn't think she's ever seen Shannon in a properly bad mood. 'I only smoke on holidays,' she says. 'Everything in moderation.'

'If that's what you tell yourself.'

'It's your fault anyway. You're the one who got me hooked.'

'Bullshit,' he says. 'I used to bum smokes from you.'

Shannon gives him another look, raises her eyebrows and leans back in her chair. 'All those drugs must have fried your brain.'

'What drugs?' Patrick retorts. 'Don't listen to your mother, Neve. She's delusional.'

Neve is about to announce that she's going inside when Shannon points to the garden. 'Is that Alison?'

They turn to see Alison in the distance, walking towards the hill that leads to farmlands. She's empty-handed, no gun in sight.

'Is she avoiding me?' Shannon asks. She turns to Patrick. 'You said she was happy for me to come here.'

'Alison doesn't sleep well,' Patrick says. 'She's probably been up for hours.'

'An insomniac,' Shannon says, taking a sip of coffee. 'Like me.'

'I didn't realise insomniacs were capable of sleeping for thirteen hours straight.'

'I took a sleeping tablet, Patrick.'

'Well, if you hadn't passed out before dinner you would have met her then.'

As Shannon leans down, stubs out her cigarette onto the gravel, Neve recognises how strange it is to see her parents together like this. Not that she was worried about them not getting along, but to actually see them together in the same place after so long is a novelty she doesn't entirely hate. After Patrick left, whenever he'd come back to Sydney for a longer stretch Shannon would take the opportunity to go on holidays, Bali or Byron Bay, so that their paths rarely crossed.

'Anyway,' Shannon says, 'what can I do to help for the weekend?'

'It's sorted,' Patrick replies.

'Surely there's something.'

'You can relax,' Patrick says. 'Get settled. Enjoy your holiday.'

'How about I make us brunch today, then?'

At that moment Neve realises how desperately she wants to be away from here—not just in bed and unconscious, but away from Alison and the baby, the house and its maze-like, illogical structure. She wants to be with her parents somewhere neutral. 'We could go out to eat,' she suggests.

'Great!' Shannon says. 'Where?'

'How about the cafe? Elixir might be working.'

Shannon smirks. 'What are his parents like, to give him such a freaky name?'

'He chose it for himself,' Patrick says, raising his eyebrows over his coffee.

'That's bold,' says Shannon. 'He's very small, isn't he? Like a wee little leprechaun. What does he do besides working in the cafe? Is he at uni?'

'There's no point anymore, Mum,' Neve says. 'Having an education doesn't mean you're going to get a job.'

'I'm fairly certain you still need a medical degree to be a doctor,' Patrick interjects.

'Neither of you went to uni and you're both doing fine,' Neve says.

'You better not be relying on an inheritance,' her father warns.

'I won't need an inheritance.'

'Won't you?'

'Humans will be extinct in thirty years anyway.'

'Bullshit.'

'How would you know? You don't even follow the news.'

'Don't work yourself into a tizzy, darling.'

'You'll be dead long before it happens. That's why you're not worried.'

She knows Patrick is only trying to wind her up, but as he and Shannon share another smug look, Neve feels herself regress ten years. She doesn't know why she bothers. Her parents will likely have the means to shoot off into space when things get really grim. No doubt they'll take her with them, but that is not the point.

'So, the cafe then?' Neve asks. Though it was her suggestion to go there, she now worries that her mother will find it to be plain and dinky. 'It's only pastries and stuff—but not made fresh. And the coffee's not very good.'

Shannon stretches her arms over her head, looks out into the grounds again. Neve follows her gaze, can see Alison at the edge of the field, now at the base of the hill. 'Should we wait for Alison to get back?'

Patrick takes a sip of coffee. 'Alison will stay here. She wants to get some work done today.'

'What work?'

'She's doing a film at the end of the year. In Belfast.'

'I thought she didn't do that anymore?'

'She doesn't. I mean, it's just a one-off.'

'Is she getting paid a lot?'

'I've no clue how much she's getting paid.'

Shannon turns back to the table. 'Just the three of us then.'

'I've got a bit of work to do as well, actually,' Patrick says. 'I'm on a deadline. The director wants a rough cut of the score by the end of next week.' He reaches out and takes hold of Neve's elbow. 'You don't mind, do you? It'll give you two time to catch up properly.'

Neve shakes her head, picks up her backpack from the ground. 'It's fine.'

She turns and heads to the house, goes down the stairs and into the kitchen. She takes the thermos out of her backpack and pours the tea down the sink. Inside and entirely alone she feels acutely swaddled by the walls, her headache still rippling, a warm pressure tightening against her already tight skin as though she is in the process of being slowly poached. She appreciated the momentary distraction of her parents but now that she is alone it comes back to her as fiercely as rage. In her head she pictures her hand pressed to Alison's belly, clawing past the skin and muscle, into the swelling balloon of Alison's uterus and squeezing it to pulp. She knows it's grotesque, that she is grotesque, but she cannot shake it, cannot get it to leave her: the hand, the belly, the womb.

She continues through the kitchen into her bedroom, and it's only when the door is closed and locked that her breathing begins to slow. As she lies on her bed and stares at the ceiling it continues to roil through her: hand, belly, womb; hand, belly, womb. She repeats this sequence until she sinks into a post-adrenaline stupor. When she comes to, her headache is gone.

# ALISON

ALISON FOLLOWS THE TRACK UP the hill, through the thick wet peat and the brown heather, until her thoughts are obliterated by her slow, steady steps. Instead of Neve's voice in her head reminding her that *Dad doesn't want another baby* (*I've never wanted a baby*, she should have responded) all she can hear is the dry wind stinging and her own breathing in and out until she reaches the summit, the view of the farmlands, the village, compact and picturesque, and, a few yards ahead, a filthy ewe idle in the yellow, tussocky field, its rear slimy with blood. By the time she returns home her knees are stiff from the decline, lower back aching, teeth furry when she licks them. The grass is tidy, the leaves swept away. A truck is parked snugly against the house. From behind the studio she catches a flicker of movement and focuses her attention on the broad young man in work boots and a navy get-up who appears. His size is intimidating; he's taller than Patrick, and also thicker, more brutish, someone very capable of pinning her down with little exertion. He looks in her direction and in a voice that is deep and gruff calls out something indecipherable before lifting up a large brown sack and heading towards his truck.

Alison walks to the house, watches the gardener pack away his tools, the ride-on mower already secured in the back. She does recognise him—they've had him look after the garden before—though she does not know his name and they've never had a real conversation. Once he is in the truck, heading down the driveway, she turns back to the house. Patrick's car is gone but the studio light is on; Shannon and Neve must be off somewhere, and Alison is relieved to have some more time to herself before they return. During the walk, Alison came to realise how much she's underestimated Neve; how observant she is, how astute. How she found out about the pregnancy, Alison has no idea. She's not showing yet, obviously, and other than the morning sickness she is much the same as she always is. It occurs to her now that she should have told Neve to keep the pregnancy to herself, that nothing will come of it. But she also seems like the type who would enjoy the self-importance afforded by keeping someone else's secret. Not that it is a secret. She will tell Patrick if he asks. And Neve is right: Patrick doesn't want another child—but

Alison knows he will make her talk and talk and talk, and, frankly, she would prefer for it to be done away with quickly, quietly, with no real disruption to their lives. It's not his business that her body has gone rogue.

There's a tapping and she looks up to see Patrick standing at the studio window. He waves, disappears, reappears at the door and crosses the grass to join her. 'What are you doing?' he asks.

'You didn't tell me the gardener was coming.'

'I only called him this morning. You did ask me to.'

'I don't like to come home to strangers prowling around,' she says. 'I nearly had a heart attack.'

'Did you have a good walk?'

'I did.'

'Shannon and Neve have gone out for breakfast. They'll be back soon.'

'Good.'

He puts his hands on his hips and his undone button strains his shirt to reveal a scruff of greying hair, his bellybutton a wrinkled gash. 'You really should have come over to say hello to Shannon before.'

'I was walking off a mood.'

'What mood?'

'I don't remember. It's lifted.'

'Shannon thinks you're avoiding her.'

'Why would I be avoiding her?'

'You tell me.'

'This is my house,' she says. 'I was out for a walk, not hiding away.'

'Would it have been so difficult to come over and say hello?' he asks. 'She knows you saw her.'

'It's not as though I won't get another opportunity.'

'She'll feel unwelcome.'

'I agreed that she could stay here, didn't I?'

Patrick's nostrils twitch and he lets out a deep exhale. She can sense him chanting some sort of mantra in his head to stop himself detonating at her, though she is the one who should be angry. It's not her job to entertain anyone. She's done nothing wrong.

'Yes,' he says. 'You did.' His face softens, and when he reaches for her hand, he notices the ring. 'Nice,' he says, raising her hand closer to his face. 'Is this new?'

She'd forgotten she was wearing it. She takes back her hand, forces off the ring and slips it into her pocket. 'When will they be back?'

'Soon.' He squints down at her. 'You look exhausted.'

'Thank you.'

'Were you up early?'

'No earlier than usual.'

'You were with Neve, then?'

'Yes,' she says. 'She wanted to go hunting.'

'She did?'

'She insisted.'

He smiles. 'I told you she finds you interesting.' He takes his sunglasses from on top of his head and slips them on to shade his eyes from the glare. 'You know what I was just thinking of this morning?' he asks. 'I don't know why, but it just popped into my head. When we went to San Sebastián—what, five, six years ago? We had that amazing stew with the prunes and rabbit and afterwards went down to the beach with all the sandcastles, and there was that horrible-looking thing washed up on the shore. It was like an alien, or some abject sea creature, and as we were leaving that group of schoolkids started kicking it, whacking its brains out with a piece of driftwood.'

Alison's skin prickles as she remembers. She hasn't swum in the ocean for years, or thought about that trip for almost as long. It's not yearning she's feeling, though. That version of herself—before she gave up work, before she moved here—was flimsy and impulsive. She was obsessed with her reflection, exercised compulsively, subsisted mostly on tea and bacon and porridge. When Patrick insisted they go out for decadent meals, more often than not—depending on her mood and how unwieldy she was feeling—she would go to the bathroom afterwards to heave it all out of her. She didn't even feel shame. Didn't even try to hide it. It felt good at the time, and now she considers it a period of personal growth, purging to rebalance the equilibrium of her humours, like an Elizabethan monk, a stoic.

Patrick continues, 'It was like some sort of amphibian crossed with a sheep, all slimy and hairy in the sand. Hideous.'

Alison yawns. 'I don't remember that.'

'Of course you do,' he says. 'It was right after we played that show in Madrid. I took a photo of it. We were telling people about it for days.'

'Maybe you were with Shannon.'

'You really don't remember?'

Alison pauses. She remembers perfectly. 'I recall going to Spain and finding a dead dog on the beach.'

He looks at her as though she's an infant. 'It wasn't a dog,' he says. 'It looked nothing like a dog.'

'It was a dog,' she says. 'I just didn't tell you at the time. You were so thrilled by this mystical-looking corpse and I couldn't bear to correct you. It was the children who killed it in the first place, you know?'

He says nothing, and Alison looks away to stop herself from grinding away at him further. Sometimes this impulse to make him suffer in small ways comes from nowhere, and she looks around for a distraction before she escalates and says something truly hurtful. There: a glint of terracotta on the lawn near the window catches her eye. Crossing the grass, she can see it's a small jagged shard of something ceramic, covered in a red film, a geometric pattern underneath. She can't figure out what she's looking at. It's familiar but she can't place it, as though her brain is suffering from a momentary electrical disturbance.

'What is it?' Patrick asks, coming to her side.

When she places the chip in the centre of her palm he bends down to look at it. 'It's nothing,' he says, reaching over to take it from her. 'It's rubbish.'

She closes her palm and snatches away her fist.

Patrick looks her in the eye for a moment before standing up straight. 'I'm going back to work,' he says. 'I was just trying to check in, but obviously you're not interested.'

She waits until he is walking back to the studio before going inside. In the kitchen, she rinses the ceramic under water and dries it on her shirt. The pattern is a heinous swirl of orange and green on an eggshell background. She sets it by the sink and fills the kettle, lights a match, and when the gas ignites it comes to her. She opens the cupboard and takes out her mother's casserole dish. Just as she expected, the shard fits cleanly in the missing slot of the lid like a puzzle piece. How did it get outside? She raises the chip to her nose. It smells of clay and she has a craving to lick it, to chew on it like she used to do with her scabs when she was small and trying to ingest some densely magicked part of herself. She puts it in her mouth but the feeling is not as she hoped. She grinds it between her molars and the ceramic chalks away, gritty in her mouth, as though a tooth has crumbled as it would in a dream predicting catastrophe.

As she picks up the dish to return it to the cupboard, there's a strangled revving from outside. Her hands are still damp and she loses her grip, the dish plummeting to the stone floor and shattering into seven or eight pieces. She hears tyres on gravel and a moment later the car appears, rolling to a stop in the driveway. Alison crouches down and gathers the larger shards, places them in the sink. She will wash them, keep them somewhere safe. Cement-like flecks dust the ground. She thinks to find the broom to sweep them up, but the image of Shannon finding her like that, hands and knees on the floor in servitude, is enough to keep her upright.

She considers going upstairs to avoid meeting her until later, but as Shannon and Neve get out of the car she stays by the window. Though she's much closer than when she saw her this morning on the patio with Patrick, she still can't get a real sense of Shannon beyond her basic physicality: short, slender, pretty. Again, Alison is tempted to retreat upstairs but decides to get it over with. She runs her hands through her hair and turns back to the stove, watches the kettle tremble above the blue flames until the doorhandle rattles.

She turns to the door as Shannon is stamping her feet on the doormat, a disposable coffee cup in one hand, a brown paper bag in the other. Alison steps towards her, unsure if she should shake hands or lean in for a kiss. Her perfume is clean and fresh, like grass and citrus, and an unfamiliar feeling sits inside her. 'Hello,' Alison says, her hands clasped in front of her. 'Did you sleep well?'

Shannon smiles. She has the whitest, straightest teeth Alison has ever seen. 'You've got a gorgeous house.'

'Oh,' Alison says. 'That's kind.'

Shannon holds out the paper bag. 'We got you a danish.'

Alison takes the bag. She places it on the counter and asks Shannon how long she's staying for, already knowing the answer.

'A quick trip. Just until Sunday.'

'That's right,' Alison says. 'Patrick did tell me.'

'I couldn't bear to be away from this one on her big day,' Shannon says, nodding towards Neve, who is hanging her coat on the hook on the back of the door, looking dour as usual.

Alison pulls at her collar, her clothes scratching. She can't stop fidgeting, and notices that Shannon has hardly moved at all.

'Well, it's wonderful to meet you finally,' Alison says, and desperately tries to think of something slightly more interesting to say. She is thankful when water begins to boil, steam wisping from the nozzle in thin, white clouds. 'Did you sleep well?' she asks again over her shoulder, turning off the gas. Having something to do with her hands makes her feel more in control of herself. It's all Neve's doing, she thinks. If she hadn't been ambushed earlier, she wouldn't be so out of sorts, so scattered. 'You didn't mind the room?'

'It was great.'

'Were you comfortable? It wasn't too cold?'

'Everything's perfect.'

Alison notices a shard of ceramic on the floor, steps on it so that it crunches under her foot. Her eyes sweep the room. 'It's dated, but it has character. We keep meaning to renovate but it's so hard to find decent people.' Decent people. God,

Alison thinks, what am I saying? When have I ever wanted to renovate?

'Mum,' Neve interrupts, 'do you still want to go for a walk?'

'I know an amazing designer in Sydney,' Shannon says, ignoring the question. 'Not much help for you, though. He did a great job of the kitchen, didn't he, Neve?'

They both look to Neve for a response, as if she has all along been an active and essential participant in the conversation. She gives them a blank look, shrugs dismissively.

Alison turns back to Shannon. At first, she couldn't quite place it, but it occurs to her now what the feeling is: she wants Shannon to like her. It feels desperate, as though she must strive to make a good impression to avoid the shame that will ricochet through her when the conversation is over and Shannon has formed an opinion that is not entirely positive.

'You're radiant,' Alison says.

Shannon looks baffled, then lets out a sudden, sweet burst of laughter.

'What's wrong?' Alison asks.

'Sorry,' Shannon says, clasping the pendant around her neck. 'That's very nice.'

'You are, though. You look very healthy.' Alison didn't realise that people could look like that in the flesh. She has the skin of a child, of a dolphin, and Alison has an urge to touch it, to feel the texture on her fingers.

'I would hope so,' Shannon says, 'considering how much money I've spent on my face.'

'Mum,' Neve hisses.

'Neve's embarrassed by me,' Shannon says, reaching over to squeeze the back of her daughter's neck.

'Well, it's normal for girls to be embarrassed by their mothers,' says Alison.

Alison expected to find the woman vaguely pathetic, for her to evoke the same feelings in her that Neve does. Instead, she feels a warm surge of affection and goodwill towards her. She *is* radiant.

'I'm making tea,' Alison says. 'Would you like one?'

Shannon shakes her head, raises her coffee cup as Alison begins to rifle around in the cupboard. Finding a packet of chocolate biscuits, she arranges them on a plate, turns back to the tea. 'The house is rather old,' she says. 'There's heating, of course, and the fireplaces, but it can become freezing if you leave a window open. It was built in the 1700s, originally, but it didn't look like this until a century ago, when the owner wanted something a wee bit grander. Until now, no one has been able to hold on to it for long. My mother thought it was cursed, because of the animals—there used to be a private zoo here, did Neve tell you?—but it's been ours for over a decade now and nothing's tried to get rid of us yet.'

When Alison turns around, Shannon has placed her coffee on the table, is tying her jumper around her waist.

'I'm boring you,' Alison says.

'Sorry,' Shannon says, looking up. 'Just a bit jet-lagged. Still out of it, I suppose.'

'You should have a lie-down.'

'Later, maybe.' Shannon picks up her cup. 'Neve and I are going for a walk if you want to join us?'

She'd like to suggest a walk without Neve, but knows there'll be time for that. 'Oh, no,' she says. 'I've far too much to do here.'

'Let's go then, Mum,' Neve says, taking her coat back off the peg and jamming herself into it. She opens the door, heaves out of it, no goodbye.

Shannon rolls her eyes at the flourish of Neve disappearing into the garden and follows her. Alison stays by the window and pretends to rinse out a coffee mug over the sink, only slightly disappointed that Shannon didn't ask what she was busy with. When they come into view she watches them tramp across the grass. They stop near a cluster of daffodils and Shannon crouches down to take a photo on her phone. Alison feels for the paper bag on the bench beside her, tears off buttery flakes of pastry and eats quickly, until her gums are stinging with sugar, the tips of her fingers sticky, all the while watching Shannon and Neve shrink to figurines. When she turns back to the kitchen it doesn't look as she remembered, her corneas coated with some sort of kaleidoscopic film. She's surprised and a little pleased to find herself feeling somewhat giddy. It's as though a warm light has descended. Everyone is exactly where they should be.

Alison brings the script down from the bedroom and reads it again on the sofa in the library. She scans the same lines over and over. It used to be easy to melt into concentration but lately she feels as if her brain is shrivelling, a dry sponge unable to retain moisture. She is looking forward to next week when her body is her own again. Bored and restless, she phones Neil and he tells her more about the project, the three young actresses she is scheduled to do chemistry reads with next week. Her daughters. As they speak, Alison has the sensation she is talking to a disembodied voice; she cannot picture him, cannot remember what he looks like, his mannerisms, whether he talks with his hands.

Her mouth is tacky and a little painful still from the danish, and after hanging up she sets the script on the ottoman and wanders through to the kitchen, pours a glass of water and heads upstairs. She stops when she reaches Shannon's room. The door is ajar, and though she only taps lightly it swings open. She hesitates in the doorway. The Georgian yellow wallpaper is brighter than she recalls. It gives the room a childish quality and she wonders if it was a nursery in a past life. Shannon has left the lamp on and when Alison steps inside to switch it off she finds herself lingering. The bed is messily made, a glimpse of pale peach pyjama tonguing out from under the pillow. Beside the lamp is a book, the brutalist font of an airport thriller, and on a small wooden chest closer to the window is a hair band, blonde hair coiled into a tight bead. Though Alison is compelled she does not touch it, but as she goes to leave she spots Shannon's open suitcase on the floor at the end of the bed. She crouches down and surveys: plain t-shirts, jumpers, a silk eye mask, a jar of multivitamins, a handful of black and white cotton underwear. She is disappointed. Nothing remarkable, nothing that tells her anything of substance.

Back to standing, she is again distracted, this time by a painting hanging on the other side of the furthest bed. Alison crosses the room. The girl is framed from the waist up, sitting down on an unseen chair, body angled to the left. The background is colourless, as though she is being painted at night in a dark room. She's wearing a blue dress, lace ruffles at the neck and on the sleeves, clown-red cheeks, hair curled and pinned back off her face. At her chest she holds a loose arrangement of long-stemmed flowers and ferns, like a rustic wedding bouquet. She must be five or six but her eyes have been drawn to make her look far older, her expression sensual and penetrating, as though she is in fact an enigmatic bride trapped in the body of this pure, beautiful child.

For the second time today she is surprised, and finds herself truly moved by the portrait. She unhooks it from the wall and exits the room clutching it to her chest. She goes downstairs, across the garden and into the studio. She is excited, not just to show it to Patrick, but to speak with him, to speak with anyone. That giddiness again.

He is behind the glass and holds a finger up, signals for her to wait. The studio is one room partitioned into two sections: on one side of the glass is Patrick's recording equipment, microphones and cables, guitars lining the wall, a baby grand in the centre, all of it encased by padded walls. The smaller section, where Alison is, has the character of a waiting room: desktop computer, stacks of papers and post-it notes, a lonesome, glossy-leafed pot plant. The shelf adjacent to the desk has a plastic tray filled with muesli bars and miniature sea salt crisp packets, a cluster of plaques and awards, beneath which is a bar fridge that turns out to be empty when Alison swings it open. She's never noticed how ugly it is in here, how plain. A sound engineer from Glasgow fitted out what used to be the worker's hut, a surprise for when Patrick moved in. He'd originally planned to commute to the city and rent out a space, but Alison wanted to show him he was welcome here. She used to do that sort of thing—kind things.

Patrick takes off his headphones and pops his head around the door. 'Hey,' he says flatly.

The painting is facing inwards at Alison's feet and she flips it around. 'Look at this painting,' she says.

He takes in it but seems uninspired. 'What about it?'

'Isn't it exquisite?'

'I guess so.'

'I'm going to hang it in the bedroom,' she says. 'Unless you want it in here?'

'No,' he says. 'You put it wherever.'

'Let's just see what it looks like.' She picks up the painting, struggling under its weight as she holds it at shoulder height. There are no hooks on the walls so she props it up on the shelf beside the tray of snacks. 'There's no personality in here,' she says. 'How can you be expected to create great art if your work environment is soulless?'

'I'm not trying to create great art.'

'Don't be modest,' she says. 'Of course you are.'

He comes to stand beside her and together they assess the painting. 'Where did you find it?'

'It was in the yellow room.'

He looks confused. 'Did Shannon not like it?'

'I don't know,' she says. 'I only just met her. How am I to know her tastes?'

'So why did you take it away?'

'Because it speaks to me, Patrick,' she says, a little irritated by his questioning. 'And it was wasting away up there. Poor thing, trapped up there all alone.'

She takes the painting from the shelf and holds it under an arm. It's surprisingly heavy, the gold frame made of a dense wood. There's a coating of grime on the top of the frame and she wipes it off with her fingertips, brushes it onto the floor.

'Is that all you wanted?' Patrick asks.

He looks so weary, and Alison feels a terrible pang for being short with him earlier. Usually when they are upset with each other, if they leave it long enough, a convenient memory fog descends and they continue on as though the particular clashing never occurred. 'I was horrible before,' she says. 'It wasn't a dog. I don't know why I said that.'

He exhales, pinches the bridge of his nose. 'It's fine,' he says. 'I know it's not your choice to have so many people coming and going.'

'I don't deserve you.'

'No,' he says. 'You don't.'

The painting digs into her forearm so she manoeuvres it onto the desk, rests it against the wall. Again, they inspect it, but it doesn't look right amid the drudgery of office supplies, the clear glass, the light woods and the sleek Scandinavian furniture Alison ordered online from a factory to replicate the studio he'd been renting in London before the move.

'It looks exactly like Neve, don't you think?' Alison asks. She'd hoped he would say it first, to validate the thought, though the resemblance is undeniable.

Patrick cocks his head, makes a noncommittal sound.

'I imagine she's dead now,' Alison continues. 'Not Neve, obviously. The girl in the painting.' She again takes the canvas, hooks it under an arm. As she reaches for the door, she turns back to Patrick. 'I think we should renovate.'

'Okay,' he says.

'Do you think it's a good idea?'

'Sure,' he says. 'Whatever you want.'

'Everything's beginning to feel so stale. And it will increase the property value.'

He looks surprised. 'You want to sell?'

'Of course not,' she says. 'It's just hard to be a lady of leisure when you're surrounded by dry rot.'

'We can talk about it after the weekend.'

'When I'm in Belfast after summer would be a good time. You can stay here and oversee it all.'

'I thought I was coming with you?'

'These are just thoughts, Patrick. We haven't decided on anything.'

She takes the painting inside, up to their bedroom. She looks for a spot to hang it but can't settle on an appropriate resting place and leaves it leaning against the wardrobe door. The girl is facing inwards at first, towards the cool, dark wood, but Alison feels guilty and turns the painting around so she can see out into the world, a new room that she may not have seen for a long time, if ever.

She's in the kitchen when there's a knock at the door. At first, she ignores it, but when it sounds again with more urgency she relents and goes to open the front door. It's Elixir standing on the stoop. His arms are crossed, hands cosily tucked into his armpits. 'Hiya,' he says. 'Neve in?'

'No,' Alison replies. 'She's out with her mother.'

He frowns. 'I sent her a text but she didn't reply.' He looks past Alison and into the house as though he doesn't believe her and Neve is standing just out of sight. 'Can I wait inside?'

She hesitates before opening the door wider. He's just a boy, she tells herself. 'If you like.'

He follows her into the kitchen. The biscuits from earlier are still on the table, untouched. She noticed him eyeing them and holds out the plate.

'Ta,' he says. He slips his phone in his pocket, leans over and takes two.

'I was just in the middle of something.' She sets down the plate. 'Preparing for Neve's birthday.'

He continues to beam at her, gumming a chocolate biscuit. She doesn't know what to do with him, where to put him. 'I suppose you can wait here—or in Neve's room, if you'd prefer.'

'I can help if you want.'

She recoils. 'I don't need help.'

'I don't have anything else to do,' he says. 'I like to be useful.'

She would rather he sit somewhere quietly or disappear completely, but she's sure he'll prowl around given the opportunity. 'Alright,' she says. 'Come with me then.'

She hadn't planned on setting up for the party, but she has nervous energy to burn off, so she leads him through the house, past the library to the dining room they rarely use. The curtains are made of a thick, heavy fabric and she tells Elixir to draw them, her voice echoing against the timber floors, the high ceilings. He does as he's told and Alison stands in the doorway and waits for the darkness to be peeled back. The light reveals the fug of dust in the room, languid motes levitating through space. It is peaceful: the only room in the house sparsely furnished and uncluttered, empty except for an imposing oak dining table pushed up against the back wall.

'Help me move this,' she says, gesturing towards the table.

Elixir walks to the other side of the table and curls his fingers under the top. They drag it along the floor until it sits squarely in the room's centre. For a time, though it was just the two of them, Patrick would set the table as if they were hosting a lavish dinner party, spend hours in the kitchen preparing the evening meal, trips to the supermarket each day. He loved making a spectacle out of eating. The thing he enjoyed most about having money, he once told her, was being able to eat out at restaurants on a whim. Sitting at a table over conversation, no television on full-blast, no microwave meals. He liked how when people got drunk at restaurants it felt festive rather than chaotic.

Elixir takes in the adjustment, hands on his hips. 'How are you decorating then?'

'Decorating?'

'It's a party, isn't it?' he replies. 'You'll need balloons and decorations and lights. It needs to be special.'

While Elixir mops the floor, Alison brings in the fairy lights from the patio. They are tacky, but every time she takes them down, Patrick hangs them back up and so she stopped bothering. She strings them along the windowsill, then forages through the house for candles and tea lights, arranges them in clusters of three. Elixir is right. Shannon's come all this way; it should be special.

'Shouldn't Patrick be helping with all this?' Elixir calls from the other side of the room, where he's started on the windows.

'Why do you say that?'

'Well, it's Neve's birthday and he's making you do all the work. Not very progressive, is it?'

'Patrick's anxious at the moment,' she says. 'I don't mind.'

He reaches down, submerges a sponge in the bucket, wrings it out in his fist. His face is sheened with sweat and the sleeves of his jumper are dark with wet. He seems to change his mind and throws the sponge back into the bucket, then he picks up the bucket and walks purposefully across the room towards her. Now that the film of dust has been removed from the windowpanes the room is bright, the sun coming through the glass and catching the gold in his bristly hair.

'Alison,' Elixir says. He stands right up close to her face and she can see the fine black hairs on the tip of his nose. 'Can I ask you something?'

Oh God, she thinks, as a hot feeling floods her. She raises her eyebrows and nods, apprehensive already.

'Why don't you go anywhere?'

'Pardon?' she replies.

'I never see you in the village anymore. And Patrick's always over at our house but never you.'

'He's not always over.' Alison steps back, but rather than giving her the space he inches closer. 'And I'm going to London next week.'

'I wasn't even sure you were still alive until recently. Me and Da hadn't seen you in ages, not for months. Maybe even a year. I thought maybe Patrick had killed you and buried you in the garden or something.'

'Well, here I am. Very much alive.'

'Da wouldn't mind if you came over, you know.'

'I'm sure.'

'He's a good guy,' he says. 'He's got nothing against you.'

The room grows warm and, dizzy, Alison turns to the window. A good guy. Yes, she supposes he is. Self-righteous, pious, saintly. Just because he's a good guy that doesn't mean she has to spend time with him. In her experience, good people are tedious, and she wonders whether Gareth thinks Patrick is *a good guy*.

Elixir puts the bucket down and water sloshes onto the floor. Alison steps back but the water has already seeped through her socks. He crouches down to clean up the spill, mopping the water with his sleeve, before she takes the bucket by the handle, prods his arm with her toe. 'Come on,' she says. 'You can help with the flowers.'

They go to the kitchen, where Alison finds a pair of scissors and empties loose onion skins from the bottom of a wicker basket, then continue into the garden. There are daffodils sprouting around the perimeter of the house, brilliant, lemony clusters of them. Alison leads Elixir to the side of the house, where they're particularly rampant, and he lowers himself to his knees, begins snipping the daffodils at angles at the base of their stems.

'Be careful with them,' she says, though he seems to know exactly what he's doing, his fingers nimble and discerning. 'And try not to pick any that are wilted. They need to last until tomorrow evening.'

'Da picks his daffodils when they're still wee babies,' he says, laying a bud into the basket gently. 'The heat from inside opens them right up.'

She stands over Elixir as he snips away merrily and is surprised to find herself enjoying his presence. He'd make a good companion, like a faithful dog, and she wonders if that's what Neve sees in him. She hears an engine in the distance and looks towards the driveway with anticipation, is disappointed when the sound fades, the car doesn't appear.

It occurs to her then that Elixir might be of use to her. Neve has probably told him all sorts of things about the lot of them, and she tries to sound off-handed when she asks, 'And what has Neve told you about her mother?'

Elixir separates a daffodil from the bunch and shrugs. 'Nothing.'

'Surely you know something.'

'Just, you know, the basics. Only just met her, didn't I?'

'Does Neve talk to you about her?'

'Sometimes. Not really.'

'What do you think of her?'

'She seems cool,' he says. 'She seems like a laugh.'

The sun shines brightly and she turns her back to it. She realises she's still wearing just her socks and can feel her feet softening into the ground. 'What is it you like about Neve?'

'I don't know,' he says. 'I just like her. She's weird.'

'Do you think I'm weird?'

He smiles. 'A little bit.'

'I'm actually very ordinary.'

He looks down at the flower he's just picked. He holds it away from his body and for a moment Alison thinks he's going to hand it to her in a romantic gesture of courtship, but instead he places it in the basket with the others, reaches for another thick, plasticky stem.

When the basket is half full Elixir gets up off his knees and presents it to her for approval. 'Enough?'

She peers into it. So much yellow. She looks out into the garden; there's a sprinkling of drooping bluebells in a clearing over by the ring of oak trees, a spray of dandelions. 'I don't know why Patrick didn't think to get flowers delivered.'

'Daffodils are lovely.'

'We can't have a room of them for a birthday party,' she says. 'It's a flower of the underworld. They're entirely morbid.'

She was speaking to herself more than him, but again he chimes in. 'My da grows flowers. All sorts. We could get some from him?'

Normally she would say no, but she can't shake the feeling that tomorrow needs to be perfect. There's been something strange about the day and she is compelled to behave strangely too. She'll wait outside with Elixir while he picks the flowers.

How long could it take? With any luck, Gareth might not even be home.

Once down the driveway they fall in step, the flowers swinging between them. As they cross through the woods, the edge of the farmlands, further and further away from the house, Alison focuses on the basket, the rhythmic, pendulous swaying, the blur of yellow petals and the black slug of a watch on Elixir's wrist. He begins to whistle, and at first the sound is shrill, but then the repetition becomes hypnotic, as though the sound he is making and the furious swinging of his wrist are working in tandem to lure Alison towards something sinister.

They cross the footbridge over the stream and the house comes into view at the bottom of the hill: a stone cottage with a blue door and matching windowsills. There's a strange pain in Alison's chest, a constricting which grows tighter the closer they get to the house. To stop her head from spinning she focuses on the garden, which is neat and particular: an army of vibrant flowers shooting from the large beds in front of the house, erect tulips and hydrangeas. The urge to turn and go home is overwhelming and she chides herself for her weakness. Imagine being too frightened of the world to pop around to the neighbours to ask a favour. Pathetic.

They are on the front path when the door swings open and Gareth appears. Alison is surprised to find she feels very little at the sight of him. Not anger, not irritation. He looks much the same as the last time she saw him this close up, at the service for Frances that Patrick and her assistant Martine organised at the small Protestant church in town. She remembers Gareth and Elixir sitting in a pew up the back, fidgeting in their cheap black suits. They weren't invited to the wake, were not bold enough to come regardless.

'Alison,' Gareth says, nodding his head at her, as though Alison dropping in is an entirely common occurrence. 'Good to see you.'

'We need some flowers, Da,' Elixir says. 'For the party.'

'Go for your life,' he says, waving his hand at the garden. 'Just not the Himalayan poppies. Those are far too special to part with.'

'Which are those again?'

'The blue ones, just there.'

As Elixir takes the basket and kneels by the flowerbed, Gareth turns to Alison, glances at her socks and then her face. 'Cup of tea, then?'

He turns and goes inside without waiting for her response, and Alison has no option but to follow.

It's too bright: the curtains are open and the fire is lit, making the room feel queasy and twee. The cloying scent of a floral air freshener goes straight to her throat like an allergen, but there's a smell hidden below the artificial lavender, the scent of other people and their lived-in things: not unpleasant, but intimate. She notices how clean the place is; dishes drying in the rack, the benchtop gleaming. Suspiciously clean, she would whisper to Patrick if he were here, as if Gareth had just gone over a murder scene with bleach. There is no division between the kitchen and the living area, and on the small, square dining table is a pile of folded laundry, the socks paired and bundled, a tidy stack of beige face cloths. She feels exceptionally large, her body swollen and taking up space. Though this is where Patrick often sets off to with a bottle of Talisker—always stumbling home late, always a nightmare to deal with the following morning—it's impossible to imagine him here, drinking on the chaise by the fire, knowing where the bathroom is and moving there with ease and without permission. She feels a sting of resentment towards him for maintaining a secret other life she does not have access to.

Gareth turns to the bench and takes the tea from the cupboard over the sink. Alison idles over to the sofa, which is crosshatched with bristly white hairs. There is movement beside the fireplace, and when she focuses she sees a pair of yellow eyes gazing back at her. The dog blinks once before lowering its head, letting out a human-like sigh, deep and exasperated. Gareth is speaking from the kitchen, but she can't follow what he's saying. He speaks quickly and his accent is thick, pitched at an indecipherable level. She wonders if that's what she sounds like; is his accent her accent? She joins him back at the benchtop, assuming it will be easier if she can watch his mouth. Like Patrick he is intense with his eye contact, but that makes it more difficult to follow.

She looks out the window. Though Elixir is crouched down and out of sight she can hear his voice now as well. At first, she assumes he is talking to himself, but then another voice chimes in. The voices are muffled and she supposes Elixir is listening to something on his phone, except that it is Elixir's voice she can hear, and then it occurs to her that it is her own voice she can hear as well, which is impossible, because she is here, inside, and is not talking.

'Alison?' Gareth speaks clearly this time and she turns to him. His eyebrows are raised, lips parted in expectation.

'Pardon?'

'How d'you take it?' He holds up the carton of milk in his hand.

'White. Three sugars.'

He places the teabag in the sink, dashes milk into the cup. He stirs the tea and clinks the spoon against the rim. 'Neve's a lovely girl, isn't she? James has taken quite a shine to her.'

Alison takes a sip of tea. It is lukewarm and oily. She tries to listen to what Elixir is doing outside, what he's listening to, but Gareth won't stop talking. 'I'd imagine it's nice for you both to have a bit of youthful energy in the house. Especially for Patrick.'

'Why's that?'

'I just mean to say that he must be enjoying having his girl around.'

'Yes,' she says. 'I'm happy he's happy.'

'And you?'

'Sorry?'

'Are you and Neve getting along alright?'

Of course Gareth would assume the worst of her. 'We get along fine. Has she said something?'

'No, not at all,' he says. 'That's good. Very good.'

'Why are you asking?'

'No reason,' he says. 'I'm just surprised to see you here, Alison.'

Elixir appears in the doorway. He wipes his shoes on the doormat and steps inside. The dog pads over from the fireplace and leans against Elixir's leg. In one hand he's still holding the scissors and scratches the top of the dog's head with the tip of the shears. One stumble and the animal will be lobotomised. 'How's this, Alison?' he asks, jiggling the basket, full with flowers.

Alison nods. 'Grand. Thank you.'

Elixir squats, sets down the basket. He wraps his arms around the neck of the dog and murmurs nonsensical babble into its pricked ear. 'Alright, then,' he says after a moment, scruffing the top of the animal's head. 'What's next, Alison?'

When the dog moans in pleasure, it is as though a trance has broken. Alison has awoken and found herself somewhere she should not be. What on earth has she been doing all morning with this boy? Why has she come here, of all places? 'I'll tell Neve to phone when she's back,' she says, taking the basket and scissors. 'She might be a while yet.'

'Do you not need any more help?' he asks. 'I can help arrange the bouquets. I'm good at that, aren't I, Da?'

She's embarrassed by his pleading and nods at Gareth. 'Thank you for the flowers,' she says, exiting swiftly before they can try to keep her any longer.

Once outside: immediate relief, as though her whole body has been infused with oxygen. She walks down the path and turns only once she's passed the gate, half-expecting Elixir to have bounded along after her. He hasn't, but the pair of them have followed her outside and are standing side by side in the doorway, Gareth's hand on Elixir's shoulder, gawking at her as she walks away.

❧

They are in the garden when she gets home: Patrick, Shannon and Neve. They've set up a badminton set—a long, slack net, metal poles sinking into the rain-soaked ground—and he and Shannon are versing each other. Patrick's jacket is draped over the back of the wrought-iron garden bench a few yards away where Neve sits, her head on her forearms, which are resting on the matching round table. Both Patrick and Shannon seem at ease as they play, athletic and deep in concentration. The shuttlecock glides—almost invisible—over the net, a white, thin-boned bird in the process of being throttled.

Alison watches Patrick lunge for a return, swear loudly when he misses. They continue to rally and Alison goes to Neve at the bench, places the basket of flowers on the table beside her. She doesn't acknowledge Alison at first, but eventually her eyes flick to the basket. 'What are those for?'

'For you,' Alison says. 'For your birthday party.'

Neve returns her gaze to the game.

'Elixir was looking for you today.'

This perks her up. She lifts her head, glances over her shoulder towards the direction Alison walked from. 'He was here?'

'Yes.'

'Why didn't he text me?'

'He said he did.'

Neve picks up her phone from the table, taps the screen and scans it briefly before setting it down again.

'He was a great help,' Alison continues, taking a seat beside her. 'Very obedient.'

'What did he help you with?'

'This and that,' Alison says. 'He's looking forward to the party. We all are.'

Neve brings the length of her thumb to her teeth, chews at the skin there. The moment to mention what happened that morning in the woods comes and goes, and Alison is glad to put it behind them. For now, she supposes, it's a small, inconsequential secret they share; it will be forgotten by both of them eventually.

'Your turn, Neve,' Patrick calls out. He is a few paces from the net, hands on his hips.

'No, thanks,' Neve says.

'Come on,' he says. 'Don't be a spoilsport.'

'I'm not,' she says. 'I just don't want to play.'

Shannon jogs around the net towards them. 'Go on,' she says, her skin glistening.

'Fine,' Neve says, and takes the racquet.

Patrick pings the shuttlecock at Neve. Her reflexes are quick and she closes her hand around it, heads to one side of the net.

Shannon sits down beside Alison. Her cheeks are flushed and she smooths back her hair, which is tied into a high, tight ponytail. 'Bloody badminton.' She exhales. 'When did Patrick become such a snob?'

'I didn't even know we owned a badminton set.'

'We found it in the cellar,' Shannon tells her. 'It's a museum down there.'

'Take anything you want,' Alison says. 'If there's something you like you should take it.'

Shannon picks up Neve's phone from the table, types in various password combinations, then sets it down again, leans back and looks over to the game. 'Does he dress like this all the time?' she asks. 'He looks like a wanker, doesn't he?'

'He thinks of it as a uniform. Says it increases his brain power.'

Shannon laughs, rests her fist under her chin, and they watch Neve and Patrick play. Neve is surprisingly adept and looks more comfortable than Alison has ever seen her. There is a chill of cold wind; she drapes Patrick's jacket over her knees, absently digs into the pockets. One is empty. In the other is a coin, half a pellet of nicotine gum, a receipt for throat lozenges with a phone number scribbled on the back. She rips up the receipt, returns the coin, pops the gum into her mouth.

Shannon is still engrossed in the game when Alison turns to her. Without thinking it through she places her hand on the other woman's knee. It feels awkward immediately, and she tries to relax her hand, make the gesture seem less forced. 'So,' she says, 'what did Neve tell you about me?'

Shannon lets out a snort. 'Neve doesn't tell me anything.'

'You're not close?'

'Neve's always been secretive,' Shannon says. 'She's nothing like me.'

'You're very maternal, though.'

Shannon considers this for a moment. 'I wouldn't say that.'

'You are,' Alison says. 'I could feel it straight away. You being here has made me feel much better about things.'

She said it in the hope that this offering of warmth would split the other woman open, invite her to confirm something vital about herself that she's suspected. But it's true, Alison feels good, better than she has in months.

'Neve hasn't been a little shit, has she?'

'Not at all.'

Shannon shifts in place. 'I honestly thought she'd want to come home by now. I don't understand why she doesn't want to start her life.'

'Is this not a life?'

Alison is only teasing, but Shannon tries to explain herself. 'I just mean that she's never had any real interest in her father,' she says. 'And now, all of a sudden . . .' She gestures towards Neve and Patrick over at the net.

Alison takes her hand from Shannon's knee. There's a dried leaf in Shannon's hair and, feeling bold, she pulls it out, flicks it into the grass.

'She'll come back to you soon. I looked after my mother for months when she was unwell. I assume Patrick told you that. Children always end up where they're supposed to. I came back to her, and Neve will come back to you.'

Shannon claps as Neve slams a shot over Patrick's head. 'Thanks for looking after her,' she says, once they resume play. 'I'm sure it's not what you wanted.'

'She hasn't needed looking after,' Alison says. 'She hasn't needed a thing.'

Over at the net, Patrick has hit the shuttlecock into a low-hanging tree branch. He is holding his arm rigid like a pole, making dainty leaps and batting at the leaves to shake it free. When it falls from the tree and into Patrick's outstretched hand, Alison clears her throat. 'You were young when you had Neve, weren't you?'

'Just turned twenty,' Shannon replies. 'Not all that young for where I grew up. Most of my schoolfriends were on their second by then.'

Alison tries to make her voice sound breezy when she then asks, 'And what about Anya?'

Beside her, Shannon stiffens. Alison wanted Shannon to feel close to her, to confide in her, to enter into a warm nest of intimacy, but as the seconds drag on, Alison is both embarrassed and irritated by Shannon's silence, her refusal to join her there. 'I've overstepped,' she says.

Shannon shakes her head. 'You haven't,' she says. 'It's just . . .'

Alison waits for her to finish. Shannon doesn't seem all that affected by the question; her face is set in a look of enthralled intensity as she focuses on the rally, as though she is simply distracted by the game and has taken no offence. Alison decides to try a different tack. 'Have you thought about having another child?'

Shannon cracks her neck to the side, reaches up to tighten her ponytail. 'I've thought about it, sure.'

Alison waits for her to elaborate but Shannon only clasps her hands and leans into the game.

'My mother liked children,' Alison says, eager to avoid another painful silence. 'Truly adored them. She always wanted grandchildren.'

'Yeah?'

'Never happened, of course. I don't think she ever forgave me.'

Leaning back into the seat, it's clear to Alison the opportunity has passed, but she is content to simply watch Shannon watching the game, clapping or whistling whenever Neve scores a point, her face still flushed with good health and vitality. For now, being beside her is enough.

After a time, Patrick's serve hits the wooden edge of his racquet and the shuttlecock sails towards them. It bounces from the iron tabletop into the basket of flowers. Alison plucks it out. The top is smooth and round and egg-pale and she presses it into her palm.

Before she can throw it back, Patrick comes over. He swings the racquet. It makes a swooshing sound in the air. 'I'm knackered,' he says.

Alison removes the jacket from her lap. 'I'd like to play,' she says.

Patrick seems amused. 'Alright then.'

Alison takes the racquet from Neve. The tape on the handle is beginning to unravel, so Alison tears it off and wraps it around her index finger, making a tourniquet at the second knuckle. She spits the gum into the grass and is first to serve. The shuttlecock slices through the air and goes right over Patrick's head. He jogs back to retrieve it, and when he returns the serve they fall into a brief rally before he misses an easy shot, reels from the overextension. He picks up the shuttlecock and takes a few steps back. He is focusing intently and grunts when he serves. They slip into another, easy rhythm.

Alison's thighs begin to itch and the splintered wood rubs against her palm. A blister is forming but none of it feels bad. She is using muscles she hasn't used in a long time. It is invigorating, her body being awoken by the blood pumping into all these neglected nooks. She feels very much alive. Something about the loosening of her muscles seems to loosen something tightly wound in her mind, a question being asked and then immediately answered. She can see their lives stretching out in front of her like a still, clear lake.

When Patrick misses another shot he presses his hands to his thighs, doubles over and calls the game. After a moment he straightens up, holds his hands to the back of his head to catch his breath.

'Don't feel emasculated, darling,' Alison calls out.

'Fuck off, Alison,' he says, breathless.

She is taken aback and glances over to see if Shannon has heard what he said, but she and Neve have stopped paying attention and are looking at something on Neve's phone, their heads pressed together. Alison's heart is large and loud in her chest. She throws the racquet towards Patrick with the intention of hitting him, sits and then lies back on the grass to recover, puts one hand on her belly and the other on her chest, and takes deep breaths through her nose. The sky is bright and the grass smells freshly cut from that morning. Her limbs are heavy. She closes her eyes and hears Patrick's voice, then Shannon's voice. Both seem far away, as though Alison has slipped into another dimension and they are back on land, behind some sort of supernatural glaze. She keeps her eyes closed. Her breathing begins to slow. When footsteps move towards her, she can tell from the gait it's Patrick, can feel him standing over her, his body blocking the heat of the sun. She has the sensation that he is about to kick her, hard in the ribs. He has never hit her before. She doubts he's hit anyone before.

There is an inhale and she waits for him to speak, waits for the kick, the crack of stiff leather against bone, which never does come. His shadow is gone; again, there is light.

Back when they first met—six, seven years ago now—Patrick was forever trying to goad Alison into tedious, intimate conversations. *What's the worst thing you've ever done? When did your parents most let you down?* In bed after sex, over salty anchovies on buttered toast in her London flat, during walks through the lowlands every few weekends, like he was trying to uncover something precious within her, something he wanted to claim for himself. *My mother's never let me down*, she would tell him. Alison knew he didn't believe her, assumed she was concealing some essential, fragile part of herself that he was determined to nut out eventually, like a challenge, a conquering.

It was in one of those early moments he told her about Anya. He was loquacious and needy, touching her, his eyes on her. She poured fingers of Scotch and they sat cross-legged on the rug like schoolchildren. After he'd rolled and smoked a cigarette he went to his small, prim suitcase and took out a battered King James Bible, opened its mulberry leather cover to remove a photograph. She was horrifically small, cradled in Shannon's arms, a tiny, swollen-eyed doll. The side of Neve's wispy child body hovering out of focus in the background, the demonic flash of a red school uniform jumper, a blur of plaid.

Alison does not remember saying anything comforting. She stared at the photograph for a long time, until Patrick passed out with his head back on the sofa, exposing the tender knot of his Adam's apple knocking at the throat.

While they pack up the badminton net, Alison slips upstairs to look for the photograph. She goes through Patrick's things, stored in one of the spare rooms: boxes of documents, books, printed email correspondences bound together with bulldog clips. She finds it surprisingly quickly. In a drawer is a manila folder, and in the folder is an envelope, and in the envelope is the photograph. It isn't just the one he showed her that night; there are three of them secured with a paperclip. In one, Patrick is serene-faced, holding Anya—who has the expression of a jelly baby: hazy, indistinct—in his arms. The last of the set: Neve as the centrepiece, the deep red uniform as Alison remembered it.

She puts the photographs back into the folder, puts the folder away. She presses her hand to her belly and wonders if it can see her hand like a shadow, feel the warmth of her palm, God-like over the womb.

The key is tucked into a sock in the lowest drawer of her bedside table. Down to the end of the hallway, then up the staircase that spirals up the turret, into the master bedroom. The bronze key rattles in the lock as though shrunken and emaciated from lack of use. It clicks into place and Alison opens the door. She flicks on the light switch. The bulb is blown but she can see clearly enough, everything as it was: the king bed in the centre of the room, the sheets in a tangle; an empty glass on the bedside table. There's a jumper on the chair beside the bed, its arms hanging loosely over the seat, sleeves skimming the ground as though lounging in repose. The jumper was Alison's, is Alison's. Soft cashmere, lurid magenta. There are Frances's flannel pyjamas and thick wool nighties in pelts on the carpet, stacks of newspapers and magazines, more clutter on the bureau. Below the window: a wooden easel, a plastic sewing bobbin, a metal pot filled with calico, a dead field mouse mummified to a crisp, twigs wrapped in gold thread, a pincushion in the shape of an apple.

Is she here? Not a ghost of her physical self, but an imprint, perhaps, or some sort of afterglow. Alison pays attention to the air and how it feels on her skin. She waits for it to grow colder, or maybe warmer, for a prickle of something, a hand at the small of her back.

She moves to the bed. The top sheet is crumpled, the fitted sheet curled at the top-right corner, revealing greyish stains on the mattress. Alison can smell the human musk of it. It almost winds her. She sits on the end of the bed and presses her feet into the floorboards. She takes the ring from her pocket and slips it back onto her finger. She rubs the gold band, but still, the air does not turn, her mother does not appear.

There is a prickling sensation in her throat and she goes to the window, unhooks the latch and pushes at the pane. It takes all her force before it creaks and shudders open. The air is cool on her cheeks. It's baptismal and she wants to throw herself into it. Instead, she sticks her head out the window and tries to get a good, full gasp of it.

For a second her mind is blissfully blank, but when she turns around there it is: the plasticine face of her mother, exactly as she remembers it. When Alison found her, the stench of death had already set in, something foul, something antiseptic. Her eyes were closed, which Alison was grateful for, but it was her mouth that she couldn't stop looking at, opened painfully wide, as though rusted apart at the hinges. She couldn't stop thinking about what had crawled in there during the night, tapped at her teeth and burrowed into the flesh of her tongue, braved the deep well of her throat to lodge somewhere dark and damp. Too scared to look properly, Alison did other things. She clipped her mother's fingernails, wrangled her stubborn body out of soiled clothes. She filled a bucket with water and soap and, with her face turned away, sponged at her skin, towelled her dry. In the wardrobe was a new pair of pyjamas, flannel with an elastic waist, and she cut off the tags, dressed her. She propped her up on her pillow, combed out her hair. She closed the door and did not look back then went downstairs to find Patrick.

Now, Alison strips the bed. She adds the sheets to the pile of dirty clothes and bath towels. What should be washed and kept? What should be burnt? Everything, probably. There's a small dressing room beside the ensuite, and Alison begins to haul everything in there. She opens the wardrobe and takes clothes down from the hangers: Frances's polyester day dresses, heavy coats, her wedding dress, yellowed to the colour of scrambled eggs. She clears the sturdy, beige garments from the underwear drawer and the shoes stacked in their boxes, the leather polished, soles immaculately tended, all of her treasures tucked away in drawers, her fabrics and paints, delicate pressed poppies, thumbed paperbacks. Alison picks up the mouse by its tail and flings it into the dressing room. She sweeps through the bathroom, gathers the cakes of soap and the shower cap, the toothbrush and shower stool, a cloudy knob of crystal deodorant, the bottles of fragrant lotions and hand creams, bath salts and talcum powder, and when she is done, she steps back and surveys her work, the hills of junk looming. There is the sum of her mother stained into the threads of her clothes, encased behind the thread-thin ribs of the mouse, the dust of her unsettled and swirling, a toenail in the bottom of a shoe.

She's barely done any cleaning for years, and now, twice in one day! The windows first, then the floor. After mopping, she wipes the grime from the bedhead, the black, wet dust. The bath is thick with soap scum and she scrubs it hard, does the same with the toothpaste in the basin, dried to fossils. She finds another mouse behind the toilet and throws this one out the window. With great difficulty, she turns the mattress. The dust makes her sneeze, her eyes itch. She empties the mouse shit from the chest of drawers and, once everything is clean, she cleans it again.

Her knees are stiff by the time she's done, bones swelling in her back, hands sore, scaly red. In the bathroom she washes off the vinegar acidity, eager to get downstairs to Shannon and Patrick. Even Neve. Alison knew she'd been dreaming of her mother for a reason. The dreams started right as Alison began to suspect something was wrong and that she could be pregnant. She used to secretly mock her mother for her blind faith in the supernatural, but now that she's felt the power of it firsthand, she feels special, chosen. *All babies are gifts*, Frances used to say. *You are a gift, Alison. You are a gift.*

She looks into the mirror, gets right up close to it so she can see her pores, the spidery veins at the sides of her nose, the hairs in between her eyebrows, the small milky lump beneath her left eye. She feels demonic: her hair wild, eyes puffy and eerily round like discs, lips thin, as though sucked back into her mouth or chewed off. Is this how I always look? she wonders. She can see nothing delicate in her face, no warmth at all.

Downstairs, she undresses. In the wardrobe she finds rows of garment bags. She is shocked by how tiny some of them are, and unzips each until she finds a dress that looks generous enough to fit. She squeezes herself into the dress. It's tight around her ribs and shoulders, but drapes over her stomach, the silk skirt cool around her legs. In the bathroom she washes her hair in the sink, blow-dries and pins it off her face. She plucks the bristly hairs from between her eyebrows, smears

Vaseline on her chapped lips. There's a toiletry bag under the sink: pale pink alligator skin. Alison unzips the bag and rifles through the sleek tubs and tubes and wands. She opens a pot of concealer, a fingerprint fossilised into the thick, matt paste. She turns back to the mirror, dabs the concealer under her eyes, at the sides of her nose, then fills in her eyebrows, flushes her cheeks with a coral blush. Curls her eyelashes, lines her eyes, two coats of mascara. The word mascara derives from the Latin word *masca*: spectre. Patrick told her that. She makes her lips red, blots on a square of toilet paper and takes in her reflection. She hasn't thought about her face this much in a long time.

❧

It's late afternoon and Patrick is at the stove, sautéing onions. Alison walks up behind him and pats him on the bottom. She's aware of her exposed cleavage, the colour on her lips. Patrick turns around, takes in the dress. He doesn't comment on her appearance and she's simultaneously relieved and disappointed by his disinterest.

'I've been looking for you,' he says. 'I thought you might have left me.'

'I've been here. Upstairs, cleaning the master bedroom. I thought Shannon might like to sleep there for the rest of her stay.' She tries to say it nonchalantly, as though the question of what to do with Frances's room has not been a source of contention.

'You did?'

'You yourself said it's a waste of space; the best room in the house not being used for anything but storage.'

'I know,' he says. 'It's a good idea.'

'It was your suggestion.'

'I know,' he repeats. 'It's good.' He lowers the gas, adds more butter to the pan. 'Where did you put everything?' he asks. 'I could have helped you.'

'I've taken care of it.'

'Okay,' he says. 'Well, thank you. She'll appreciate it.'

'I feel embarrassed now,' Alison says, opening the fridge. 'Making her sleep in that awful children's room. A rickety old single bed! What was I thinking?'

'Shannon's very low maintenance,' he says. 'I'm sure she didn't even notice.'

'Of course she noticed.'

'Well, either way, she'll enjoy having more space.'

Empty-handed, Alison closes the fridge. 'Where is she?'

'Gone for a walk with Neve.'

'Another one? When will they be back? I want to show her the room.'

'Soon.'

'Maybe I'll just move her things up there myself. She won't mind, will she?'

She leans over the stove. The onions are clear and glistening. She's barely eaten all day but the smell of it doesn't give her an appetite. It's as though the baby is full of nutrients, keeping her sated, that they are symbiotically keeping each other alive. She hasn't felt nauseous since this morning with Neve in the woods, that final purge expelling the poison from her for good, exorcising her of something rancid.

Patrick stirs then rests the wooden spoon over the side of the pan. His eyes are wet-looking and rimmed red from cutting the onions.

Alison reaches for the spoon and continues to stir. 'Shannon's wonderful, isn't she?' she says. 'Not at all what I expected.'

'Hmm,' Patrick says, smashing a garlic clove with the back of a knife.

'I don't know why on earth you left her.'

He glances at her side on. 'Really, Alison?'

'What?'

'She left me.'

'Did she really?'

'You know this.'

She knows he's right, but every time he's told her the story she gets a slightly different version. 'Yes,' she says. 'But you seem the type who would retreat from that sort of situation. It makes more sense in terms of your personalities.'

'Well,' he says, frowning into the garlic, 'I'm not that type.'

'All I'm trying to say is that when we met, you weren't in a particularly good state of mind. And that was right after the two of you separated.' He doesn't respond and she continues. 'It just seems like something you would have done.'

Patrick takes the spoon from her hand. 'I wasn't in a good state of mind because my daughter died and my wife left me.'

It's as though she's been struck. She didn't mean to hit a nerve, and remains frozen by his side as he scrapes the minced garlic into the pot, stirs. He moves back to the table, to where Neve's birthday card is laid out, and sits down. It's not yet written in, but there is a draft version beside it on a notepad, variations of the same message, things crossed out, repeated.

'She's a good mother, isn't she?' Alison is met with silence. 'Neve's lucky to have her.' She waits for him to look up and see her face and know she isn't trying to provoke him.

He ignores her and focuses on the card. Alison stirs the pot so that the garlic doesn't burn. She lowers the heat on the stove, joins him by the table, presses her thigh to his arm. Tucked below the notebook is Alison's script.

'Were you reading this?' she asks, reaching for it, trying to reset the mood.

'Nope.'

'What's it doing in here?'

'I don't know.'

'Someone's been reading it. It's confidential.'

He rolls his eyes. 'No, it's not.'

It's opened to a scene close to the end of the first act and she squints to skim the lines, trying to make sense of her notes in the margin. They're near illegible. She doesn't remember writing them, doesn't even remember thinking them.

When Alison places her hand on his shoulder, her touch seems to soften him. The nib of his Montblanc hovers over the paper and he exhales as though releasing a great tension deep within his body, tilts his head back so that his ear nuzzles against her wrist. 'Neve will have a good time tomorrow, won't she?'

'Yes,' Alison says. 'Why wouldn't she?'

'I wonder if we should be doing more for her. Maybe we should have let her decide how to spend the day. We've forced a party on her when she didn't want it.'

'You don't want to spoil her.' She squeezes his shoulder, traces a crease on his neck with the tip of a finger, making the reedy muscles flutter involuntarily.

He takes her hand, strokes the back of her knuckles. 'It could be a disaster. We hired a Michelin-starred chef, for God's sake. It's not Neve at all.'

'Stop your worrying. It won't be a disaster.'

'How do you know?'

It all rushes into her at once: Frances and the chanterelles, everything cleaving together, something cresting inside her. 'Because,' she says, 'I have something planned. An announcement.'

Patrick puts down the pen. 'What kind of announcement?'

'It's a surprise.'

He raises his eyebrows. 'Neve hates surprises. Always has.'

'It's not for Neve,' she says, picking up the script again. She leans down and kisses him on the forehead, which is damp and cool. 'It's for everybody, darling.'

She pours herself a glass of water, finds a multivitamin in the pantry. It's expired but she takes it anyway. Soon, she'll need to see a doctor: get bloods taken and an ultrasound; take iron supplements, folic acid, vitamin D. She needs to start looking after herself. Already she's been so careless, about so many things, but she doesn't let herself feel guilty. There's been enough of that already. She's carried it around inside herself like rot.

# SHANNON

FOR ALL THREE FLIGHTS SHANNON is wide awake: Sydney to Singapore, Singapore to Heathrow, Heathrow to Edinburgh. Twenty-seven hours in transit, none of which she remembers with any precision, not the meals nor the trashy rom-coms, the vodka, lime and sodas that went right to her head. After landing she is wrecked but her senses grow wildly alert when she leaves the tarmac and is back on steady ground; the fluorescent lights in the airport bathroom haloing around her, the smell of urine crusted to the underside of the toilet bowl. Her exhaustion is too deep to be uncomfortable and she fumbles through the routine of brushing her teeth and running a wet wipe over her face and neck, reapplying moisturiser and eye cream. She knows they are waiting for her in arrivals but she takes her time. Let him wait, she thinks. Let him wait.

She will still be jet-lagged by the time she flies back home. A four-day trip; almost as much time spent in transit as on land. She's never been to Scotland before but there'll be no time to sightsee. Not that she wants to. She doesn't like the cold. She doesn't much like the outdoors anymore. Neve has sent her pictures of the house and it looks completely uninviting. She hopes the weekend passes quickly and she can finally get on with her life.

The plane ticket was a drunken impulse buy; she was three cocktails deep when her new work friend Spence asked her about the mythical Patrick. He is a filthy gossip and probed, then was horrified by her answer, which is why she usually skims over the earlier details of their relationship whenever anyone shows interest. She hadn't even realised the trip fell over Neve's birthday until she opened the invoice on her laptop the following morning and the dates glared back at her, the previous night's conversation returning to her in mortifying fragments. She remembered Spence's face in the bar when she told him about the piano lessons and the sleepovers, and how ever since she feels as though her life belongs to him. There were things she told Spence she'd never told anyone, that she hadn't thought about for decades. She wondered where it came from, why it chose to rise to the surface at that particular moment.

She could have cancelled the trip—she hadn't messaged Neve or Patrick to let them know her plan—but there was something niggling away at her, a voice telling her to go. It's not that she wants to punish him. They were married, after all—are still married, in fact. They had children together. Any reasonable person would simply send an email or make a phone call, but she knew she'd find excuses to put it off, and off, and off . . .

She is tense as she queues for passport control. Though she chats effortlessly with the Border Force officer, inside is a slow and steady seethe. She feels powerful, like she is on a mission which will bring about a great, furious reckoning. Past the baggage claim, out to arrivals. And just like that, all that anger she's been holding on to since she booked the ticket and really started thinking about things (although, she realises now that she's been turning things over for much longer than that, at least since Anya), all that tension, dissipates. There is Patrick, as lovely and striking as ever. She lets herself be folded into him, his festive prickle, the smell of him hallucinogenic. She feels herself let it all go, that thick, sludgy build-up in her body. Here: the two people she loves the most. Neve holds her hand in the back seat for the long, flat drive. Shannon lets herself enjoy it while it lasts. She lets herself forget why she is there. Lets herself forget what he has done to her life.

Shannon passes out in Neve's bed soon after she arrives, but the following morning they drive into the village for bitter Americanos, walk through the fairytale moss of the woods, the wind scraping at her face, arms linked with Neve's until her daughter shrugs her off. Though drained, Shannon wants to suck up as much of Neve as possible. She was never like this back in Sydney. When Neve was born, Patrick mocked the kinds of women who were obsessed with their children. How small their lives must be for their babies to become the centre of things. Patrick found it middle class and embarrassing. He had more money than anyone could ever need, three times over, yet considered himself to have the authenticity of the working class, to be above gender reveals and babymoons, an inverse sort of snobbery. His disdain towards trendy parenting practices must have worked, because living with Neve was like having a quiet, self-reliant roommate. She came out fully formed, and for that Shannon was secretly proud, but she knew it had nothing to do with either of them. They didn't quite know what to do with her so they didn't do anything, and suddenly there she was, a complete being who barely needed looking after.

Though Neve doesn't question Shannon's newfound neediness, she gives her little in return, is vague about what she does all day long, what she thinks of Alison, how she's getting along with Patrick. So mostly Shannon talks. Neve nods politely at the right times as Shannon rambles on. She asks questions, but absently, like she is doing her mother a favour and doesn't particularly care about her answers, the way you would talk to a small child only just capable of having the most basic of conversations. Shannon thinks Neve seems smaller here. She's lost weight, yes, but it is more profound than that, as if a delicate layer of bone has been shaved back. There is something off about her, something unfamiliar and distant. Shannon has an unshakable feeling that after she flies home on Sunday she'll never see her daughter again; Neve will continue to shrink right down into something hard and unmovable, unreachable and lost to her for good.

'How are you really?' Shannon asks. It's the day after she arrived. That morning they walked for a long time and both have blisters on their heels. Neve has made tea and they are on opposite ends of the sofa in the library, their socked feet lightly touching. 'Are you having an okay time?'

'I've told you already,' Neve says. 'It's fine. It's good.'

'Is Dad spending time with you?'

'Yeah,' she says. 'Enough.'

'I've barely seen him.'

'You haven't even been here a whole day.'

Shannon recognises something snarky in her daughter's voice, but when she glances over, Neve's face is empty. Shannon thinks back to when Neve was in primary school. She hated school camp, and every year Shannon would get a call late at night from Neve, who would be inconsolable, crouched in the bathroom whisper-crying into the phone. Shannon loved getting those calls. She anticipated them; the absolute confidence that they were coming made her giddy. She loved hearing her daughter's raw distress, the opportunity to properly soothe her. Neve showed little emotion at home towards either of her parents, but knowing that there was this fierce part of her that wanted to be somewhere familiar made Shannon feel hitched to Neve. So often she thought that Neve could just drift away at any moment, but those phone calls were proof that despite Neve's apparent ambivalence towards her, at her core her daughter loved her, needed her. Until now, at least.

'What about Alison?' Shannon asks. She met Alison briefly for the first time that morning. It was anticlimactic. She looks more like Patrick in real life than in pictures on the internet; far more eccentric, far less polished. It's only after seeing Alison in person that she can understand it, her and Patrick. She seems unknowable, unpredictable; deeply, uncomfortably odd.

'What about her?'

'She's stunning, isn't she?' Shannon takes a sip of tea. 'I mean, I knew she would be, but in person she's gorgeous.'

'I guess so.'

'She's weird, though, right?'

'All actors are weird.'

'It's not that,' Shannon says. 'She's awkward.'

Neve shrugs. 'Maybe she's jealous.'

Shannon snorts. 'What would she be jealous of?'

'Of you, obviously.'

Ridiculous, Shannon thinks, and looks to the fireplace: the burnt logs in the pit, grey flecks of ash. 'She's lovely. She is, really. A bit unsocialised, though.'

She wants to latch on to something hefty, something with a bit of meat to it. With Patrick, their few, brief interactions have been jokey and membrane-thin. She's been trying to figure out how to talk to him properly. It is why she's here: to address it head on, hold him accountable. 'Do you know where Dad and I met?' she asks Neve.

Neve shrugs, scratches her nose. 'In Wantarra.'

'Yeah,' she says, 'of course. But do you know how?'

'Swimming, I think. Or something. I don't know.'

Shannon's voice comes out in a register higher than she is familiar with. 'How'd you know that?'

'I don't know. You must have told me.'

'I don't think I told you that.'

'Dad then,' her daughter mumbles. 'I don't know.'

Shannon sips her tea. She is grateful that Neve has never seemed curious about her and Patrick, about how they met. Shannon feels a headache coming on. She imagines hot concrete against her thighs, ant bites, sunburn.

There's a flash of something at the window. Shannon's first thought is that it's an animal, something dark and large and vaguely humanoid, and she startles and makes a small, pathetic noise in the back of her throat, sloshes Earl Grey over her hands. She doesn't have her contact lenses in, but after she sets down her cup and dries her hands on her leggings she looks again properly to see it's only Patrick, standing outside peering in at them. He taps at the window then disappears, and a moment later he announces himself from the doorway. 'What a pair of lazy cats,' he says.

Shannon cranes her neck around so she can see his face. 'I'm on holidays,' she says. 'I'm allowed to be lazy.'

'What are you gossiping about then?'

'I don't gossip.'

'I love gossip.'

'I know you do.'

'Tell me then.'

He enters the room and gently pushes their feet aside, sits between them, his arms drape around the both of their shoulders, pulling them closer. His fingertips graze Shannon's neck. It gives her goosebumps. He'll be able to feel them flare up like a rash, and she is angry at her biology for betraying her so shamelessly.

'I like Alison,' Shannon says. She turns to face Patrick. 'I really do.'

'She's been behaving herself.'

'How does she usually behave?'

'She's far crueller.'

'Poor thing.'

'It's a compliment.'

'No, it's not,' she says. 'I hope you don't say that to her face.'

'She knows she's mean,' he says. 'She revels in it. She likes to make people feel bad.'

'Don't be so dramatic.'

'I'm being truthful, Shannon.'

'You probably just give her the shits,' she says. 'Imagine being stuck out here with no one but you to talk to. I'd want to torture you as well.'

She didn't mean it, but knows it sounded spiteful. He doesn't jab back, lets the comment disintegrate. 'She has Neve now as well,' he says. 'They're getting on famously, aren't you, Neve?'

Neve nods, takes a sip of tea. Shannon waits for him to turn back to her, but he stays angled towards Neve. 'Shall we do something, daughter?'

Neve's hands are around her mug. She presses the rim against her chin, looks up at him, sleepy-eyed and slightly suspicious. 'Like what?'

'Let's play a game,' he says, standing abruptly. 'I need some exercise. I feel fat.'

He looms over them. The cuffs of his pants are rolled too short and Shannon can see a thin flash of ankle. Recently, Shannon had been sleeping with a man far younger than herself who wore his clothes like that: ankles and wrists on display, provocatively, like he was showing off cleavage. He took finasteride pills to stop his hairline receding and Shannon once found a pot of La Mer in his overnight bag. Despite Shannon's strict Pilates schedule, her rotation of salon appointments, he was by far the vainer of the two of them. As they all eventually did, he began to disgust her, and she imagined suffocating him with a pillow while he snored, slack-jawed, beside her. He was the one to end things, over text, gutless.

The three of them trudge into the daylight. Patrick leads them to a small cavity attached to the side of the house. He jemmies open the stiff, paint-chipped door and it opens creakily. The smell of it is mould and coolness, a crypt. They descend a small flight of stairs to a room full of junk: old furniture, stacked cardboard boxes, a pair of rusted bicycles. 'Maybe there's a ball,' Patrick says. 'Or a cricket bat!'

The cellar is brown with dust, and with little enthusiasm, Neve begins to sift through things while Patrick plunges into the dark. Shannon sneezes three times in succession, and goes back up the steps for clean air. She can feel dust in her lungs, particles of it clinging like spores onto the damp tissue of her insides.

After a few minutes Patrick makes a gleeful sound and comes back up the stairs, emerging into the light with his arms full, Neve trailing behind him. They follow him onto the grass. Shannon sneezes again. They wait for him to shake out a dishevelled net, his white shirt streaked with dirt.

'Go set it up, Neve,' he says, once the net is untangled.

Neve squints up at him. 'You're the one who wanted to play.'

'Do as you're told, daughter.'

Neve takes the net and poles, trudges over to a patch of grass. 'Here?' she calls out.

Patrick gives her a thumbs-up and she begins to erect the net. He crouches down and takes the racquets out of their square wooden cases, taps them on the grass to shake off more dust. They are old-fashioned, the frames also made of wood, the strings the same stiff, grey wire of a cello.

'Daughter,' Shannon says.

'Hey?'

'You called her "daughter".'

'Well, she is my daughter.'

'I've never heard you call her that before.'

'I don't know what to tell you,' he says. 'She's my daughter. Unless there's something you'd like to tell me?'

'I'm not having a go.'

He stands up straight, plucks the strings of one racquet before handing it to her, keeping the other for himself. 'How's everything, then?'

'Everything's great,' she replies. 'The same.'

'Have I passed the test?'

'What test?'

He looks at her sceptically. 'Well, you're here to check up on me. Make sure I'm not being a deadbeat.'

Shannon scoffs. 'I'm here for Neve's birthday,' she says. 'It's her eighteenth. It means something.'

'I'm sure that's why you're here,' he says, eyebrows raised.

'Don't be such a narcissist,' she says. 'I'm here to be with Neve.'

She sees a flash of pain on his face. She's offended him again and it wasn't even on purpose. 'I've never said you were a shit parent,' she says. 'I've never even thought it.'

Running his hand through his hair, he notices the dirt on his sleeve. He rubs at it with his palm, spits on his fingers, rubs again.

They watch Neve as she sets up the net. She moves slowly and deliberately, everything precise. Stepping back and measuring with her eyes, making things line up. 'God, she's quiet, isn't she?' Patrick says. 'Was she always this quiet?'

Shannon doesn't say anything. She doesn't want to talk about Neve.

'Maybe she's depressed,' he continues. 'Do you think she's depressed?'

'That's Neve,' she says. 'This is what she's like. You know that.'

Shannon looks sideways at Patrick. His hands are on his hips and he's watching Neve intently still. That's the closest they ever get to acknowledging what they both knew to be true. If they said it out loud it would be a betrayal, like horrible, malicious gossiping. When Shannon fell pregnant with Neve, the first thing Patrick said was that having a baby at her age was bohemian; any younger would be trashy. He asked if she was considering a termination, but Shannon knew that if she had the baby, Patrick would be tied to her for life. At the time, she was so in love that the thought of Patrick changing his mind about her and disappearing again made her physically ill. When Neve was still an infant, they had long, romantic conversations about the type of person they hoped she'd become, but as she grew it became obvious that she'd gone rogue, spitefully, as if on purpose. Recently, Shannon wonders if they are being punished. The universe's way of telling them that, actually, they were wrong; they shouldn't have had children, or not together at least. And perhaps that's what Anya was as well: another sign telling them they'd made a terrible mistake. Whatever it was they had was punishable. They were being punished.

Patrick is still watching Neve. Shannon used to be able to guess at what he was thinking. He isn't as complicated as most people assume, but everything here seems to be off kilter. Patrick especially—with his slicked-back hair, his crisp, ironed shirts—is different here. When she imagined this trip over the past month, she'd pictured a grand, dramatic confrontation, had rehearsed her speech in her head on the plane over, but now it all seems melodramatic and perhaps even unnecessary and she cannot think of what to say in its place. 'You've been avoiding me,' she says, when she needs to say something.

Patrick lets out a sharp, exasperated laugh, but still, he doesn't look at her. 'You're kidding.'

'No.'

'What do you think we're doing right now?'

'It's like you can't be bothered.' It's not what she wanted to say. She doesn't know how to be direct with him. She feels like a schoolgirl, nervous and mortified by her own existence, expecting someone older and more intelligent to take pity on her and fill in the gap, steer the conversation in the right direction.

'Okay,' he says with irritation. He doesn't ask her to clarify and picks at a piece of splintered wood on the rim of the racquet.

Her hands are hot. She presses them against her cheeks before taking a breath. Now, she thinks. Do it now. 'I've been thinking about something. I think I should say it.'

He waits a moment. 'Yeah?'

'It's about when we were in Wantarra. When we first started going out.'

Another pause. 'Go on then.'

She sighs. 'Not with Neve here.'

'You're the one who brought it up, Shannon. If you have something to say, say it.'

'Let's go inside for a minute. Can we?'

'Don't tell me then,' he says. There's a sneer in his voice, a glimmer of contempt she's never heard from him before. 'I don't want to know.'

'Are you serious?'

'I honestly can't be bothered, Shannon. I know what you're going to say.'

This surprises Shannon; maybe he *has* been avoiding her. 'Okay,' she says. 'What am I going to say then?'

He bounces the racquet against his knee, stares straight ahead. In front of them, a tree branch cracks and drops gently to the ground. They watch it fall, settle in the grass. 'You're going to accuse me of something.'

She feels a roiling deep in her bowels. It's as though he's blocked her from going any further. She feels sick, and then desperately stupid. He knows her too well; his territory marked all over her. She's covered in his scent, in his hot, wet piss.

He doesn't wait for a response, does not give her a chance. 'Come on, then,' he says, and just like that a switch is flicked, everything forgotten or pushed down somewhere inaccessible. It is like he is saying: *Now is not the time; there will never be a time. I have not done anything wrong.* He picks up the shuttlecock and strides out onto the grass. When he reaches Neve he devours her in a hug, kisses the top of her head, looking over at Shannon as he does so, making sure she is watching: *See what a good father I am; see how well it's all turned out.* He lets Neve go and stretches his arm, whacks the shuttlecock over the net with all of his force, the entire angry knot of his wiry body coming loose. It goes spiralling, spiralling, spiralling into the tree.

Shannon decides to put off bringing up Wantarra again until later, and dinner that evening is pleasant, for the most part. Patrick is in a better mood, and Alison is charmingly bratty, so much so that Shannon thinks she could easily be the youngest of many siblings, though she knows that is not the case. They talk about sweet, gentle Nick—Patrick's best friend and old band mate—whom Alison has only met once but does a remarkable impression of, sad-drunk and pining over a different woman each week.

'I saw Nick last month,' Shannon interrupts. She hadn't planned on bringing it up, had even told Nick not to tell Patrick they'd spoken. She didn't want to give Patrick the chance to come up with some smooth, neat justification. 'We had drinks.'

'How was he?' Alison asks.

'Miserable, as usual,' Shannon says. 'He's the one who told me about Jock, all that shit that happened in Thailand.'

'Right,' Patrick says. 'I didn't realise you were in touch.'

'He's Neve's godfather,' she says. 'Why wouldn't we be in touch?'

'What else did you talk about then?'

'Nothing worth mentioning. He's sending you a present, Neve. Said to tell you happy birthday.'

In fact, they had talked about Patrick mostly, at length. Shannon and Patrick and Wantarra. Shannon barely knew Nick back then. Nick barely knew Shannon. They orbited each other, never quite connecting, which, in hindsight, was probably Patrick's doing. Nick apologised, nonetheless. He said she seemed older back then. He said he didn't realise it was going on, not in any way he could clearly discern. He thought she had a crush, that Patrick felt sorry for her, was letting her be a hanger-on.

'You should meet Gareth while you're here,' Patrick says to Shannon. 'He's a lot like Nick.'

Across the table, Alison laughs. 'He's nothing like Nick.'

'Well, he makes me miss Nick less then.'

'Remember when we first moved here, Patrick?' Alison says. 'Gareth would be over every other day, nosing around, demanding to see Frances.'

'He wasn't demanding,' Patrick says. 'They were friends.'

'She was completely demented by then. She could barely communicate.'

'He was just being neighbourly.'

'He didn't even know her.' She turns her full attention to Shannon. 'It was all very strange,' she says conspiratorially. 'He makes me feel quite uncomfortable, actually. There's something not right about him.'

'He's nice,' Neve says, tracing her fork along the plate. It is the first time she's joined the conversation all night.

'He's not *nice*,' Alison says. 'He's a cretin, weaselling his way in with you, Patrick—and now you too, Neve!'

Patrick turns and stage-whispers to Shannon, 'Alison gets worked up about Gareth. I think she might have a bit of a thing for him.'

'That's absurd, Patrick,' Alison says.

'Is it?'

'He called the police on us,' she says, thumping her hand down on the table emphatically. Her eyes are feverish and Shannon realises Alison is enjoying herself. 'And you've just gone ahead and forgiven him.'

'He thought he was doing the right thing.'

'Why did he call the police?' Shannon asks, finding it hard to keep up.

Alison stares at Patrick. It is clear she's not going to be the one to explain. Patrick sighs, which morphs into a strained chuckle. He picks at the corner of his napkin, folds it into a square as he speaks. 'He was concerned about Frances, before she died. He thought Alison was unhinged.'

Alison takes over. 'He was trying to get Frances to put him in her will. He was probably planning on swooping in the minute she died.'

'She's joking,' Patrick says to Shannon.

'I'm not joking,' Alison says. 'His bags were already packed!'

Shannon is enraptured by the back and forth; again, she can see how they must be together, with no one else around. There is a spark there, something tense and volatile. She has a brief, sickening image of them in bed together, bovines consuming each other. 'Well, it sounds complicated.'

Another pause. The clinking of a glass. 'I spoke with him today, actually,' says Alison.

'I didn't know he came around,' Patrick says. 'You should have come to get me.'

'He didn't,' she says. 'I went to see him.'

'What?' Patrick looks startled. 'Where?'

'At his home, of course,' Alison replies. She motions in its direction, as though the cottage is visible through the walls.

'You went over there?'

'Why do you sound so surprised?'

'I'm not surprised,' he says. 'It's good. It's great.'

'We needed flowers for tomorrow,' is all she says.

'And . . .'

'And his house reeks like a crematorium. Plus, his dog is hideous.'

'Well then,' Patrick says, 'those are excellent reasons not to like someone.'

'It was interesting to see where you always disappear to,' Alison says. 'I still don't understand what you see in him, though. You're not at all alike.'

Shannon wonders what it would be like to be on the receiving end of Alison's wrath, her radiating disapproval. She has the sense that Alison would be able to sniff out unworthiness, write someone off based on nothing but a hunch. She feels sorry for Gareth and has an urge to defend him. 'He can't be that bad, can he?' Shannon asks. 'Neve seems to think he's alright.'

Alison seems taken aback, lowers her fork and addresses Neve directly. 'What exactly is it you like about him?'

Neve looks up from her plate and gives a defeated half-shrug. A pink rash begins to stretch up her throat like a handprint. 'I don't know,' she mumbles. 'Elixir likes him. And he gave me a job.'

'Well, of course Elixir likes him,' Alison says. 'Gareth's his father. He has to like him.'

'You didn't like your father,' says Patrick.

'My father was a beast.'

'What's your point, Alison?'

'No point,' she replies after taking a bite of food. She points the prongs of her fork at Neve. 'Don't tell Elixir any of this,' she says. Her mouth is full, voice muffled. She swallows. 'Actually,' she continues, 'tell him. I couldn't care less.'

'Gareth is a lovely man,' Patrick says to Shannon. 'I'm very fond of him.'

'Well, it seems I've been overruled,' Alison says. 'Invite him to your party, Neve.'

Shannon tries to catch Neve's eye, but her daughter is trying, it seems, to look everywhere but her mother's face: the plate, her nails, the high plaster ceiling. Across the table, Alison leans back in her chair, as though she has completed a vigorous workout and is drained of all energy. She looks up at Shannon and smiles, her face bright and full of warmth. And where is Patrick during all of this? Oblivious to all things; unshakable, and as slippery as oil.

They'd eaten late and the conversation soon slows. Neve goes to bed first, then Patrick retreats outside to the studio. He kisses Alison full on the mouth on his way through, and they don't speak again until he's left the room, until they hear the back door lurch closed, a gust of cold, the quiet. A minute later, his studio light flicks on through the window and, like a signal for them to commence, they gather the plates and glasses and take them into the kitchen. When Shannon makes a start on the dishes Alison appears at her side, takes the plate she is rinsing from her hands. 'Patrick will do it in the morning,' she says, discarding it into the sink so carelessly that Shannon is surprised it doesn't shatter to pieces. 'He's good at that sort of thing.'

'What sort of thing? Cleaning up?'

'Following orders.'

Alison pours Shannon another glass of wine and directs her into the library. They sit across from each other, Shannon on the sofa, Alison on the high-backed wooden chair. The fire was lit before dinner and the dying embers look volcanic, flecks of pulsing lava. Alison undoes the stumpy braid from her hair, shakes it out, then ties it into a low, loose bun. They haven't been alone together yet and Shannon can't think of what to say. She is good with people, knows how to find a common ground, but Alison doesn't seem receptive to her in that way.

Shannon gazes over at the portrait of Patrick and Alison on the wall beside the fireplace. The painting itself is technically impressive—or so she supposes; what does she know about art?—but she is amused that they consider themselves to be as important as aristocracy, worthy of being preserved in the annals of history.

'Great painting,' she says.

Alison glances over to see what Shannon is talking about. 'It doesn't look a thing like me.'

'You don't think?'

'I look deformed.'

While Shannon was just being polite when she complimented the painting, the more she looks, the more taken she is with it. Though beautiful, Alison's own, real-life face is too particular to be intimidating or even enviable. Her features are large and distinctive, yet somehow elegant and striking in concert, like an Easter Island statue or a Picasso. The painting captures her force and makes her look Amazonian compared to Patrick, whose narrow back is turned to the artist. His proportions are wrong, but perhaps that's intentional. He looks slight and inferior and unworthy of being paired with someone so commanding.

'You look like you,' Shannon says. 'You look beautiful.'

Finally, Alison turns to look at the painting properly, gives herself a chance to reassess. 'I loathe it,' she says. 'Patrick organised it. He tries so hard but he has no aesthetic sense.'

Shannon is surprised by this, and somewhat vindicated. Patrick—who, in Sydney, would evaluate her outfit before they went anywhere they would be photographed, dispersing his arbitrary style rules like an expert; would ask her what wine she wanted with dinner, and then order what he preferred, the heaviest red, even if she was having fish—has no taste.

'Don't tell him I said that,' Alison adds. 'He's so sensitive he'll probably take the painting down and slash it.'

Alison sips her water, places it on the coffee table, then crosses her legs. At some point she'd slipped her socks off and a single toe pokes out from beneath the hem of her dress. She looks out the window, the illuminated studio a yellow, dazzling cocoon, and then turns to Shannon. 'Do you think you'll be a mumsy or a crone?'

'Sorry?'

'When women reach a certain age, they either become warm and soft—a mumsy—or harsh and sharp—a crone.'

Shannon is rattled by the question. She wonders if it is a trick and her answer will reveal something essential about herself, will allow Alison to divine the palm lines of her life. 'Which are you going to be?' she asks, playing along.

'A crone,' Alison says.

'How can you tell?'

'My mother was a crone,' she says. 'It's all in the genes.'

Alison holds out her hands. Her fingers are long and thin. The tips of her nails translucent, like raw scallops. 'They look like skeleton fingers,' Alison says. 'They look like an X-ray. It's like I'm gazing at my own death.'

'What will I be, then?' Shannon asks, already knowing the answer. She considers her own hands: small, plump paws.

'You'll be a mumsy,' Alison confirms. She takes Shannon's hand and examines it. 'Definitely a mumsy.'

From what Neve had told her, from what she'd read online, Shannon expected Alison to be cold and intimidating—which she is—but it's her oddness that is most unsettling and makes Shannon feel dull and without personality. She often felt that way around Patrick too, as though the deep core of her is fundamentally conservative. If not for him she has no doubt where she'd be: back in Wantarra, having never left. A nine-to-five job and a mortgage on an estate house. Average body. Terrible hair. There'd be no Neve, or there'd be a sort of Neve made with the DNA of someone else: a sturdy, oafish tradie, someone simple and undemanding. None of Patrick in this alternate Neve, not even a speck. She'd have had more children. A different rendering of Anya, one compatible with life. She would have known different kinds of pain.

'Is your mother still with us?' Alison asks.

Thinking about Debbie, especially now, makes Shannon feel drained. 'Yes,' she says. 'She's back home. In Wantarra.'

'Neve's never mentioned her,' Alison says. 'Nor Patrick. I thought she might have passed.'

'She's alive alright. She's outrageous.'

'Do you not get on?'

Shannon is not angry at her mother, for any of it, but something hard chips away at her regardless. 'Oh, we get on okay,' she says. 'She's a nut but we get on.'

'Wantarra's far from Sydney, isn't it?'

'It's not close.'

'Would you move back?' she asks. 'To be nearer to your mother?'

'Sydney's home now,' Shannon says. 'I wouldn't go back to Wantarra to live. It's miserable—surely Patrick told you that?'

'I mean, if you were to have another child,' Alison says. 'You'd need the help. Patrick said you don't have family in Sydney.'

'I have Neve.'

'But Neve's here.'

The wine has made Shannon woozy, her face relaxed. She wonders if they always drink this much, or if it's just because she's here, because it's an occasion. It seems as if someone is always putting a drink in front of her, topping up her glass. She doesn't know the time, but has the feeling the night has stretched out and been impossibly long already.

'Look at you,' Alison says, as Shannon stifles a yawn. 'I'm sure you want to sleep.'

'I'm wide awake actually,' Shannon replies. 'I'm all out of sync still. You go to bed, though.'

'Oh, I don't sleep.'

Shannon sips at her drink, looks around the room for something else to cling on to. 'How's that coming along?' Shannon asks, spying what she assumes is the screenplay on the other chair. 'Patrick said it's a pretty big deal.'

'Not really,' Alison says.

'He said he and Neve are going to go to Ireland with you.'

Alison looks over at the script. 'I'm not going to do it, actually.'

'Right,' Shannon says. 'I thought . . .'

'I was never going to do it. I got carried away.' Alison leans over to pick up the script and leafs through it. 'It doesn't interest me anymore,' she says. 'And I was never any good at it, really.'

Shannon thinks about complimenting her, mentioning one of her films, but Alison is right. She wasn't very good. Alluring, yes, but one-note and incapable of true transformation. She seemed to always play the same version of herself, over and over, until each performance was an imitation of the one previous.

'And what's the point, anyway?' Alison continues. 'I mean, really, what's the point of it?'

'It's art, I suppose,' Shannon says.

'It's farcical when we'll all be dead before long.'

'You sound like Neve.'

'Well, Neve's a smart girl.' She tosses the script back onto the side table. 'There are more important ways to spend a life.'

'Do it for the money then.'

'I have money,' Alison says. 'Plenty of it.'

Shannon feels the familiar ripple of shame. After Patrick left he still sent her money—for child support, yes, but far more than was necessary, far more than she and Neve needed. There was no formal arrangement, no court-ordered alimony. She was paid well for a TV show from a few years back—soon after Patrick finally moved out—that mostly involved completing masochistic obstacle courses in a bathing suit and withstanding hours of mental torture, but she burnt through it swiftly, as though the money was dirty and needed to be laundered as quickly as possible to get it off her hands. Recently, she finished her training and has started leading a few classes a week at the gym, but her weekly pay is a fraction of what Patrick continues to funnel through. At least Alison had worked for her money. At least she'd earnt it in a noble, pure way.

Unfolding her legs from beneath her, Shannon realises she is tired. Exhausted even. If she doesn't leave now the night will continue on. It will be endless. As Shannon stands, begins to say goodnight, Alison grabs hold of her elbow. 'I left something in your room,' she says, rising and taking the lead towards the staircase, up to the master where Shannon had moved in to that afternoon. Shannon follows Alison, watching her hair, which has fallen out of her bun to sit lumpenly at the nape of her neck. Shannon has an urge to reach out and touch it. When she was a child she loved Debbie's hair: dirty blonde, smelling of sweat and coconut. Shannon would play hairdressers: wrap a tea towel around her mother's neck, spritz her hair with the spray bottle Debbie used to iron her work uniform, tease the hair with a fine-tooth comb, adorn it with butterfly clips and glittery scrunchies and set it with hairspray. The stray hairs floated around her and she would wrap the yellow threads tight around her fingertips until they started to pulse. She wanted to be a hairdresser, all through school. When had she decided not to? She hadn't thought of that in ages.

Alison lets them in to the master and turns on the light. For something to do Shannon goes straight to the window, jams it open. The outside is dark and a cold breeze comes in. When she turns around Alison is hovering and Shannon apologises for the state of the room. 'It's a mess,' she says, which isn't entirely true. Her sleek Samsonite suitcase is pushed against the wall. A sports bra is hooked over the handle of the bathroom door. The bed is made, but sloppily, Neve's birthday presents piled in the centre, purchased from the airport gift shop and still in their shopping bags: silk pyjamas, a pair of navy Ugg boots, a tennis bracelet she knows Neve will hate. None of it is to her daughter's taste. Shannon doesn't even know what Neve's tastes are.

Alison moves to the bed and grazes her hand on the quilt, then idly reaches for a bag, squeezes the package and continues to assess the room. When Shannon relocated upstairs, the room smelt clinical, of bleach and vinegar. Neve had helped her put on fresh sheets, held the stool steady as she replaced the light bulb. When Neve went downstairs Shannon opened the wardrobes—empty—and then the dressing room beside the ensuite. She thought it would be as stark as the rest of the room, but it was piled high with the chaotic junk of a hoarder, of someone's private history. She had the feeling that she'd seen something she shouldn't have, felt embarrassed as she closed the door.

Alison walks over to the ensuite. The tap is dripping. Shannon has placed a cup beneath it to catch the water, but the cup is now full and the water is lapping over the sides and into the basin. Shannon has left a wet towel draped over the side of the bathtub. She is sure she's left a used tampon by the sink and hopes that Alison won't go in any further, is relieved when she shuts the door and turns back to Shannon.

'I'm sorry if I've been strange tonight,' Alison says from the doorway. 'We don't have company very often.'

'Oh,' Shannon says. 'You haven't been.'

Alison nods slowly, seems to be deep in contemplation. 'Have you seen her?'

'Seen who?'

'My mother,' Alison says. 'I thought you might have seen her.'

Air catches in Shannon's throat. The woman in front of her suddenly looks unsteady and fragile and slightly deranged. She looks like an older version of the same quietly unstable character she played over and over in her films, finally leant into madness, beginning a sharp descent. Shannon doesn't know what to say. She wonders if she should go and get Patrick. Alison must have noticed a look on her face, because something sparks inside her and she is back to normal. 'Nothing like that,' she scoffs. 'I'm not insane.'

'I know you're not,' Shannon says. 'I didn't think you meant—'

'Her spirit is what I mean to say, I suppose,' Alison says. 'But I don't think that's quite the word for it.' Shannon can't tell if Alison is joking, or if she has actually lost her mind. 'You'll tell me, though, if you do?'

Assuming now she is being serious, Shannon tries to match her solemnity without laughing. 'Yes,' she says. 'I will.'

Satisfied, Alison nods. 'I'll let you sleep then.' She assesses the room again, and again makes no attempt to leave.

'You needed something?' Shannon prompts.

'Pardon?'

'You said you left something up here.'

Alison glances around the room, turns to Shannon and smiles. 'It's not urgent,' she says, stepping towards Shannon and wrapping her into a hug. 'I'll get it later.' Their bodies slot together awkwardly and Shannon is stunned by the sudden gesture of intimacy. There is something rigid about Alison's body. It's like holding a mannequin, Shannon thinks, as she relaxes her limbs and tries to retreat from her embrace. Alison follows suit and lets go, but rather than stepping back she leans in and kisses Shannon gently on the side of the mouth. Shannon is taken aback but does not pull away. It is as chaste as kissing a nun or a grandmother, lips dry, mouths closed, but for those few seconds something electric passes between them. Like a neglected child, Shannon is flattered by the attention, by being singled out and seen by someone remarkable, and is overcome by a pounding echo of hollowness when Alison steps back and drifts through the door as though nothing astonishing had occurred.

Shannon stands paralysed for a moment. The residual thrill she felt from the kiss has evaporated completely now that Alison is out of sight. She shuts the window and sits on the bed. Feeling generous, she looks around and tries to intuit something otherworldly around her. But the room is just a room. The air is only air. The light bulb has heated up and is shockingly bright. The rest of the house is softly and warmly lit, but up here it's as fluorescent as a hospital ward. If there were ghosts, *spirits*, Shannon thinks, they wouldn't be up here with her. They would be latched on to Alison, trailing her like disciples.

Shannon removes her jewellery and places it on the bedside table. When she shakes her hair out of her ponytail her tight scalp softens. She massages her cheeks with her fingers, presses into the muscle knotted at her jaw. She'll wait until morning to shower but needs to brush her teeth, wash her face. She stands, but the act of moving to the bathroom seems immense and she sits back on the covers. Above her head, the light burns brighter. She can feel a migraine coming on. Something about the hot whiteness of the light gives Shannon a pang of homesickness for the glassy Australian sun. Small desires begin to come to her in an upsurge: the citrus scent of her own hand soap, a long, salty swim in the ocean. What she wants, she thinks, is a good cup of coffee and to *really* sweat, to be surrounded by people, to feel suffocated by them. But that would not be enough. She wants to go back further, to be watching *Home and Away* on the couch with Debbie, her head in her mother's lap as the cat scratches at the flyscreen, mosquito coil smoking at their feet. She wants to be propped up beside the bathroom sink, her mother brushing her teeth, the taste of bubble gum and iron as she spits foam. Debbie combing her hair for lice eggs, doling out worm tablets, pulling splinters from her palm. (The light is making her delirious now; she can feel fingernails scratching the surface of her brain, a fiery ball of coal nestled in its centre.) Further still, to before speech, before sight and touch, to before she had a mind, before she had a body. Back to when she was just a cluster of cells, a possibility, and there was no one burrowed under her skin like a tick, sucking away, sucking away.

Shannon had heard about Patrick's father from her cousin, who had gone to boarding school with Patrick in the city.

He'd hung around Wantarra for a few years after graduating high school; three younger siblings, schoolteacher father, stay-at-home mother. He'd moved to Melbourne to start an arts degree only to drop out after a semester when his father died. An accident on the highway, the brutal combination of dusk and a kangaroo. When he moved back to Wantarra, Patrick got work accompanying the school choir on piano and giving private tuition for cheap. Of course, Shannon knew of Patrick long before that—everyone knew of Patrick. The gangly spectacle of him among the church choir, dressed in white at the Carols by Candlelight. The profane mural he painted out the back of Quan's Chinese Takeaway. But when she saw him at the pool a few months after the funeral, it was as though the tragedy had transformed him into the most alluring thing in existence. She'd seen him with girls before—women, she supposed: his hand deep in the back pocket of their jeans, them clambering into his lap on the gum-stained lounge at the cinema. But that day he was alone, which to Shannon, made him seem fragile and accessible. She wanted to bundle him up, stroke his hair until he fell asleep in her lap. She'd never had that feeling before. She'd never had the feeling of just wanting to be near someone, of needing nothing in return.

Shannon watched him from the edge of the pool, her razor-nicked legs burning, the wet cement scorching her heels as she smeared bull ants into the concrete with her thumbnail. Patrick had settled himself on the grass by the chain-link fence that bordered the car park, stretched out on a towel with a paperback and a notebook, a biro tucked behind his ear. He wasn't in his bathers, hadn't even taken his shoes off. Every so often his littlest sister or young cousins would scramble from the pool towards him and take an orange wedge from a Tupperware container. As they ate the fruit, Patrick would squirt sunscreen from a fat tube, slather it on their shoulders and backs, then they'd race back into the water like raucous ghosts, squealing and white-smeared.

He was there the next day, and the day after that. Every afternoon, on his child-sized beach towel, baggy t-shirt, combat boots, which on the third day he'd taken off and lined up neatly, one sock poking out of each opening. Shannon took it as a sign, his shoes being off like that. Today he was a little more open to her. His toes were long and thin. He kept flexing them, digging them into the grass, as if they had minds of their own and were calling to her. Telling her yes.

On the fourth day, Shannon arrived earlier than usual, set up her own towel close to his, made sure he could see her. Though it was hot she didn't swim. She didn't want someone to take her spot, for someone else to be closer to him than she was.

She'd packed a glossy magazine, *Dolly* or *Girlfriend*, lay on her stomach and pretended to read it. When he opened his container of orange wedges she mustered all her courage and called over to him. 'Give me one of those?'

He looked at her and held out the container, lazily swatted the circling flies. She scuttled over on her knees, took the orange and ate it right there, the juice dripping down her wrists. As she threw the rind into the bushes, wiped her sticky fingers on the lycra of her bathers, she could feel his eyes on her but didn't return the look.

'I know you,' Patrick said eventually. It was the first thing he ever said to her, and still she remembers it. *I know you.* She thought his voice would be baritone-deep, like how he sang, but it was light and musical and soft.

'You do?'

'Yeah,' he said. 'You're Mikey's sister.'

He was talking about her friend Bessie. They didn't even look alike. Bessie was tall. She had breasts and hips and double piercings in her ears, the skin there always crusty with infection. Compared to her, Shannon was thin like a boy, bony and straight. Sexless.

'Nah,' she said. 'That's Bess.'

'Right,' he said, but he looked at her like he didn't believe her, as though she was, in fact, Bessie with the infected piercings, the breasts and the hips, and was trying to fool him into thinking she was someone she was not.

Patrick glanced towards the pool, then back to her. She could feel him looking at her shoulder, her forehead, her ear.

'My dad's dead too,' Shannon said.

He didn't seem surprised. 'Yeah?' he replied. 'How?'

She said the first thing that came to mind. 'He drowned.'

'Shit.'

'Yeah,' she said. 'It's shit.'

'Where?' he asked. 'Where'd he drown?' He glanced back at the water, as though hoping she would say: *Here. Right here. He died here.*

'At the beach.'

He raised his chin. 'Like Holt.'

She didn't know what he meant by that. Her dad wasn't actually dead; he lived up in Rockhampton with Eleanor and the twins, babies still, soft as finger buns. 'Yeah,' she agreed. 'Like Holt.'

He told her he'd be going to the showgrounds that night, that she could come, or not, and at twilight they met up by the Caltex and walked the rest of the way there, him on the road, her on the footpath. They shared a stick of fairy floss and a dagwood dog dipped into tomato sauce. It gave her heartburn. She wasn't even hungry. She couldn't imagine she'd ever be hungry again. He told her about his job, how his mother had taught all of them piano but he was the only one who stuck with it, he was the only one with any real talent. At the end of the night he looked at her with kindness and kissed her on the forehead, lips oily from the deep-fry batter, and left her under the queasy lights of the servo to make his way home alone. She felt like she had been blessed. Her mother had never taken her to church, but Shannon had seen the girls from St Mary's before Easter and it was as though ash had been smudged on her forehead by someone holy. She kept touching it, that sacred space where she'd been anointed by grease.

Shannon had got good at nicking make-up from the pharmacy. She thought it made her look older—thick eyeliner; pink, frosty lip gloss—but looking back now at photographs, she realises she looked every bit her age: her large, toothy mouth; hair tinged green from soaking in chlorine all summer hanging lankly down the sides of her face. Freckles, also greenish; skin peeling off her nose. And her body—her nothing body. That was the end of Christmas holidays, and a few weeks later she started back at school, convinced Debbie to let her have piano lessons if she gave up netball. She called her father in Rockhampton and asked for an electric keyboard as an early birthday present, assembled it in the lounge room beside the television. Patrick came over every Tuesday afternoon. Some nights after a lesson Debbie invited him to stay for dinner. They'd eat at the table and then watch television together, the three of them, and Debbie would ask Patrick for a shoulder rub because her neck was always tight from being on her feet all day at the fruit and veg shop. She sat between his feet on the carpet and leant back into him, eyes closed, moaning in a way that made Shannon hot with disgust or jealousy as he dug his beautiful fingers into the soft pink flesh spilling over her bra straps.

'You're a good boy,' Debbie would say. 'What did we do to deserve you?'

While her mother snored on the couch, Patrick would lead Shannon into her bedroom. At first it was just kissing, then kissing and him touching her, then her touching him, and after a few weeks he positioned her on the floor and pulled aside her underwear. Though Patrick was gentle it always hurt. She liked watching his eyes glaze over, his long fingers wrapped around her head like he was cupping a precious stone as he heaved into her, always sweating by the end of it, even in winter, even when it was cold.

She started going over to his place most weekends, told Debbie she was sleeping at Bess's. Patrick had moved out of his mother's house by that point and was leasing a shoebox above the newsagency, right across from the high school. He played gigs at the local hotels on weekends with Nick and Darren, sometimes crammed the three of them and their gear into the Lancer and drove to bigger cities, the regional centres. Shannon asked if she could come along, but there was always an excuse.

He moved to Melbourne with the boys the week Shannon started year nine. Berlin after that, then London, which was where things blew up. He called her every few months, sometimes more but mostly less. The week she dropped out of high school she packed up her Barina and drove the eight hundred kilometres down to Sydney. She got a job as an orderly in a hospital, then an aged-care facility, then back to the hospital on reception. Patrick's calls became less frequent—a year apart at one point—but whenever they talked, a cheque would arrive in the post afterwards; enough to cover her rent for the next few months, enough to pay for expensive haircuts at a salon in Surry Hills. She bought an ivory leather couch, expensive lingerie, a treadmill. She got a tattoo of a shark at the base of her spine and shaved her head, then grew it back and dyed it with peroxide. She got her teeth fixed, breast implants, a nose job. During one of his phone calls Patrick told her he had a girlfriend whom he was serious about: a lanky, Danish photographer who had shot their second record cover. The day it was released, Shannon walked to Westfield and bought the CD in Sanity. She read the lyrics in the liner notes, which made her feel as though she'd had a life that slipped away. It was Patrick who had made her existence magic and worth living. Her life now was easy and free but unremarkable, ordinary. She never thought to question why he didn't leave her alone.

It wasn't for another few years that the band moved back to Australia. Patrick and Nick, really; the rest were interchangeable, a constant rotation of men—always men, and always the same kind of men, who would tolerate the pair's insularity, their cattiness, until they no longer could. At first Patrick was embarrassed to be home, but they'd fallen into bad habits overseas and were too ambitious to let it all come apart. He phoned Shannon the day he landed, and after her shift at St Vincent's they met at a scungy pub on Darlinghurst Road. He looked terrible. Rake-thin, skin scabby and dry, his lips the bloodless colour of a chicken thigh straight from the deli. Erratic, though there was nothing unusual about that. A few months later Patrick bought the terrace in Elizabeth Bay outright, no mortgage. Within a year, Neve.

It was simple really, the way it all came together in the end. When Patrick too told the story of their togetherness, that first chapter no longer existed. It was sterilised clean, a blank white haze of years that melted against the hot, summer concrete. There was no swimming pool, no orange quarters, no piano lessons. Patrick's hand was never hot on her thigh, never nestled into her crotch as she practised arpeggios. There was no carpet-burn red up her back, no string of bells ringing by the window. No purple-feathered dreamcatcher, no glow-in-the-dark stickers on the ceiling, fantastical constellations, shooting stars, three thin slices of moons. There was no Cabbage Patch doll discarded under the bed to bear witness to it all.

And so, Shannon is here twenty-five years later, after two children and a full life together, which was, up until the end, mostly beautiful, to ask him why he had decided to do that, to take her girlhood and twist it into something mucky and shameful; why, on that hot afternoon at the pool, he didn't just give her an orange quarter and return to his book.

## NEVE

FROM THE BATHROOM WINDOW, NEVE watches the caterers pile out of the van. There are three of them: two women plus a man, all dressed in black slacks and crisp white shirts. Alison appears in the driveway and greets them, her poppy-coloured dress blistering in the light, her fleshy arms bare. Neve didn't expect her to make an effort and feels a surge of something; affection, perhaps, or maybe guilt, though neither of those seem quite right. Before yesterday, Neve had only ever seen her in the same two pairs of beige pants belted at the waist and oversized woollen jumpers, but she has poked through the wardrobes upstairs and found them full of lovely things: intricately stitched, architectural dresses, proper formal gowns protected in garment bags. Even Neve could tell they were expensive and beautiful artworks.

She opens the window but the sound of the conversation doesn't carry. The man must be in charge, because it's him that Alison talks to as the women unload trays and boxes from the back of the van and take them into the house. Neve closes the window and squeezes the wet tips of her hair into the sink. She's just out of the shower, and the small fan-forced heater blows hot against her ankles. She is hungry and wants something to eat, but doesn't want to talk to anyone, Alison especially. So, even though it's still light outside, just past four, and the party won't start for hours, she towel-dries her hair, smears deodorant into her pits, changes into the new dress which hangs limply from a coathanger on the back of the door. She sifts through the scant selection of make-up she keeps in a small plastic crate beneath the sink: a cakey foundation, shimmery eyeshadow, a pink-and-green tube of mascara. She rubs the steam from the mirror with her fist to reveal the grey moon of her reflection and begins to goop things onto her face with no particular finesse. She's watched videos on the internet—how to do a cat eye, how to contour your face to give the illusion of sharp cheekbones and a thinner nose—but when she tried it out on herself it looked sloppy and cartoonish. She doesn't know why she bothers and is embarrassed that she's bought into the capitalist notion that her own face is less than, but she ploughs on regardless. It doesn't take her long, and by the time she's finished she looks roughly the same, yet somehow a more desperate version.

As she neatens up her toiletries, her phone vibrates from on top of the toilet cistern. She opens the message: it's Elixir, asking if he can come over early. She hasn't heard from him since they returned from Edinburgh the day before last, and was beginning to worry that Alison had said something to scare him off during their bizarre little morning together yesterday. Neve replies quickly, then checks herself in the mirror one final time before heading back to her room to wait for him. She can hear clattering from the kitchen and catches sight of Alison as she passes. Her back is turned as two of the caterers unpack an electrical contraption from a cardboard box. On the table is a spread of ingredients: skinny Dutch carrots, fat-leafed artichokes, half-a-dozen tiny bird carcasses, fine enough to chew right through the bones.

Alison holds an onion in her hand. 'She doesn't eat meat,' she says. 'I only just found out.'

In her room, Neve sits on the corner of her bed and plugs her phone into the charger. She reaches down and pulls her suitcase out from under the bed, unzips one of the smaller pouches on the front. After checking the door is properly shut she takes Alison's pregnancy test from the pocket. Neve knows it's filthy and invasive, that she should throw out the test, should never have taken it from the rubbish in the first place. She would be mortified if Patrick or Alison found it, had known she was keeping it tucked away like some mucky memento. And yet. She lies back on her bed and rests it on her stomach, the tip facing upwards towards her head in a straight, talismanic line. She practises breathing slowly and deeply from her diaphragm and attempts a quick meditation, but her mind keeps wandering. Though she tries to put it out of her head, she finds herself contemplating the pregnancy test and her inability to throw it away, the compulsion she feels to check it multiple times a day. It gives her the same sense of profound shame she felt when she first started menstruating in primary school. Instead of sanitary pads or tampons, which Shannon kept supplies of in the bathroom, she instead chose to stuff her underwear with toilet paper, wads and wads of it, so full it felt as though she was wearing a thick, ragged nappy. There was so much of it clotting out of her she'd have to change the toilet paper several times a night; the blood was like a rapid and she barely slept because of it, and for those three or four torturous days at school she was always finely attuned to the chaos happening beneath her skirt. She grew out of it eventually, but even now there is a wide, spacious gap when she tries to understand why exactly she had done that, why she chose to make herself suffer in that particular way.

She presses the tip of the test into her bellybutton, pushes down until she can feel an uncomfortable pressure against her intestines. She'll throw it out today, she decides. Right now. But at that moment there's a sound at the door and before Neve can put away the test, Elixir swoops right in. 'Happy birthday, Nevey.'

'How did you get here so quickly?' It's only been a couple of minutes since he asked to come over. She brushes her hair from her face and can feel a slick of moisture on her skin, her throat thickening.

'I was well on my way when I messaged you,' he says. 'Da wanted me to help wash Bingo so I skipped off early.'

He shrugs out of his backpack and tosses it on the floor. He's brought his sleeping bag as well, though Neve didn't know he planned on staying the night, and throws that down too. She can smell it, the musky, masculine funk of it. It takes until he's sitting beside her on the bed to notice the test clutched in her hands. 'What you got there?'

Neve doesn't reply, but squeezes tighter in the hopes it will explode or disappear and she won't have to answer the question. Elixir squints, looks closer at what she's holding. As he comprehends what it is, repulsion flashes across his face, and then a look of mild horror. 'Are you . . . ?'

'No,' she says, standing and closing the door. 'You idiot. Of course not.'

'But,' he says, clearly confused, 'you thought you were?'

She jams the test back into the suitcase and slides it under the bed before he can get a good look at it.

'Well?' he prompts.

Neve is speechless and coughs to buy time.

Elixir waits another beat. 'You shouldn't keep secrets from your best and only friend.' He stares at her, leans his face in close to hers and begins poking her on the side of the arm with his index finger, jackhammering into the muscle.

Neve tolerates it for a moment, thinking of what to say to get him off her back, and remembers an article she read about a colony of Mennonites in Bolivia. She tells him the story, how each night, or every few nights, men from the village would creep out of their homes where they lived with their wives and children and mothers and diffuse animal tranquilliser through the windows of whichever house to drug the women and girls who lived there. They'd break in while they were comatose—old ladies, little girls, pregnant women, their sisters, mothers, daughters. It went on for years and years. The women never remembered a thing in the morning. They'd sleep right through it and wake up in pain or naked or sometimes bleeding and think it was the devil.

'Jesus,' Elixir says.

'But it wasn't the devil,' Neve continues. 'It was all these men they knew and trusted. Religious men. And the women—the girls—had no idea it was happening to them. They woke up with no memory of it.'

Elixir fiddles with the silver ring hooked to his septum. He doesn't look as horrified as she'd expected. 'So, what then? You're pissing on a stick to make sure you're not being raped in your sleep? There's no one around except for me and my da. Or your da.'

'I don't think I'm pregnant,' she says. 'I'm not an idiot. I'm just, you know . . .'

He finally leaves his nose ring alone and sniffs, his upper lip curling in an unattractive, gummy way. 'Can never be too sure, I suppose.'

It wasn't entirely false. The story had made her feel truly and sickly distressed when she read the article a year earlier. It started softly, like the bloom of a headache, but the more she thought about it the more unnerved she became. For a few strange months, whenever the first sign of her period made her breasts ache and her belly bloat, she would feel a seismic wash of dread begin to descend over her. When she couldn't bear it any longer, when she was convinced she would never be able to concentrate on anything ever again until she knew for sure, she went to the supermarket a suburb over, hid a test in a shopping basket among bottles of Powerade, bags of grapes, tubs of Greek yoghurt. She'd wait until Shannon was out for the evening and then urinate on the stick in the bathroom, set the timer on her phone and wait on the toilet seat, a concrete block still pressing down on her that didn't shatter until the negative test beamed like an orb of pure relief in her hands. Until the next month, when it all started up again. But of course, she didn't tell Elixir any of this.

Neve smooths out the skirt of her dress. She spots a yellow stain near the hem. It's already seeped deep into the threads; it's probably been there for years; some stranger's filthy DNA. She looks back to Elixir. 'Just don't tell anyone,' she says. 'Don't, like, bring it up during dinner or anything.'

The bedsprings creak as Elixir shifts his weight. 'What'll you give me?'

'What do you mean?'

'Well, if I'm going to keep your secret you'll have to give me something in return.'

His smile is mischievous and Neve doesn't think he's being serious, but she plays along regardless. 'What do you want then?'

He pauses and seems to consider it deeply. 'I don't know.'

A stillness falls over them. Elixir presses his hands onto his knees and cups them. Neve assumes he's still thinking about what he hypothetically wants from her, until he asks, 'So, have you?'

'Have I what?'

'You know,' he says. 'The story about the Bavarians.'

'Bolivians,' Neve corrects. 'But it wasn't a story. It actually happened. I wasn't making it up.'

'No, I mean have you, you know . . . done it?'

Neve feels her face go warm. The answer is no, but any allusion to her having a body is an unacceptable invasion. Before she has a chance to sputter out a response or change the subject Elixir continues quickly, as though trying to swallow back what he just said. 'You don't have to answer. It's just, I've never got that vibe from you.'

She realises their thighs are touching slightly, shifts to create a gap between them.

'See!' he yelps, almost levitating up off the bed. 'This is what I'm talking about. You're always trying to wriggle away from me.'

'I'm not wriggling away. I just moved my leg.'

'Trust me, Neve, I'm not interested.'

She's sure she's misheard him, because the next thing he does, without warning, is lean in and latch his mouth onto hers, his hand reaching for the back of her head. His lips are dry at first, and she feels his tongue slip out, just for a second, an eager little lizard testing the waters before retreating back into the safe cave of his mouth.

Pulling away, he takes his hand and pats her on top of the head. 'See?' he says. 'That wasn't so bad.'

Neve sits still, facing forward. It is as though it happened to someone else, like she'd clinically observed someone doing something vaguely out of the ordinary, content to sit back and passively take it in. 'You're such a pest,' she says, because she knows she has to say something. 'You can't just kiss people without asking.'

'I know,' he says. 'I'm sorry. I just wanted to see what your reaction would be.'

She takes a moment to consider if she feels violated, or used, or betrayed in some way. But there's nothing there, nothing like that. She can feel a cramp forming in her left foot. Her wrist itches; she scratches it. A seed from the multigrain toast she had at breakfast is lodged in a back molar and she tries to work it out with her tongue. She truly couldn't care less. 'Well, this is it,' she says. 'Very underwhelmed.'

Elixir gets up off the bed, crouches over his backpack. 'So,' he says, rifling through its contents, 'where's Alison?'

She was wondering how long it would take for him to bring her up. 'Didn't she let you in?'

'No,' he says. 'The door was open. I could only see the servants.'

'They're not servants.'

'If you pay someone to come to your house and wait on you hand and foot then they're servants.'

'Well, you're getting served like the rest of us.'

The sentence spits out of her but Elixir waves away her defensiveness and stands up, now holding his phone. 'Servants, caterers, whatever.'

Sitting cross-legged, she angles herself to face him, leans back into a pillow. 'What do you want Alison for, anyway?'

'No reason,' he says, sitting down beside her.

'Are you still recording her like a pervert?' she asks. 'Is that what you were doing with her yesterday?'

'No,' he says. 'I mean, yes, I was, but I was also helping her.'

'Why would she want help from you?'

'We literally cleaned all morning,' he says. 'Don't get jealous.'

'I'm not jealous,' she says. 'It was just a question.' He's tapping on his phone and she cranes her neck to try to see what he's doing. 'So, did you find anything out?'

'Nothing interesting.'

'Yeah,' Neve says. 'Because she's not interesting.'

Elixir continues tapping away. 'You don't even know the half of it.'

'Let me listen to it then.'

'Alright,' he says. 'The quality's shite, though.' He fast-forwards for a few seconds, presses play and holds the phone between their ears. It's a fuzzy, elusive sort of sound at first before Alison's voice cuts through, an Australian twang scratching at her accent, as if these past few years with Patrick has rubbed off on her but its effect can only be picked up via the twitchy magic of technology. It takes Neve a second to realise that Alison is talking about Shannon, asking Elixir about her, but when she leans in closer Elixir turns off the recording and tosses the phone onto the bed.

'Why were you talking about my mum?'

'Alison brought her up. She was asking me what I thought of her.'

'What did you say?'

He shrugs. 'Said I liked her.'

'What else did you talk about?'

'Nothing.'

'Did she talk about me?'

'Don't remember,' he says. 'Don't think so.'

'Let me listen to the rest.' She leans over him to take the phone but he yanks it out of arm's reach.

'It's, like, two hours long.'

'You should delete it then,' she says, 'if it's not important. And you know it's illegal to record someone without their permission? It's a felony. You could go to prison for that.'

'It could be good for something, eventually. For the project.'

Again, Neve feels that pang of guilt. Alison has let them into her home and they're treating her like a specimen, digging into her, picking her apart.

'Oh!' Elixir goes back over to his backpack, unzips the front pocket. 'Your present. I forgot.'

'You didn't have to buy me anything.'

'It's your birthday, you dummy.' He hands over the gift. It's a small package, the size of an apple, wrapped in recycled Christmas paper. She turns it over in her hands. 'Are you going to open it?'

The gift is heavy and glass-hard. Elixir beams at her.

'Later,' she says. 'With everyone else.'

'I don't want you to open it with other people around,' he says. 'I'll be embarrassed. They'll make fun of me.'

'Fine,' she says. 'I'll open it.' And then, as an afterthought: 'Thank you.'

Carefully, she peels back the paper. It felt like glass because it is—a bottle of perfume; small and plump and amber-coloured. The glass is cool and smooth. She reads the label and raises the spray nozzle to her nose, inhales. It's floral but acrid; something about it is not quite right. She's not sure if the perfume has gone bad or whether there's something wrong with her senses. She's always loved the cold, raw smell of butchers and fish markets.

Elixir watching her, she sprays it on her wrists and mashes them together. 'You really didn't have to buy me anything,' she repeats.

'I didn't buy it.'

'Don't tell me you stole it.'

'No,' he says. 'It was my mam's.'

At first, she is confused, thinks he means it was just the same kind of perfume his mother wore, but then she looks closer at the bottle and sees that the golden liquid doesn't quite reach the top. There is a scratch on the side of the glass, a slight crust around the base of the nozzle. 'I'm skint, as usual,' he continues, 'but I had to get you something.'

There is an ache in Neve's collarbone; a sick, panicked feeling stretching over her. The greasy colour of the perfume makes her think of fluid leaking out of something long dead, of embalming. The spot on her wrist where she sprayed the perfume begins to hum, as though someone invisible and predatory is puffing their hot breath onto her skin.

She forces a smile and puts the bottle on the shelf beside the lamp. 'Thank you,' she says again. She surreptitiously rubs her wrists on her blanket to stop the perfume seeping into her skin. This is the first physical evidence Neve has had of Elixir's mother's existence. There's nothing at his house to suggest she ever lived there; no photographs, no feminine knick-knacks. Neve doesn't know where Elixir's mother is, doesn't even know if she's alive. Presumably, it's something bad. Prison. A drug habit which has rendered her useless. She's never asked, and though Elixir has mentioned her in passing once before, it is a threshold Neve cannot quite manage to cross. She knows it's the type of thing you're supposed to ask a friend about, but the distance between thinking the question and asking it out loud seems immense. She could ask Patrick, but she finds the not-knowing makes Elixir far more interesting.

'Do you like it then?' Elixir asks.

'Yeah. Of course.'

'Knew you would.'

Neve is thankful when, a moment later, Elixir announces he needs the bathroom. She takes the glass of water from beside her bed, splashes it onto her wrists. As she pats her skin dry with the blanket, she notices Elixir's phone at the end of the bed. She hasn't heard the toilet flush yet and snatches it up. The battery is overheated and vibrates in her palm, hot and fuzzy. Neve types in his passcode, which she's memorised by sight, and goes straight to his voice recorder. She finds the most recent recording, labelled with yesterday's date, and deletes the file, tosses the phone back on the bed. She hopes Elixir notices and she hopes he is mad.

They decide to lie in the sun before it gets dark. They grab jumpers and a blanket and go outside to a soft patch on the lawn, the last of the afternoon light like burnt butter. Neve's mood is no better. There's that heavy sense of dread she can't shake. In a few more hours her birthday will be over but the baby will remain; Neve will still be the same self.

Patrick is standing in the studio entrance on his phone. He raises his hand when he sees them, hangs up a moment later and wanders over to where Neve is setting down the blanket. 'The chef here?' Patrick asks, gesturing to the van parked in the driveway.

'Yep,' Neve says. 'Inside.'

'Good,' he says. He slips his phone into his pocket, straightens up his jacket. 'G'day, Elixir,' he says, squeezing him on the shoulder. 'We're really pleased you're joining us.' He turns back to Neve. 'Having a good birthday?'

'Yeah.'

'Where's Alison?'

'Inside, I think?'

'And Mum?'

'Resting. I don't know.'

'Well,' he says, 'I'm done for the day. I was thinking we could have a little aperitif before the main event. Kick things off.'

'Okay.'

'Elixir, mate,' he says. 'Go find Shan and Ali, would you? And grab a bottle of bubbles from the fridge. The Dom Perignon, if it's chilled.'

'Yes, sir.' Elixir beams, turns and jogs inside, while Neve and Patrick sit down on the blanket. Neve takes off her boots and crosses her legs, Patrick lounging on his side.

'Are you looking forward to the party?' he asks, taking his sunglasses from his breast pocket and slipping them on.

Neve plucks a piece of grass from the ground and shreds off a ribbon. 'Guess so.'

Patrick readjusts his jacket, wriggles to get comfortable. 'Alison's put a lot of effort into this, you know, Neve. She's organised the caterers, everything.'

'I thought you did all that.'

'We both did.'

She doesn't believe him, but says, 'That's really nice of her.'

'Yes,' he says. 'It is. She's really trying, you know. To make you feel welcome. Shannon, too.'

'She seems to really like Mum a lot.'

'Everyone likes your mum.'

'Yeah, but, like, it's a bit weird, isn't it?'

What's weird is Alison and Elixir talking about her mother. They don't even know her. They don't know anything about her. If Elixir wants to stalk Alison around the house then fine, but she doesn't know why Shannon needs to be a part of it. Again, she feels a sting of guilt for coming here in the first place, for leaving her mother, for choosing her father. She couldn't bear it if Shannon tried to persuade her to come home; how awful it would be to have to reject her again.

'Alison's enjoying the female company.'

A piece of her hair flies into her face, sticks to her lip balm. 'I'm a female,' she says, removing the strand from her mouth.

'You know what I mean,' he says. 'An adult. A friend. She gets lonely. Alison pretends to detest anything with a pulse, but she doesn't really. She's actually quite sensitive, under all of that hardness. You'll see that side of her eventually.'

Neve plucks another blade of grass. One of the caterers, the man, emerges from the house and walks to the back of the van, opens it and takes out a cardboard box. They watch him, but he ignores them both and keeps his eyes on the gravel, goes back inside with the box on his hip.

'Hey!' Patrick says excitedly. He raises his sunglasses onto his head, and Neve can see her reflection mutated in his watery blue eyes. On anyone else the paleness would be sinister. 'I just remembered. Alison has a surprise for you.'

'What kind of surprise?'

'If you knew then it wouldn't be much of a surprise, would it?'

Neve hadn't asked for gifts. Usually, Patrick transfers a grand into her bank account for birthdays and Christmases, sends a card in the post with a long, heartfelt note that makes Neve embarrassed and glad he's not there to see her read it. 'Animal, vegetable or mineral?'

'I couldn't possible say,' he says coyly.

'Will I like it?'

'I don't know,' he says, then pauses. 'I don't know what it is, actually.'

'Right.'

'Act surprised when she gives it to you, though,' he says. 'She'll be cranky if she knows I spoilt it. She was very secretive about the whole thing.'

'Okay.'

He whacks his hand on the blanket enthusiastically. 'Well,' he says, 'let me see it then.'

'See what?'

'Let me see your surprised face.'

Neve is frequently baffled by how inconsistent he is towards her; how swiftly he switches between confiding in her and then treating her like an infant. She stares at him with contempt, but his face is so earnest that she feels a rare flash of pity towards him. For the first time she considers the possibility that maybe her father is lonely too. Who does he have out here aside from Alison? He's used to living in cities; in houses and apartments and hotels full of people. Years of touring, always Neve and Shannon to come back to, the glaring streetlights, traffic at all hours, tourists, fans, groupies probably. Neve remembers when she was little, before Anya, and Nick came to stay, ended up moving into a spare bedroom for two or three months. He and Patrick stayed up late watching videos on the laptop, jamming softly in the living room. Red wine. The occasional joint. Toasted sandwiches at midnight. Blocks of Cadbury Dairy Milk, like schoolgirls at a sleepover. Patrick had cried the night Nick packed his things and moved back to Clovelly, back to his girlfriend, and fell into a brief and superficial depression for the days following. He must really love Alison a lot, Neve thinks, to give all that up.

He's looking at her expectantly and she relents, contorts her face into an expression of performative surprise. She knows she looks stupid, but Patrick seems thrilled. She feels foreign and brand-new. She feels like a hobby. Maybe he does want a baby, she thinks. Maybe they both need something to fill the space they've hollowed out for themselves here. Something to stop the relationship from atrophying; someone else to pay attention to them so that they don't collapse inwards and turn on each other.

Elixir comes from the house, crystal flutes spiked between his fingers. When he gets close he calls out: 'Alison gave me this.' With his other hand he holds out a knife, stout with a thick white handle. 'Don't know what it's for.'

'Ah,' Patrick says, sitting up. 'Brilliant.' He rubs his hands together, takes the knife from Elixir's outstretched hand.

As they stand, Shannon and Alison exit the house: Shannon with the champagne, Alison carrying a large, silver dish. They make their way over to Alison and Shannon at the table on the patio. Elixir lines up the flutes. Shannon pops the cork off the champagne and then fills them, each thick with a top layer of foamy bubbles.

The dish Alison has set down is filled with oysters, two dozen or so, nestled on a bed of cloudy ice. After they cheers Patrick takes the knife and a barnacled oyster. 'Couldn't you get the chef to do this?' he asks Alison.

'They're not slaves, Patrick.'

'Isn't that what we're paying them for?'

He turns to Neve. 'Ever shucked an oyster, Neve-bean?'

Before Neve can reply, Alison takes the knife and oyster from his hands. 'Let me do it, darling,' she says. She holds the oyster in her palm, jabs the knife into the lip of the shell. It makes a clean popping sound and she shimmies the blade along the base and then flips the top shell off, hands Neve the oyster. 'This one's all yours,' she says. 'Happy birthday.'

The oyster is plump and glistening. Alison takes a wedge of lemon from on top of the ice, squeezes the juice onto the oyster cupped in Neve's hand. The lemon spurts and stings the irritated hangnail on her thumb. She can smell the tang of salt and sea water, acidic lemon juice. Neve doesn't even like oysters, but she unsticks the mollusc from the shell and reluctantly slurps it down without chewing, everyone watching her, their champagnes fizzing. When Neve puts the shell down, everyone beaming at her still, their faces morphed by shadows in the dimming light, someone begins to clap—Elixir probably, but Neve cannot be sure. It catches on. They put down their flutes, the four of them applauding her, as though she is at the centre of some sacred ritual, on the precipice of transforming into somebody else.

It's getting dark now, and colder. Neve takes a sip of champagne and it chills her teeth. She places her glass on the table and the conversations resume. Her hands are sticky and she sits down on a chair, a little dizzy, a little fearful of something she cannot identify. She finds her mind barrelling forward and she cannot reel it in. She can see the top of Alison's belly from across the table. This time next year everything will be different, and it disturbs her.

Across the table, Shannon and Patrick chat loudly and continuously over the top of each other in a cacophony, Elixir chiming in every now and then, his contributions mostly ignored, which he doesn't seem to take personally. He is smiling and engaged and obviously thrilled just to be there, as though he's been welcomed into a special club, which, really, he has been. Beside them, Alison continues to quietly shuck the oysters and arrange them over the ice, the swift movements practised and mechanical, her large hands strong and elegant and as capable as a fisherman's, luring them all out to sea.

Neve was mortified when Patrick told her they had hired a chef for the dinner party. It seemed old-fashioned and pretentious, like the idea of a dinner party itself. She would have been just as happy to go to a pub in the village, or have Patrick cook something at home, or—better yet—ignore the day completely. Neve doesn't care about birthdays. She doesn't like the attention, and it's not as though they are special; everyone has them, consistently. But her father has always been like this. Extravagant and prone to excess. Whenever he visited her in Sydney, he took her to expensive restaurants she didn't have the palate to appreciate. A few years ago, he flew up to see her on his way back to Scotland from Melbourne, where he and Nick had been honoured at an award ceremony. On a Friday afternoon he met her at the school gates and they walked to a cafe close by, sat at the outdoor wicker tables, red-and-white-striped tablecloths, a white plastic daisy in a vase, the plane trees lining the street stark and elegant. An elderly homeless woman in a thick, leopard-print coat stopped by their table and asked them for change. Patrick gave her a fifty-dollar note from his wallet. His coffee came out lukewarm and he sent it back.

The restaurant that evening was close to home, dimly lit and small but crowded and prickling with energy. Patrick said the food was spectacular, as if that would mean anything to Neve. The specials were handwritten onto pieces of thick cardboard tacked up on the walls. The scent of lemon myrtle misted from the ceiling. They sat at a table by the window and Patrick selected a scattering of dishes from the menu: glazed miso eggplant; crab and chicken dumplings; a whole, grilled snapper, its demonic head hard and crispy, as if millennia-old and embalmed. Even though she was still in her school uniform—her straw hat in her lap, bulky backpack between her feet—when Patrick ordered wine the waiter filled both of their glasses.

Neve didn't miss her father all that much when he moved out of the terrace and then swiftly overseas, but she appreciated how seriously he took her whenever he reappeared for those concentrated bursts. While her mother chatted constantly and inanely, her father asked her real questions, asked her what she thought about the world, what music she was listening to, whether she had read this or that book. She wasn't what he expected, that much she knew. Though he'd never said it, he thought she should be wilder, more exuberant. Neve was well aware that she was dull and overly internal. She wasn't charismatic like her parents and had developed a theory that when two people had a child, if they both had a particularly potent quality, then that quality would be stamped out in the progeny, some kind of neutralising of genetics. But her father seemed intent on digging away at her nonetheless, as though trying in vain to uncover some part of himself in her.

That night they talked about the Russian Revolution, which Neve was studying in modern history that term. She opened her phone and showed her father a series of photographs taken at the Romanovs' last ball at the Winter Palace in St Petersburg. An artist had restored the images to colour, and there was something ethereal and haunting about the enormous, bejewelled headdresses, the unsmiling, melancholic faces, as though their sullenness was brought on by a mass psychic premonition of what was to come. Her father was very keen on Rasputin; that's why she showed him the photos. They'd talked about him before, about how his weird, prolonged death could all be explained by science, which Patrick refused to believe. He was completely fanciful, interested in the idea of things rather than trying to understand the thing itself. Neve was mystified by how willing he was to suspend disbelief. He wasn't logical at all. She truly didn't understand why so many people were so obsessed with him.

'We should go,' Patrick said, pinching a limp piece of bok choy between his fingers.

'Where?'

'To Russia,' he said. 'We should go.'

Neve shrugged. Her father had made similar suggestions before. Reykjavík to see the aurora borealis. Jerusalem for Gethsemane and the Cenacle. He was calling himself a non-Christian follower of Christ at that point. He was drawn to the idea of mystical, powerful men, and especially liked the idea that to a certain type of person he was one. He never followed through with any of their travel plans, but Neve wasn't bothered. She knew he got carried away, that his tendency to get worked up and then let her down wasn't malicious.

'Moscow's incredible. The Kremlin, St Basil's. And the *pelmeni*!' He kissed his fingers. 'You'll love it, Neve-bean. I promise.'

'You're so busy, though.'

He'd been composing back-to-back film scores for the previous two years, churning them out like pulp fiction. 'Not that busy,' he said. 'Come and stay with me and Alison for a few days at the house, then we can fly over together. Spend a week or two. A month even. Alison can come too. She's dying to meet you—you know that.'

'I want to,' she said—and it was true, she desperately did—'but I have school.'

'Christmas holidays then.'

Neve took a bite of dumpling. The inside of it was scalding. She tried to swallow it down, but the steam poached her tongue and Patrick mistook her silence for a no. 'Once you turn eighteen, alright? For your birthday.'

She sipped wine slowly. Patrick finished the bottle, ordered more dumplings. He knew the chef—or the chef knew him—because he came out with each of the dishes to talk them through what they were eating, what was seasonal and what region the produce had been sourced from. Everything was beautiful: beautiful native plum, beautiful duck. When he brought out the second round of dumplings, he pulled up a chair and Neve sat dumbly as the two men talked over each other, gripping each other's forearms. On the chef's recommendation, Patrick ordered a sticky dessert wine, glistening like rosin in the crystal glass, while Neve slipped off to the bathroom to scroll on her phone.

They finished dinner—a five-hundred-dollar meal, on the house—and walked back to the terrace. Shannon was away at a girls' weekend in Byron Bay. Neve said she was fine to get home by herself, that she'd see him for breakfast in the morning, but he was drunk and affectionate by then, his arm draped around her shoulder. Fireworks crackled in the distance but she couldn't see them through the trees.

Once home, they lingered at the gate. Neve didn't want him to come inside. The space was hers and Shannon's now, warm and girlish, all of it clean and gold and rosewater pink, and she did not want him to intrude on their cocoon. He hadn't been there since he'd left five years earlier. When he was in town, he seemed to make a point of never coming over; meeting Neve on the opposite side of the city, having a taxi drop her home from his hotel, as though there was a radio-active barrier that physically prevented him from coming close.

But that night, whatever usually held him back was absent. He seemed fixated on getting himself inside and Neve could not deter him. Though almost manic on the walk from the restaurant, he became quiet as she opened the front gate, fumbled over getting the key in the door and shutting off the alarm system, Patrick's hands in his pockets, acting casual as if simply returning home after a long day at work.

Once inside, Neve hovered by the window. She was conscious of the smell; sweet vanilla, the straw musk of the mouse cage. The sawdust began to rustle and she walked over to it, stuck her finger through the bar and hoped he would say something about them. Patrick loathed mice. When he first moved out Neve's initial response was to be thrilled because she knew Shannon would have no choice but to relent. But she grew bored and resentful quickly. The smell of them was noxious, and whenever she held them they released hot urine into her hands. It felt intentional. She had the sense that they hated her and the power she wielded over them. In return she was repulsed by their chalky yellow teeth, their red, ghoulish eyes, their greedy mouths as they suckled the sipper bottle she never remembered to refill. They had passed their life expectancy twice over, which, considering how neglected they were, Neve found unnatural and disturbing.

Patrick walked through to the dining room, up the stairs to the second level, reappeared ten minutes later, just as Neve was contemplating whether or not to go check on him. He went over to the piano, opened the lid and began to play something jaunty. It was out of tune; neither Shannon nor Neve played and it was only there for aesthetics. He made a mistake, which seemed to throw him off. When he closed the lid the notes continued to reverberate in the air like church bells.

As he continued to stalk through the house Neve wondered if her mother would be able to tell he'd been there. Whether she'd be able to feel his presence; his thick, black energy. Not that she'd mind, Neve thought. Her parents talked on the phone all the time, probably more than Neve and Patrick did, and got on better than anyone else she knew. Argumentative but teasing, like siblings, as if all their conversations were one circular, continuous interaction that gave them vitality, which was why she was often confused by the fact they were no longer together. She assumed it was to do with Anya, though she'd never asked outright or even interrogated it deeply. In her memory, Anya was born and the next week her father was gone, but in reality there was that slow, sickly year in between.

Neve opened the door to the balcony and asked if he wanted tea. He didn't respond. She felt like he was searching for something, which was confirmed when he came back to Neve in the lounge room. His eyes were vacant and he rubbed his temples with his fingers. For a moment Neve thought he was about to pass out. He rocked back and forth slightly, as though trying to find his balance. 'I feel like I'm grasping at something,' he said cryptically. He sat down on the sofa and rested his hands on his knees. There was a shimmer of sweat across his forehead. Neve didn't know what to do. She was terrified he would start to cry. She wanted to call her mother. She wanted him gone again.

His phone rang in his pocket and he ignored it, then rose and went back to the kitchen, unable to settle. He helped himself to a glass of water. Neve watched him from the other side of the kitchen island, separated by the slab of vast, white marble. He stood in front of the fridge. On post-it notes, Neve and her mother kept a list of the books they'd finished. Her mother mostly read things recommended by Oprah: emotionally manipulative tomes; self-help books about wellness and gut health. There was a scattering of wedding invitations, a grocery list, a leaflet for a day spa pinned to the chrome with a wooden Pinocchio magnet, his red boots dangling from pieces of white cord, as though his shoes were directly attached to his bones.

'We should go to Wantarra,' Patrick said, finally seeming to remember she was there. 'See your gran.'

'I went last year with Mum,' Neve replied. 'We go there a lot still. For Easter and stuff.'

'We'll go again,' he said. 'I'll bring Alison.'

Neve shrugged. 'Yeah, okay.'

'It'll be great,' he said. 'We can go to the Rocking Horse, have a swim in the quarry. We can drive out to Muldoon. I bet your aunty Terri still has the quad bike.'

Patrick walked past her, back into the lounge room. Neve trailed behind. She was tired but didn't know how to tell him to leave. He went back over to the piano. On its top was a vase of sunflowers and a thick soy candle, its wick intact. He picked up the candle and sniffed it, then turned to Neve and asked, 'Where are my photos?'

'What?'

'My photos,' he said. 'Don't tell me Shannon's chucked them.'

He opened a cabinet drawer beside the piano and rifled through it. Neve understood now what it was he was grasping at. Those awful pictures, like something from a horror film. He walked over to another cabinet and opened another drawer, pulled out a box. He flicked through the photographs until he found what he was looking for.

'Look, Neve,' he said. 'It's your sister.'

Neve nodded. 'Yeah,' she said. 'I know.'

'Come look at her.'

Neve stayed by the French doors which opened onto the balcony. She looked out into the night. There was the moon, the bridge flickering through the trees. The button from her school skirt pinched into her waist, but she couldn't bring herself to adjust it as Patrick sifted through the rest of the box and picked out three or four more photos. He put the lid onto the box, slipped it back into place in the drawer. Without speaking he tucked the photos into his breast pocket, smoothed his palm over it, as though incanting something, absorbing the essence of the photos into the tight, hardened space of his chest cavity.

When he went back to his hotel Neve felt cowardly for not telling him to leave the photographs behind. They didn't belong just to him. They were her mother's too, and Neve had just let him take them. She took out her phone to call him and demand he bring them back, but as she typed in the passcode she lost her nerve. She knew she wouldn't be able to bring herself to confront him. He knew this also. He knew she wouldn't be able to demand anything of him and that's why he did it. Just like her mother, she was under his thumb. Defeated, she put down her phone and took off her shoes and socks, unbuttoned her skirt and fingered the red dent in her hip. She felt the largeness of the house around her. Its stillness. Frightened, she turned on all the lights, made sure the front door was locked and the alarm was set before going upstairs. She padded into her mother's room, stripped back the doona and climbed into the bed. The sheets were cold. They smelt like a drycleaners. She reached on top of the headboard for her mother's weighted eye mask, heavy with magnets. The silk was also cold, and when she slipped it over her eyes she kept them open so that all she could see was a calming, fleshy pink, sunset pink. Neve was wide awake now but all she could think to do was wait for sleep to take her.

The following morning Neve walked the long way to Patrick's hotel, passing the Saturday markets. On impulse, she bought a bouquet of sunflowers the same as they had at home. Patrick would be gone tomorrow, but she didn't think of that as she handed over the correct change to the vendor, and it wasn't until she got to the hotel that she considered that flowers were a weirdly intimate, almost sensual thing to gift her father. Why did she even feel the need to bring him anything? He should be the one giving her gifts. As she stood under the awning of his red-brick, Art Deco hotel she considered stashing them in a bin or lobbing them into the bushes, but when a stylish, elderly couple with matching cropped haircuts walked past and eyed her with suspicion, she realised she was lurking and pressed the intercom.

'Stunning,' Patrick said, when she handed him the flowers. They were already beginning to retreat shyly into themselves and he placed them flat on the bench, did not seek out a vase. He didn't mention his theft last night and Neve didn't either. They'd decided on a swim before breakfast, and while Patrick went to the bathroom to change, Neve scanned the room for the photographs of Anya, but everything had been neatly put away, out of sight.

The interior of the lift was brass and dark wood with temperamental buttons, and they shuddered down to the facilities on the ground floor. A pool, deep and glowing, a bubbling spa and a steam room, glossy white tiles. They disrobed out of their hotel dressing-gowns and her father went straight for the steam room. The door was clear glass, and as Neve took off her watch and tucked it into her folded gown she could see Patrick through the lightly fogged screen, eyes closed, head resting against the back wall, his hair slicked with sweat already.

There was only one other person in the pool, an older, stocky man in goggles swimming laps. He ignored Neve as she descended the metal steps into the water. It was heated to an unpleasant temperature, and she dunked her head under, bounced up and down a few times before beginning slow laps up its length. She was an average swimmer and mostly persevered for the feeling at the end of it: the jellied muscles, the exhaustion, the appetite and how good food tasted after. Though the water made her feel uncoordinated, she soon settled into a comfortable flow. She opened her eyes under water and the chlorine made them sting, but she didn't mind it. More people entered the pool area, vague shadows at the cusp of her vision whenever she surfaced to draw breath. She kept going until she felt everything retreat. She was in another realm, an underworld, and what was happening above couldn't be accessed, had nothing to do with her.

And yet, the longer she swam, the worse she felt. There it was again: those pictures slicing their way in. She'd once read about a man who braked for a kangaroo on a highway. He went head first through his windscreen, and years later the tiny fragments of glass started to work their way out of his forehead, minuscule slivers revealing themselves after all that time. That's how Neve felt: like the glass that had edged in was now edging out. She often fantasised about diving head first into the shallow end of a pool or onto a sandbar in the sea. It seemed a practical and swift way to deal with what wouldn't leave her; one violent, heaving surge to render her helpless. The thick, sticky memory of Anya was always there: the cold car ride after Nick picked her up from school, the antiseptic light at the hospital. Shannon sweaty and fat and reeking of something foul. Anya, pressed against her mother's heavy breasts, looking so alive Neve couldn't quite believe what they were telling her. Neve remembered sitting beside her mother and prodding at its little chest, so sure she could see movement beneath its translucent skin, and then recoiling when her fingertip brushed over its fingernail, like a flake of dried milk. The realisation that what she was touching wasn't alive felt epiphanic. Was everyone else delusional? The baby wasn't a baby. It was a corpse. They were kissing and cuddling a corpse.

By the time Patrick arrived, straight off a plane from Tokyo, her mother seemed to realise the baby was no longer a baby. Neve sat quietly on a chair in the corner doing her homework: mathematical drawing, the compass grinding into the grid paper. Her mother was quiet; Anya far from them both, now swaddled and lying in a crib, a knitted beanie on her bare scalp. Her name wasn't Anya then. Back at home, where she already had her own bedroom, as much presence as someone who already existed, they'd simply called her the baby. Neve couldn't remember when Patrick had chosen Anya, whether he and Shannon had even discussed it, or whether he'd just bulldozed ahead with the name and snatched the decision for himself, as though the baby was his and his alone.

After a while Patrick unpacked his camera from his suitcase and fiddled with the lens. 'Go,' he said to Neve. He took her homework from her lap, grabbed her by the arm and moved her closer to the crib. 'Pick her up.'

Neve ignored him, licked the inside of her cheek, poked her tongue into the puckered flesh. Never in her short life had she so strongly wished to be elsewhere. Despite her resistance Patrick snapped the photo, then handed Neve the camera and told her to take a picture of him and Anya together. He picked her up from the crib, sat down on the end of the bed, Shannon behind him. He touched her fingers, the size of cat litter pellets, gently stroked along the suggestions of a nose. He gazed solemnly into the camera, tilted his head, chin raised. After decades of practice, he knew his angles well.

Neve couldn't tell for how long she'd been swimming when she felt someone enter the pool. There was a disturbance in the water, the force of it lapping waves into her. Something knocked softly against her arm. She shrugged it off and kept going, but a moment later the same something grabbed at her neck, at her hair. She was at the shallow end and stood up, the water level at her hips, and wiped the wet from her eyes. The man swimming laps was gone and in his place was a child, maybe two or three years old, with dark, fine hair, floaties strapped around her twiggy biceps. The girl bashed her fists in the water, giggled at the disorder she created, shrieked with delight like a wildling, something slight but utterly feral.

Neve couldn't look away from the girl's grabby hands, her legs kicking furiously. There was something deep in the pit of Neve that made her panic. She felt it between her legs, a deep pulsing. Her body turned hot. Though the ceiling was high the space felt exceptionally compact. She was large and swollen. She felt something detach, her skin ripping from muscle ripping from bone ripping from whatever essential part came beneath that, and watched a version of herself drift towards the child, lift her out of the water, position her on the side of the pool, on the tiles, slippery, wet. She could see it like a fresh memory, or else her body and her mind had become separate entities, and she was watching herself from above. It wasn't rage, wasn't even close, but a bubbling urge to wield power, the understanding that things wouldn't feel *right* until the girl's body was defiled, degraded. She imagined how she would hurt the child, do things worse than hurt.

Another shriek jolted her out of it and she came back to herself, dizzy and nauseous, could taste burnt coffee in her mouth, bitter and metallic. Neve looked around for Patrick. The door to the steam room was open but he wasn't in there, nor was he in the spa, or relaxing on one of the deckchairs by the pool's edge. Neve hurried out of the water, scraping her knee on the rough cement as she did so and smearing the dots of blood with the heel of her hand as it rose to the skin's surface. She crossed the cold, slippery floor and opened the door to the steam room, sat down on the tiled bench, right where Patrick had been. It was only then that she could feel how strong her pulse was, so quick and vital it was sore in her throat. The heat of the steam room was astonishing already and she found it hard to get the air into her lungs, which she knew she needed if she wasn't going to faint. She waited for the sputtering of the steam, a fresh burst of heat to enter her body.

Behind the glass she had a perfect view of the girl. She was playing a game now. Her eyes were scrunched closed as she gnashed her baby teeth, reaching out her stiff claws, pretended to be a predatory animal, a shark or a crocodile. There was the girl's mother, playing along half-heartedly. Of course, she had been there the whole time, in a chic, black one-piece, her silky hair swept into a bun, dewy olive skin, a lovely, symmetrical face. Unaware of Neve and what had started ticking away inside her.

Neve remembers when it started. It wasn't even that bad at first. She'd see a random child at the park or in the supermarket and have an urge to pinch them on the thigh or dig her nails into their wrist. They weren't deliberate, malicious thoughts. Out of nowhere they would float in and land, almost like hallucinations. But soon enough it escalated. The thoughts started to turn, to intensify. She had horrific visions of luring the unlucky child away, imagining how far she would be able to take it if given the chance. Her whole life she'd done as she was told, done the right and sensible and good thing, but suddenly there was this sly but powerful element needling away at her. Pinching became slapping became strangling became slicing. The girl in the pool squealed and Neve wondered what would happen if she was alone. If the mother asked Neve to watch her for a minute while she went to the bathroom, or turned her back to take a phone call. The glass began to fog; gradually the girl disappeared. Neve started to sweat, around her hairline at first, above her top lip, drops of it slinking down her chest until her skin was drenched and she was covered in a slick coating of untenable, adult shame, of disgust at what her body told her it desired, of the terrible thing that had slowly begun to erupt.

They finish the champagne and open another bottle in the soft dim of candlelight. The night smells of jasmine, like

Sydney in August, and gives Neve a sugary, artificial headache. Patrick is rowdy now, his voice reverberating through the crisp air. His fingers are gripping Shannon's bicep and he's emphatically struggling to get something out, Elixir laughing at whatever it is he is trying to communicate, his face cracked open, teeth glowing like drops of milk. Neve has never made him laugh like that.

Across the table from Neve, Alison is quiet. A hand rests against her stomach, the gesture absent and instinctual. She is leaning back into her chair watching on, her smile serene, and she looks genuinely contented, matriarchal, as though they are all her children gathered before her, and she has no pressing reason to speak to them but is simply basking in their presence, confident in her knowledge that she is deeply loved and valued. There's something arrogant about her, Neve observes, to have done nothing but to be welcomed by them all, to be folded so easily into Neve's family. To be the one to sit at the head of the table.

There is a cooing in the trees. The ice in the oyster dish has slowed its melting; slim, sparkling, pebbles now. Alison takes her glass of champagne, close to full, and swills it around, sets it down without taking a sip. It's her first glass and she hasn't touched the oysters either, though she shucked the lot and passed them around for everyone else to share. The shells are scattered around the table, little rotten ears listening in like spies.

It's clear to Neve now that Alison isn't actively trying to hide the pregnancy, yet no one else has noticed the obvious, what is right in front of them. Idiots, she thinks. She pushes her chair back and slips inside, mumbles something about going to the bathroom. As she passes the kitchen, the chef is busy over the stove, another of the caterers is fussing with a set of flat, white dishes laid out on the table. The girl who caught her eye earlier is slouching against the wall beside the walkway. Her face is shaped like a cadaver's: androgynous and hard.

Neve smiles apologetically without meeting her eyes. She goes to move past her into the hall but the girl straightens, steps towards her and blocks her way.

'You the birthday girl?' she asks. Her accent is harsh, like Gareth's. She's standing too close and Neve can smell raw garlic seeping from the girl's pores, which are large and brown on her fleshy nose.

'Yeah,' Neve says.

The girl looks her up and down. Like Neve, she is plain, and Neve gets the sense that, in her, the girl has seen something grotesque that she recognises in herself, but all she says is, 'Happy birthday then,' and turns back to the kitchen.

Neve heads into her bedroom and shuts the door. She is grateful to be alone for a moment, not to have to pretend she is enjoying herself. Crouching, she pulls her suitcase from under the bed. She gives herself permission to wonder what will happen once Alison gives birth, but the thought fills her with dread. She slips the pregnancy test into her coat pocket, then goes out the front door and sets out towards the road. She wants it gone, wants it out of her room, out of the house. The bins are way down the drive and the gravel crunches beneath her feet. She is worried they will be able to hear her from the patio, but when she turns they are still huddled around the table like a coven. The air is cold and stings her nose, dry from the wind. She buries her hands in her pockets for warmth and continues on until she reaches the end of the driveway. Past the bins is the light from Gareth and Elixir's cottage across the road and down the hill, a thin billow of smoke somewhere in the distance. With the day close to gone the hills are the deep green of wet moss. The starkness of it makes her homesick for her room back in Sydney—the electric-coloured birds, the majestic autumn. The heat and the light and the sound. She stamps down the longing for familiarity. This is her home now. She will not be going back.

She passes by the bins and heads towards the woods. If she's gone too long, someone will notice and ask questions of her, so she quickens her pace. She is looking down at her feet, and when she glances up she screams: up ahead are two bone-coloured, luminous entities, monstrous and as tall as she is. Her first, split-second thought is that they are ghosts—spirits of those captive zoo animals prowling the woods for eternity—but when she shines her phone light, she sees they are solid and motionless; the concrete lion statues Gareth and Patrick had taken from her room the day she moved in. She presses her hand to the mane of the closest one. It is cold, hard. The air rasps in her throat and she is so stunned it takes a minute for her to remember why she is out here. She tests the dirt with the toe of her boot. It seems soft enough to dig into easily and she squats down on her heels, bunches the skirt of her dress around her thighs so it doesn't drag in the soil. She is on edge, can feel something hovering close by, watching, though she knows she is alone out here. With her hands, she begins to paw the earth. It is cold, the dirt as well as the air. The sun is down now. She can't see much beyond her hands and the looming statues, the moon-glow of the pregnancy test which she has placed on the ground beside her, the fistfuls of dirt becoming invisible as soon as they fall from her hands. The dirt is grainy under her nails and she wishes she had gloves or a shovel, but there is no time for that.

Once the hole is a decent size, she places the test into the ground. There, she thinks, and feels a weight lifting, feels better in her body. Without the test burrowed into the house like a curse, there is a chance the baby will just slip away, cease to exist, as though the positive test is the only thing keeping it alive, and once it's gone, the baby will be gone too. She wants to say something out loud, some sort of a prayer or affirmation, but she cannot think of anything meaningful and so instead she conjures Alison clearly in her mind and continues to fill the hole, to bury the bone of plastic, and fixates on the morning in the woods with the mushrooms, touching her hand to Alison's stomach. Hand, belly, womb. Hand, belly, womb.

Down the hill: the choke of Gareth's car heaving towards the road, the dim flash of headlights. For a moment she and the lions are lit up: the violent blue of her dress, the churned earth cold and clinging to her hands. She stands and smooths over the dirt with her foot, inhales cold air into her throat and out again.

# ALISON

THE BACK DOOR OPENS, FOOTSTEPS loud on the gravel. Alison assumes Neve has returned from the bathroom but it's only the brusque, older woman bustling from the house to tell them the first course will be served shortly. They begin to gather themselves. Shannon blows out the candles and tips the melted ice onto the grass while Patrick belches loudly, takes the champagne bottle and glugs what remains. If it weren't for the baby Alison would have taken it for herself and enjoyed getting properly legless, something she and Patrick rarely do anymore, at least not together. But soon that will change. Not the drinking, of course, but the feeling of connectedness. Alison's nerves toss with anticipation in her gut, something she has not felt for years, not since she and Patrick were falling in love.

Without warning, Patrick raises his arm and smashes the bottle onto brick. The sound of it is painful; Alison thinks of a bone shattering and her elbow throbs with a phantom agony while Shannon jolts and knocks over a just-extinguished candle. Hot wax drips onto the table in globules, lit up by the inside light shining through the windows, and hardens to pearls almost instantly in the cold.

'What did you do that for?' Shannon snaps at Patrick.

Patrick throws the neck of the bottle into the dark grass where it lands noiselessly. 'I'm christening it.'

'Christening what?'

'The evening,' he says. 'The future. Our beautiful daughter.'

It's an insincere toast; Patrick hasn't realised that Neve is not even here.

'But the bottle was empty,' Elixir says. 'And we're not on a ship.'

'Don't be so literal.' Patrick grabs him by the ears and shakes his head side to side. 'It's dull, dull, dull.'

When Patrick lets go, Elixir crouches down and begins to pick up the pieces of broken bottle. He grins at Alison, palms glistening with glass, as Shannon, who had been collecting oyster shells into the ice bowl, bends to help him.

'Leave that,' Alison says to Shannon. 'We're celebrating. We'll do it in the morning.'

As though she hadn't spoken, they continue to collect the glass, Shannon's head down, her slow hands shaky. Patrick, who had slipped into the dark, now snakes up behind Alison and places his hands on her shoulders, startling her at first with their firmness. They are weights and she feels at peace despite the edge creeping into his voice, the force of his touch. She hasn't seen this side of him in ages and there is a blade of aggression glinting off him that she hadn't anticipated. He leans over and presses his nose into her hair, breathes heat into her ear, and a surge of warmth filters through her body. She wishes her mother were here to see her like this, remembers the dreams and knows that Frances is right beside her, or very close by.

As she leads the way to the dining room, she goes over the plan in her head. The whole process of childbirth is a large fissure of knowledge she doesn't possess and she'll need help. Tomorrow she'll call Martine and ask her to come and stay for a few weeks, have her organise for a doctor to come to the house to avoid hospital until further down the track. When the time comes, she'll request a caesarean, have it taken straight out of her quickly, no pain, no trauma. Sedated entirely, perhaps, leaving no substantial memory of it. She'll announce it after dinner, when things are winding down, and before Shannon leaves tomorrow they'll discuss when she'll be back, how long she can stay for next time. Alison will want her here for the birth, obviously, but maybe she can fit in a small visit before that too.

Earlier, to distract herself, Alison had arranged the bouquets and the dining room is heady with their scent; three triangulating as a table centrepiece, small posies clustered on the mantelpiece. A petal has shed from a mouth-coloured tulip and she takes it from the table, crushes it into her palm, which smells like oyster, salty and rancid.

'Where's Neve?' Shannon asks as she enters the dining room behind Patrick. Her dress is tight and shows off her body, which is that of an athletic teenager, her arms carved of marble.

'She can't be far,' says Patrick.

'She's been gone for ages.'

'Elixir, mate, go find her, would you?' asks Patrick.

Elixir glances up from his phone, the screen emitting a blue glow. He looks irritated by the request, and for a moment Alison thinks he's going to whinge and refuse, like a spoilt baby, but out he slinks.

Alison takes her seat. The cutlery, napkins and wineglasses are laid out, small bowls stacked with smoked chestnuts and sprinklings of pink rock salt for the amuse bouche. Patrick reaches for a chestnut. The champagne has turned his hands clumsy and he begins to gnaw at the nut with his front teeth. 'Pesky little bugger,' he says, placing the gnarled chestnut back on a side plate as the server enters with a bottle of wine, waits obediently by the door until Patrick waves her in.

Quietly and efficiently, the server begins to fill the glass at each table setting, one arm bent rigid behind her back. Alison doesn't think to stop the woman as she fills her glass, and when she is done, the server turns to Patrick, seeking approval from the person who is paying her. She makes a strange bowing motion, as though she is some sort of obedient Victorian maid, and then exits swiftly.

Alison takes Patrick's hand. He lets her hold it loosely for a moment before reaching for his wine and turning himself around in his chair and fixing his attention on Shannon by the window, trying to close its jammed joints.

'What were you saying before,' Patrick calls out, 'about Debbie's new man friend?'

She yelps, skin nicked on the latch as it shutters down. 'I already told you everything.'

'Tell me again. Tell Alison.'

Shannon comes over to the table, sucking the cut on the side of her thumb. 'Mum's seeing this man who has a kid, a bit older than Neve, who was in a rugby accident a few years ago. Completely paralysed.'

'Can't move a muscle,' Patrick says to Alison. 'Can't even speak.'

'They couldn't look after him at home,' Shannon continues, 'and the only place that would take him is this old folks' home. He's surrounded by dementia patients four times his age. And this guy Michael—Mum's boyfriend, whatever—hardly ever goes to visit him. He says it makes him too depressed.'

'How fucking grim is that.' Patrick shakes his head. 'Poor kid.'

Shannon shrugs. 'At least Mum's got someone. At least she's not lonely.'

'Sounds like a bit of a bastard if you ask me.'

'He's not that bad.'

'Imagine leaving your child to rot in one of those places.'

A look of indignation ripples over his face, emphasising his flabby lips, the nut of his chin—the same lips and chin gestating inside her, Alison notes. Though she is glad that Patrick will have the chance to be a father again, a part of her wishes the baby was all hers. Or, that the baby could be hers and Shannon's and have none of Patrick's genes. Better yet: comprised entirely of Shannon's DNA.

'I'm sure he's doing what he can,' Alison says.

Patrick scoffs. 'I'm sure he could do a bit better than that.'

'How can we be expected to know how to take care of someone properly?'

'Common sense?' he replies. 'Human decency?'

'And who have you taken care of, Patrick?'

'I take care of you.'

'Do you?'

'In some ways, yes. It's reciprocal, I would hope.' He turns back to Shannon. 'I should call her.'

'She'd like to hear from you,' Shannon replies. 'She loves you. You know that.'

'Tomorrow. You'll have to give me her number before you leave.'

'It's the same number it's always been.'

'I'll call her,' Patrick repeats.

'You should.'

'How is she really?' Patrick asks. 'Has she asked about me?'

'She's fine,' Shannon says. 'She's the same. She doesn't understand what Neve is doing here. She keeps asking about her and I don't know what to tell her.'

'Your mother doesn't value travel,' he says. 'She wouldn't understand it.'

'How would you know what she values?' Shannon asks. 'You haven't spoken to her in years.'

'From what I remember, her idea of a holiday is a P&O cruise around the Pacific islands.'

'That's travel, isn't it?'

In the past, whenever Patrick has spoken of Shannon to Alison, he's been nothing but positive, never a bad word, but there is a condescension to how he addresses her and Alison wonders if he's intentionally trying to put her offside or if she's got under his skin.

'Your mother sounds like a smart woman,' Alison says, smiling at Shannon. 'Who wants to be a tourist? It's tedious.'

When Neve reappears, Elixir following, her cheeks are flushed, eyeliner watered under her eyes. She looks as though she's been properly roughed up.

'Where've you been?' Shannon asks, standing up. She rubs at Neve's face with her thumb. 'I'm sorry, but you look like shit, darling. Your gran wanted me to send photos.'

'I was just in the bathroom,' Neve says, ducking out of Shannon's reach.

'Right,' her mother says slowly, sceptically. 'Is everything okay?'

'Yes, everything's okay.'

Shannon grabs Neve's hand; the girl's fingernails are mooned with soil. 'What on earth have you been doing?'

'I said I'm fine.'

There's a bite to it; Shannon looks wounded and retreats, while Neve slips into the remaining seat and straightens a fork, ignores the fact that everyone is watching her, waiting for an explanation. She glances towards the door and, as if summoned, the servers appear with the first course. Once the plates are down the young, plain one announces what they are about to eat: artichoke and pancetta, oyster cream. It looks like extremely finessed slop, strange fleshy flaps poking out of its beige crevices, and to Alison it tastes bitter and wrong. She eats quickly, washes away the aftertaste with wine. A few sips won't hurt.

The chatter picks up again. The state of Neve is forgotten as Patrick launches into a story about his twenty-first birthday. It was right after his father died and everyone was trying to mask how depressed they all were. His mother had organised a special dinner at home—roast pork, chocolate mud cake, cherry liqueur. All three of his sisters pooled their money and bought him a guitar, red bow tied to the neck. His mother cried when giving him his father's chess set, and he and Nick left right after cake, drove to the bottle shop and bought a six pack of Carlton Draught, a bottle of Stone's Original Green Ginger Wine, and took them down to the quarry, where they gave each other stick-and-poke tattoos.

'My poor mother,' Patrick says now, his face in his hands. 'What a little shit I was.'

Neve looks confused. 'What tattoo?'

Patrick smirks and rises, reaching for his belt buckle.

'Don't you dare,' says Shannon, but Patrick was bluffing, is already sitting again.

Alison turns to Neve. 'He has a smiley face on his arse. This droopy, demonic thing.'

'Nick has the same one,' Patrick says.

'Not anymore,' Shannon says.

'How would you know what's on Nick's arse?'

'Don't be crass. He told me he got it lasered off.'

'Ha,' says Patrick. 'I'll believe it when I see it.'

'And when will that be?'

'Funny you should ask,' Patrick says, raising a finger. 'I've been thinking it's time to head back home finally.'

'What?' Neve asks, her cutlery frozen mid-air. 'To live?'

'Maybe we'll settle there for good,' he says, gesturing towards Alison. 'I've been considering it for a while, and Alison was talking just yesterday about renovating and selling up.'

Alison stays quiet, sits back and lets him entertain himself. He'll never leave her; he'll never ask her to leave.

'Are you kidding?' Neve asks. Her face is grave and she looks to Shannon in a panic.

'Of course he's kidding.'

'Why is that so ridiculous?' Patrick asks.

'What the hell would you do there?'

'The same thing I do here,' he says. 'Except I'd do it in better weather.'

'The weather's shit,' Shannon says. 'Don't you read the news? Everything's on fire.'

'I miss swimming.'

'There's no water, Patrick.'

'I feel a pull,' he says. 'I feel like I'm being called back to a more innocent time.'

'And when was that?'

'Childhood. When my father was alive. Back when I was a harmless idiot. Back when I knew nothing.'

'You're still an idiot,' Shannon says.

'Less of an idiot,' he says. 'I would hope.'

'Where's this coming from? You hate Wantarra.'

'I never said I hate it.'

'When was the last time you were back then? When was the last time you saw your sisters? Your mum?'

'I see them all the time.'

Shannon laughs. 'Bullshit.'

'It's not bullshit,' he says. 'I see them via the screen. We're in constant communication.'

'Oh, piss off.'

'Well, I've no idea who to believe,' Alison interrupts. 'Patrick's never even invited me to Wantarra.'

'For good reason, darling.'

'And what's that?'

'You'd crisp up and die.'

'I'm not a witch, Patrick.' She is tired of the conversation and ready to move on, is relieved when Shannon, who must have the same idea, claps her hands together ceremoniously, leans over in her chair and resurfaces with a large paper shopping bag.

'Presents then?' She hands the bag over to Neve, who takes out the gifts slowly, examines each with care. Her smile is pained as though she is trying to deflect the attention with her teeth. 'I hope they're okay,' Shannon says. 'You're hard to shop for.'

'I know,' Neve says. 'I'm sorry.' She slips a tennis bracelet onto her wrist, fingers a caramel slip of silk and then wraps it back in its tissue paper.

Patrick is next: airfares to Italy in summer. There's no actual ticket, just its verbal offering. He reaches across the table to grab Neve's hand and kiss it. 'A week in Florence, *bambina*, just you and me. I'll spoil you rotten.'

As Alison takes another minute sip of wine, Patrick puts away the rest of his drink in one swallow and thrusts the glass down. 'Time for speeches?'

'No,' says Neve.

He waves her off. 'Do you remember your shower socks, Neve-bean?'

Elixir cocks an eyebrow. 'What are these shower socks, then?'

Neve recoils. 'Can you not, Dad?' she pleads, as Patrick rubs his hands together with glee, does a drumroll on the table.

'So,' he begins, 'for a few years when Neve was a little bugger she developed this wild fear of having her feet touch the bottom of the shower, and as a consequence, whenever she went for a wash she wore this filthy pair of socks. For years this went on! She'd put on her little socks: scrub, scrub, scrub.' He does a cleaning motion as he says this, washing his armpits with an invisible bar of soap. 'Pop out of the shower and then wring them out for next time. They were mouldy and grimy; completely dank.'

'That's disgusting,' says Elixir, crinkling his nose, turning to Neve for her response.

But Neve's face is now devoid of expression. She seems to be observing the anecdote mildly, detached and uninterested, as if listening to a story in which she is not the subject.

Patrick continues. 'Except,' he says, pausing for effect, holding up a single finger and letting the silence linger, 'one year—how old were you? Nine? Ten?—she went to camp and forgot to pack her sacred shower socks. And of course, she couldn't shower without her shower socks. So, each night after dinner she would go into the cubicle with her towel and her soap. As the water was running she'd change into her pyjamas, wet her hair a bit, and then come out announcing to the other girls how gloriously refreshing the bore water was, filthy little thing.'

Neve takes a final mouthful of food, chews with intention, sets down her cutlery.

'That is literally so disgusting,' Elixir says. 'I bet you smelt like a sewer.'

'Worse than a sewer. One of the teachers phoned Shannon and told her she needed to teach Neve about personal hygiene.'

Elixir cackles, and Shannon reaches over and squeezes Neve's hand as Neve inspects her empty plate.

Patrick leans back in his chair, looks to Shannon, then to Alison, then back to Neve, who mutters something under her breath. Patrick's expression darkens. He seems to expand, absorb whatever energy is pulsing from the room until it bloats him right up. 'What was that, Neve?' he asks, cupping a hand to his ear.

Neve's already flushed face reddens. 'Nothing.'

'Don't be hostile, Neve,' Patrick says. 'It's unpleasant.'

Feeling a wave of tenderness towards Neve, Alison turns to Patrick. 'You're embarrassing her,' she says curtly.

'It's a milestone,' he replies. 'She's supposed to be embarrassed. Baby pictures, humiliating stories, all that rigmarole.'

'Well, it wasn't a good story. No one's amused by it.'

Patrick laughs. 'You have no sense of humour, Alison. So serious all the time, just like your mother. Gareth told me she was the most humourless person he's ever met.'

It is so spiteful, what Patrick has said, that it leaves Alison speechless. She holds Patrick's gaze and is grateful when Shannon interrupts. She seems to be the only one of them who knows how to have a civil conversation. 'Was your mum born here?'

Alison composes herself. 'No, actually. She was born in Australia.'

'What are you on?' Patrick exclaims, his brow furrowed in irritation. 'No, she wasn't.'

She ignores him and continues. 'My father was a general in the army and posted to New South Wales early in his career. That's where he and my mother met, in a town a few hours west of Sydney. They married and moved back here a few years after.'

'She didn't have an accent.'

'How would you know?'

'I lived with her, didn't I?'

'You barely spoke to her. You're repulsed by the elderly.'

Patrick sets down his knife and fork, arranges them neatly on his plate, and then rises calmly from his seat. The chair legs grind against the floorboards.

'Even I knew that about Franny,' Elixir says, ripping into a piece of sourdough as Patrick leaves the room.

The casual way Elixir speaks about her mother with his small, puckered mouth makes Alison flinch, and she wishes it was just her and Shannon having dinner. That everyone else would disappear and leave them in peace. 'Who's Franny?' she asks, playing dumb.

'Duh,' he says, smearing smoked butter on his bread. 'Frances. Your mam.'

'No one called her Franny.'

'I called her Franny.' He stares at her as he eats his bread, a conceited little grin on his face, lips shiny from the smoked butter. 'Da too. We both called her Franny. She called me Jimjam, right up until I stopped coming over to see her. She always remembered me, even when her brain was all scrambled egg. Did you know that, Alison? That she remembered me?'

Though his expression is benign, his lilt pleasant, there is a hostility that Shannon must sense because she interrupts before Alison is forced to respond. 'Where's your dad now, Alison?'

'Oh, we haven't spoken in years.'

'Did he hit you or something?' asks Elixir.

'No, he didn't hit me. He never touched me.'

'What then?'

Neve hisses Elixir's name across the table, but he ignores her, props his fist under his chin, as though he is simply humouring her. Alison reaches for her glass for something to do with her hands. She doesn't understand why everyone is suddenly so fixated on her family. Patrick, Elixir. Even though she knows Shannon's question was an act of kindness, she still feels ganged up on. She sighs and pretends to be bored by the question, exaggerates the story. 'After I started making real money he sold an interview to a tabloid about how desperate he is to see me. He claimed to be living in squalor; a disabled pensioner who lost his legs to diabetes, abandoned by his family. Always hamming things up, playing the victim.'

'That sounds hard,' Shannon says.

'It's the only interesting thing about him, really.'

'Hard on you, I mean.'

'It was good riddance,' Alison says. 'He didn't deserve my mother.'

Before Elixir has another chance to say something invasive, Patrick returns with another bottle of wine, already uncorked. 'Isn't that the caterer's job, Patrick?' Alison asks.

He ignores Alison and tops up his glass. Then he leaves the room, taking the glass and the bottle with him.

They'd been in Scotland not quite a year when Alison's mother died. It was her rapid decline that prompted the move, and after Alison's return, Frances miraculously plateaued for a few months before giving in to the tangle that was rotting her brain. Compared to London, it was eerily quiet. Patrick would bore easily, was eager to get away from the house, to feel like he was still a participant in the world. Alison too felt stifled. She didn't recognise who her mother had regressed into, and it was as if her every decision was being dictated by the whims of a stranger. Her mother was so demanding, so irritating with her relapsed way of communicating: childish and bluntly mean, the look of bewilderment whenever Alison was short with her in return.

Alison knows it sounds wicked but she resented the burden of looking after Frances. At that point she was in the depths of her giddy infatuation with Patrick—they'd been together not even six months—and to get away from the house, they'd pack salad sandwiches and cheese and fruit and go on strenuous treks through the moors, or take the car and go on day trips to St Andrews, Stirling, Pitlochry. One afternoon they drove to Edinburgh and, after a long lunch of bread and mussels, still lazy from pints of ale and not yet wanting to head home, they made their way to the medical museum on George Street. The building was scattered with tourists but they went unrecognised, paid the entrance fee and made their way to the pathology collection on the upper level. They held hands for the first few minutes as they wandered through the cases of specimens: diseased and deformed body parts pickled in chemicals, bulbous tumours, spines horseshoed by scoliosis. Alison was interested in a detached way, but could not recognise herself in any of the specimens on display. At what point did the body lose its humanity and become an artefact? They were looking at corpses, she supposed—dismembered, grotesque slices of them—but the presentation made them alien and impassive, as if the various body parts once housed souls, but the souls abandoned their physical vessels at the moment of dissection. She wondered how medical students felt when preparing for their first autopsy: was the cadaver too abstract to evoke any emotion, or did it feel like a thrilling transgression, slicing someone apart? The former, most likely, though Alison assumed all doctors, like actors, must be somewhat sociopathic. She made a mental note to tell Patrick to donate her body to science.

Patrick took his time, taking photographs with his SLR, though the sign at the entrance said it wasn't permitted. They drifted apart from each other and Alison reached the back of the hall quickly. In one of the last cabinets was a display of skeletons tracking the development of a fetus in utero. There were five or six of them positioned upright, lined in order of height—like a deconstructed babushka doll, it seemed to Alison at first, before they took on a militant formation, soldiers preparing for battle. An army of half-born humans engaged in warfare, their spines rod-straight.

When Patrick found her out by the lift half an hour later, she asked if he'd seen the skeletons. It was the first time Patrick had seen her properly rattled and he chose that moment to tell her about Neve's delivery, how the trauma of it was so great that it broke her collarbone as she was wrenched out of the birth canal by forceps. The injury went undetected for weeks. Patrick and Shannon thought they'd produced some sort of devil, the crying and screaming so unrelenting that Patrick said he understood how mothers could leave their babies to poach in hot cars, hold their soft heads under water, smother them out of sheer frustration. When the paediatrician figured out the problem and reset the bone, administered painkillers, the transformation was immediate. Patrick was grateful she was no longer in pain and for the peace that descended, but said that he no longer recognised her, quiet and pliable. He had nightmares that somewhere in the chaos of the second hospital stay she'd been swapped out and this strange new creature was some sort of devious changeling, an imposter trying to extract love from them. He wondered if that was why Neve was so difficult to connect with: she blamed them for her very first experience of life being agony and retreated from them both as punishment.

It is this Alison thinks of as she stands in the doorway to the library. Patrick is by the window and puts the wine bottle down on a side table. The aromatics from the kitchen have wafted through the walls, will seep into the furniture and carpet and wallpaper and bother her for days. Her stomach tilts. It's been almost two days of good health. Alison hoped the morning sickness had passed, but there is a sudden gush of nausea, a sharp pain. Her body feels large and full of fluid, a water balloon at the point of eruption.

She stays in the doorway and waits for him to turn and acknowledge her. 'Patrick, darling, you're spoiling things. Come back to the table.'

'Just give me a minute,' he says. She expected him to be spiteful still, but his voice is soft and weary.

'I'm not sure why you're cross with me.'

'I'm not cross,' he says. 'I just need a second.'

She enters the room and stands beside him, joins him in looking out the window, which only shows their reflections. 'You're sulking.'

'I'm not sulking.'

'You knew where Frances was born,' she says. 'I should be the one cross with you for forgetting. For talking about Frances with Gareth, of all people. You remember how he treated me before she died.'

'You embarrassed me out there.'

'You're sulking because you're embarrassed?'

'There are all these things you keep to yourself. All these little mysteries you hold on to.'

She baulks at the hypocrisy. The nerve of him to accuse *her* of being secretive. 'You keep things to yourself.'

'You know everything.'

'I didn't know about Shannon.'

Alison regrets it as soon as it comes out: Patrick hadn't known she knows, and she'd planned on keeping it that way.

He hesitates before answering, and when he does his voice is cautious and masking alarm. 'What didn't you know?'

There's no way to retract, to stitch up what has now been split open, and so she continues. 'I didn't know how old she was.'

He lets the words linger for a moment, then turns to face her. He looks at her as though she's the enemy, trying to catch him out. 'What did she say to you?' he asks. 'What have the two of you been talking about?'

'She hasn't said anything.'

'Then why are you bringing this up all of a sudden?'

The intensity of his eye contact is intimidating and she turns to look at the wall of books to compose herself. Maybe it's for the best that everything is being put on the table. You shouldn't bring a baby into the world with shame festering. 'You never told me she was a child.'

He scoffs, puts his hands on his hips. Defensiveness pulses from his chest, his chin jutting out to distract from his weak jawline, which he usually does only when he's in the company of men. 'She wasn't a child.'

Alison chooses her words carefully, knows he is on the precipice of an outburst. 'You told me you got together in Sydney. You told me you barely knew her in Wantarra. But that's not true, is it?'

'It wasn't like that.'

'Wasn't like what?'

'Wasn't like what you're implying.'

'What am I implying?'

'I was practically a child myself,' he says. 'Dad had just died . . .'

'I'm not mad,' she says gently, and really, she means it. 'You don't have to explain yourself to me.'

'I don't give a shit if you're mad,' he says. 'There's nothing to be mad about.'

He sounds severe still but Alison can see he is shaken. He takes another glug of wine, turns to grab the bottle and begins to top up his glass.

'Please calm down,' she says, 'and come back to the party. We can talk about this after dinner.'

He lets out a rickety exhale and turns back to her. He seems haggard now, his confidence sapped away; an overgrown boy craving maternal reassurance. 'I'm worried she's going to do something stupid,' he says, his voice cracking. He's still in his jacket and the room is warm; a trail of sweat glistens on his upper lip, trickles down his Adam's apple. 'We were in a relationship, for God's sake. It wasn't anything predatory, and now she'll try to twist it and make it into something foul, something lecherous.'

Alison didn't expect him to admit to it outright. She didn't expect him to be so open about something he's evaded for so long. 'It will be fine, Patrick,' she says, eager to soothe him and get back to the party. They can deal with this later; right now, there are more important things. 'She's a reasonable person.'

'She's going to do something stupid,' he repeats. 'She wants to punish me.'

Alison shakes her head, though she knows it very well could be true. She's felt tension between him and Shannon, an uneasy vibration when they are in a room together. It could be mistaken for attraction—there is still a flicker of chemistry sparking between them—but she realises now that Shannon is at the edge of something formidable. 'What did she say?'

'Nothing,' he says. 'She tried to bring it up yesterday before we played badminton but I didn't give her the chance. I welcome her into our home and this is her response. To threaten me.'

'She hasn't threatened you.'

'How long have you known about this?' Patrick asks.

'For some time.'

'Who told you?'

'I truly don't remember, Patrick. There were rumours, I suppose. No one seemed too concerned.'

'You never asked me about it.'

'It never came up.'

'Because there was nothing to tell.'

The truth is they'd been together for close to two years before Alison figured it out, interrogated the timeline and how things didn't quite add up. Then she went looking and found photographs. Nothing nefarious, just sweet, romantic pictures of the two of them together. Alison was shocked by how young Shannon looked, how young she was. She felt repulsed and confused and trapped. They'd buried Frances months before and her flat in London had just sold. Suddenly, she could see Patrick how someone else might: slimy, depraved. In that moment she knew she'd made a terrible, terrible mistake by bringing him here.

Patrick reaches into his breast pocket for his phone. He presses the button on the side and it lights up. There are no messages, just the day's date imposed over a picture of Shannon and a much-younger Neve, their cheeks pressed together, eyes squinted, an orb of sunlight radiating from the tops of their heads. She's never been bothered by the photo before, but it suddenly strikes her hard and she has an urge to take his phone and toss it out the window.

'I should call Marie,' he says, scrolling through his contacts. 'Nip it in the bud.'

'You don't need to get lawyers involved. Shannon's not going to take this any further.'

'That's why she's here, isn't she?'

'She's here for Neve.'

'I bet she's been recording me this whole time, trying to get some sort of confession on tape.'

'And did you?'

'Did I what?'

'Confess.'

'I have nothing to confess to. It was completely consensual.'

Alison knows she's done a good job of excluding Shannon from the narrative she tells herself about Patrick, and now she tries to conjure herself at twelve, thirteen, though she does not recall having any interest in men—in boys—at that age. When she was a little younger than that, nine or ten, an older neighbour—still a teenager, still in school, gangly and pockmarked and utterly ordinary—put his hand inside her underpants, scratched around a bit. He didn't look at her face to gauge her reaction, just concentrated on his own fingers working away inside of her, Alison's thick, woollen skirt around her bellybutton. She didn't like it, but it didn't feel bad. Perhaps it should have. Perhaps it felt bad in some part of her body she did not have access to.

'I knew something was wrong with her,' Patrick says. He leans against the wall, then lurches upright again, unable to be still. 'Whenever we've spoken these last few months she's been cagey. She's been cold.'

She can see he's spiralling and takes his hand. It remains limp. 'Let's go back to the party.'

He closes his eyes and inhales through his nose, his brow wrinkling fatly, like the neck of a pug.

'She's your family, Patrick,' Alison says. 'She's not going to try to destroy you. She loves you.'

To temper his panic, she presses her hand to his spine, the hard knots of bone bulging through the damp fabric of his jacket like a rosary. She gets a bodily response this time and he lets her turn him around. Something twists in her belly, another swell of the nausea she's been trying to keep at bay. Her mouth is still sour and, as a cramp in her pelvis twitches, she remembers a dream from some nights ago: a cluster of babies hovering like balloons, their lungs filled with helium, limp umbilical cords serving as strings, keeping them tethered, stopping them from floating upwards and knocking their fontanelles against the plaster ceiling. She presses her stomach lightly into his. It will be easy to go back to the table, take his hand and hold it against her, make the announcement. At Alison's age and entirely unplanned, it's a miracle. She tries to think only of present-day Shannon: beautiful, funny, warm, confident. She thinks of the baby and how much good it will do for all of them.

She lets go, steps back, smooths down her dress, stands a little straighter. 'We're going back in, Patrick,' she says firmly, taking the wine bottle, walking to the door. 'Everyone is waiting.'

Back at the table, the plates have been cleared. There are footsteps, a murmur of voices, then the servers enter the room and plate the main course. The small knot of poultry swims in a pillar-box red sauce, vibrant puddles of green oil polka-dotted over the vast white plate, some sort of grey ash sprinkled over everything. It looks like a crime scene, like crass pop art. Alison loads a fork. The meat sits in her mouth, wet and solid as clay. A sharp pain whips through her back and she lets out an involuntary gasp. She has an insistent desire to contort her body for relief. The cramp came in a wave, passes just as quickly as her throat opens and she swallows, continues to pick at her meal. Nobody has even noticed that anything was wrong.

Elixir, having scoffed his food, has started to record a video on his phone. He's not even pretending to be polite anymore, leaning back on the legs of his chair, licking sauce off his fingers. It's as though he now considers himself a part of the family and no longer needs to be on good behaviour, riffing off Patrick's crassness, helping himself to wine.

Alison avoids looking into the camera, even when she can feel the lens on her, Elixir's eyes boring into her face. Head down, she tries to get as much food into her as she can before the cramp becomes unbearable, another furious clenching. When the server clears the table, pours more wine, Alison loses count of how much she's already had and takes a sip. The wine is cool and buttery and she hopes for it to dull her senses, but instead something deeper, hotter, contracts inside of her. She closes her eyes, everything red behind the lids.

And then Patrick is calling her name, asking what the matter is. 'You don't look sick,' he says, back of his hand to her forehead after she mumbles something about feeling unwell.

She rises from the table, excuses herself and heads towards the staircase. Halfway up the stairs it overwhelms her again. She staggers to the bathroom, but before she reaches the toilet she is sick on the tiles, the rich soup of food retching out of her. Woozy, she lowers herself to the floor before she loses her balance, pressing her cheek to the tiles until another wave hits. She cradles the ceramic bowl. On and on it goes, her throat scraped raw, stomach scooped out like a soft-boiled egg.

When there's nothing left and she's retching up clear bile, she lies down again and flitters on the edge of consciousness. When she opens her mouth to call for Patrick, all that escapes is a needy moan, barely audible, and she draws her knees up to her chest. Is this how I die? she thinks. Undignified as a drunk, sprawled in her own sick. The fact that she is now able to think and not simply feel her body coming loose alerts her to the possibility that the worst of it may be behind her. She mentally checks herself: yes, she is capable of sitting up without something menacing ripping through her insides; yes, she can make her way to standing. She grips the towel rack for support. Yes, she thinks. This is fine. I am fine.

There's a dampness in her knickers and she is mortified to think she's wet herself, but when she hikes up her dress and pulls them to her knees she sees it is not that at all. There is a shadow of sweat at the edges of her underwear, yes, but also a dark puddle of blood, and when she reaches down, the colour on her fingers is blackish red and glossy as a new coin, smears of something silver. There is a ringing in her ears as another throb penetrates. An ice pick chisels into her back. She sits on the toilet seat and kneads her fingers into her belly, feels another ripe clot slip out of her. She doesn't need to look between her legs to know the blood in the toilet water is brown and grey and clotted like a mussel; a soft knot of brainless, silken tissue.

Five minutes pass, ten minutes, and eventually the pain recedes to a dull ache. The door is still wide open and she wonders what it means that Patrick has not come to see if she's okay. She is relieved he will not see her in this state, that she will not have to explain herself, explain what has happened. She yanks a scrunch of toilet paper from the roll and holds it tight in her fist. She needs to go back to the party but there is a stickiness keeping her grounded. A little while longer to sit with her body, which is now as light as dust, bound to no one. She feels a deep pit opening up, which she knows she will descend into if she doesn't block what is happening and get on with things. Yesterday, the idea of her having a baby was absurd. She has no right to be upset that as soon as she changed her mind, came around to the idea, it was taken away.

But she is not surprised. As her mother used to say, babies are blessings, and neither she nor Patrick are particularly deserving of good things, of blessings. All they deserve is each other.

She musters her strength and does what she can to clean herself up, wipes up the sick, flushes the toilet. She removes her underwear and rinses it in the sink. Footsteps, not light enough to belong to Patrick. They are loud and intentional, warning of their incoming. Alison's legs are wobbly and she has the sensation of seasickness, as though she is on a small boat in the midst of a violent storm. Her hairline is damp, an amphibian coating of clamminess all over.

To her relief, it's Neve who appears tentatively in the doorway. She peers into the bathroom without expression, oblivious to the wretched smell, or perhaps just kind. 'Dad told me to come find you,' she says. 'We're about to cut the cake.'

Only now can she see Patrick reflected in the girl: the solemn eyes, the gangly legs, the bullish nostril tic. This recognition gives her a surge of appreciation for Neve—Alison can trust her, she could even love her, given enough time. She is glad she is here; not just in the bathroom, but in the house to stay, for as long as she likes. Alison opens the door wider to let her in but Neve remains where she is. Her eyes move downwards as Alison feels it trickle down the inside of her thigh and calf. There's not much of it, but blood does not belong there, outside of the body.

Alison holds ice to Neve's ears. She pricks a dot in the centre of each lobe with the felt-tip pen she told Neve to fetch along with a lighter and a cup of ice. Shannon has left a pair of earrings beside the sink, dainty silver studs with sharp ends, and Alison holds the bar of each over the flame. Neve pulls her hair back and sits up straight, closes her eyes and, without warning, Alison punctures the left earlobe. It has the sensation of working through gristle, and takes more force than she thought it would. Neve's body braces, though she keeps her eyes closed tight, the veiny lids spasming, and does not make a sound. Alison is more forceful with the right ear and the stud shoots through with a satisfying pop. Both lobes are a queasy pink with the swell of blood.

Alison steps back while Neve observes herself in the mirror, turning her head one way, then the other. She knew Neve had been hesitant, but Alison was aggressive in her insistence and did not give her a chance to refuse. *It's your birthday present*, Alison had said, Neve too timid to decline.

Neve nods decisively, thanks Alison, then stands. 'I'm sorry,' she says.

'Sorry about what?'

'You know . . .' She glances at Alison's belly, her legs, back up to her face.

Alison wants to cry. She wants Neve to come to her and hold her, or go and get Patrick, explain to him what has happened. She wants to be coddled, to be put to bed and stroked and taken care of for once. Instead, she shakes her head. 'Nothing to be sorry about.'

Neve hesitates. Her eyes narrow, as if she is trying hard to remember or articulate something difficult and precise. She looks so much like Patrick; it's as though a transformation has taken place and Neve has only truly become his daughter once she's come of age. It's strange, Alison thinks, how nothing can happen for a long time but then, suddenly, everything at once.

Neve exits without a word, closes the door behind her. Alison finds paracetamol in the medicine cabinet and swallows three pills. Her gut is heavy and she makes her way to bed. She takes the dress off and stuffs it into a plastic bag, knots it. It is not worth cleaning and keeping; the stains won't come out. She kicks it under the bed but even through the plastic she is sure she can smell her insides on the fabric. She crouches down to retrieve it, throws the bag out the window. Perhaps a fox will take it in the night, sniff out the blood and rip through the plastic, shake it between its teeth until the material disintegrates to tatters, and take the scraps back to its lair.

She slips on fresh underwear, sticks down a sanitary pad and climbs between the sheets, lies flat on her back. There is a pressure on her chest, a feeling of pure terror squeezing at her lungs. What is she scared of? She cannot name it, but it is something close and malevolent and cunning. She is too frightened to close her eyes and stares at the ceiling until faces swirl in the peels of paint. She thinks of the baby crawling through the pipes, pulling apart wetly, like tissue paper. Tomorrow,

Shannon will be gone and things will carry on, as they've always done, as they always will do.

Alison remains frozen in the dark for what seems a long time, until Patrick stumbles in. She watches him clatter around, take off his pants, slide in beside her.

'Shannon,' he whispers. She can smell something syrupy on his breath and imagines the cocktail of liquor burning through his stomach lining, his liver scarring. He touches her face and she is careful not to flinch. 'It's me,' he says. 'It's just me.' He jams his fingers into her hair, scratches her scalp and mumbles something inaudible, his breath hot and ticklish in her ear. She waits for him to try to hitch on top of her. It might distract from the ache, and she would like to see his panic when he wakes in the daylight to his groin rusted red, crusty like a disease. But he goes slack. He rolls onto his back and soon he is asleep.

Sometime before daylight the dream comes back to her: her mother in the bathtub, flimsy as crepe paper, that strange orange light of her mouth. Alison never used to dream of her mother—not when she was alive, not even in the weeks after she died and the loss felt surreal. Back when Frances was unravelling, Alison wondered if it was possible for a person to be suspended between two worlds: her mother's ravaged body almost gone and the spirit of her already elsewhere. Alison wonders if that's what made it so easy. Her mother—her real mother—was already gone, and the husk she had to bathe and feed and medicate was a stranger she did not know and felt no love for.

No one could deny that Alison was good to Frances at first. When she and Patrick moved in, Alison brought with her a determined energy and was attentive and kind: fresh sheets the moment they were soiled, a clean nightgown each morning. Meals prepared with care and patience as she tried to make her mother eat. It didn't last long, and the descent towards neglect was gradual, as easy as breathing. She pretends it's a blur her mind has blacked out, that she cannot remember that period at all, but it couldn't be clearer. She remembers everything. She remembers letting the carer go and delaying the slow, laborious ascent up the stairs to the master bedroom, how it was like climbing a treacherous mountain you know you will be pushed off once you reach the peak. She remembers leaving Frances alone for longer and longer. The baths in the tub becoming birdbaths by the window. The meals becoming a little blander: scrambled egg, mashed potato, creamed corn. She remembers being constantly startled by her mother's slightness, the insidious creep of malnourishment, and spooning olive oil straight into her mother's mouth. She remembers Frances opening up obediently, getting a taste of it and gurgling and pursing her lips, turning her head in stubborn refusal; how, more than once, Alison pinched hard at the scruff of her neck, swore and called her cruel names like you'd do to a disobedient toddler or mutt who is not capable of telling others of your small act of violence. She remembers prising her mother's mouth open, jamming the spoon between her lips, as though Frances was livestock being fattened up for consumption. She remembers the dim glaze of her mother's eyes repulsing her, remembers aching for her to drown in it, for the oil to coagulate in her throat and finally end it. Yes, she remembers. And remembers. And remembers the police arriving for a welfare check—Gareth's doing—and Patrick, who had arrived home from Brighton that morning, letting them in, answering their questions politely and thoroughly, showing them up to Frances's room. She remembers the visit being jovial and brief, without incident, and how on their way out one of the officers turned to Patrick sheepishly, pulled out his phone and asked for a selfie. Even after that, after what should have been a wake-up call which rattled some decency, some humanity into her, she couldn't bear to look at her mother, couldn't stand to be near her pathetic body, her liquefied mind.

Patrick must have known, he must have, but he let her carry on doing what she did. While Frances waited for Alison with the patience of a saint, they sunbathed nude on the grass, mouths stinging with malt vinegar, slick with fish-batter grease. They touched each other with the energy of curious children while Frances lay swaddled in bed, or in the chair by the window, useless, vegetative, waiting for her, watching. Who could she tell? There was no one but Alison. Her world was microscopic. Her perfect mother. Saint Frances.

Alison can hear footsteps. Terror in her chest. Faces on the ceiling. She gasps and grabs hold of Patrick's cold wrist beneath the sheet before remembering it is only Shannon up above, climbing into her mother's bed.

## NEVE

THEIR ANKLES ARE ENTWINED, ELIXIR'S skin hot and moist as just-buttered toast against hers. He is snoring lightly, left hand tucked in the front of his pants. It takes a few moments for everything to come back to Neve, and when it does—despite her headache, her rust-dry mouth, the hot gush of her earlobes—her chest opens as she remembers.

Neve wants to be alone with this new feeling of power surging through her, a low-key euphoria at risk of plunging if tainted. She didn't want Elixir to stay over, did not want to be close to him or anyone, but she closes her eyes, content to doze with that luxurious space inside her. She's never felt more powerful. She willed the baby gone, and it happened. It actually happened, and it was because of her.

She lies like this for a while longer until a stark image descends: Alison sprawled on the bathroom tiles having bled out, a slow shutting-down of organs, her body blue and limp. The cavity inside Neve closes. She feels iron pumping through her, can actually feel the extreme discomfort of it slugging through her bloodstream.

Neve heads into the kitchen, expecting . . . what? Some sort of carnage? But there is only her mother at the table, scrolling on her phone. Her suitcase is by the door and she's in the same outfit she arrived in: leggings, sneakers, jumper. Neve listens for voices but the rest of the house is silent.

'Sleepyhead,' Shannon says. 'How are you feeling?'

Neve goes to the sink, faces the window. Outside it is gentle and green. 'Have you seen Alison?' she asks, trying to make her voice sound as soft as the sun haze lighting up the grass.

'No,' Shannon says. 'Why?'

Neve grunts dismissively. If Alison had haemorrhaged to death, she would know about it by now. She turns on the tap and washes her hands in the sink. The kitchen is cleaner than Neve has ever seen it. All that remains from last night is a single clove of peeled garlic left on the windowsill, shaped like the severed tip of a thumb, drained of blood, appliance-white.

Neve stoops down to drink water straight from the tap, wipes her mouth on her hand and opens the fridge. Her birthday cake sits on the top shelf, sad and deflated, the cream veined with raspberry coulis. The air is ice and she inhales it into her lungs.

Soon, Patrick appears in the doorway, holding a bulky painting to his chest. He rests the painting against the sink without looking at either of them, but his presence confirms to Neve that nothing heinous has happened during the night. He's showered and dressed: white shirt, suit jacket with an ostentatious brooch on the lapel, some sort of glittering scarab. His hair is combed back, black and slick, bags under his eyes. He looks as greasy and unwell as Neve feels.

Patrick grabs the car keys from the empty fruit bowl. 'We should hit the road,' he says.

'What's that about?' her mother asks, looking at the painting.

Patrick smirks. 'That,' he says, 'is for you.'

'What for?'

'It's from Alison.'

Shannon shoves her phone into her handbag, moves towards the painting, squats down so that she is eye level with the girl. 'What am I supposed to do with it?' She presses her fingers to the canvas, to the girl's face: creamy and cherubic. The black of the background is sinister: black-hole black, tarmac black. Neve imagines it hanging on the wall in the terrace. It would look horrifying.

The three of them stare at the painting.

'Is she still coming to the airport?' Shannon asks, turning her head to find Patrick, who is unhooking a coat from the back of the door.

'She's feeling crook.'

Shannon looks to the painting again. 'I should go up and thank her.'

He shakes his head. 'She said to tell you goodbye.'

Shannon picks up the painting. 'You're sure she wants me to have it?'

'It's a gift,' Patrick says. 'You'll hurt her feelings if you don't take it.'

'How am I supposed to get it on the plane?' she asks. 'It won't exactly fit in my hand luggage.'

'You're a grown woman,' he says. 'You'll figure it out.'

'You should go,' Neve says from the doorway of her bedroom. 'We're about to take Mum to the airport.'

Elixir is just stirring. His eyes are slits and he smiles at her lazily. The bulge of his pants front is stiff and, though Neve looks away, he doesn't try to cover himself.

'I'll come,' he says, finding his shirt tangled among the sheets, slipping his arms into the sleeves. The thought of his body stewing in her bedsheets suddenly disgusts Neve, and she has to bite her tongue to avoid saying something cruel. Instead, she shrugs, turns away so he cannot see the curl of repulsion on her face. She pulls a jumper over her dress and hurries outside to where Shannon is loading her suitcase into the boot. She slams it shut as Neve climbs into the back seat, the painting propped on the seat beside her like an extra passenger. Patrick has already started the engine and is fiddling with the sound system, plugging his phone into the cable. Something loud and noxious blasts from the speakers, the screaming of someone hateful. It's familiar but she cannot place it.

Once Shannon is buckled in Patrick shifts into gear and edges towards the driveway. Neither asks after Elixir. They probably don't even remember he spent the night. Neve turns to look out the rear window but he doesn't emerge from the house. She would have liked to see his forlorn expression as he realises they're leaving without him, the pathetic slump of his shoulders, his slow turning away.

Patrick and Shannon are quiet on the drive. Neve supposes they are both hungover and tired from lack of sleep, but there is a prickliness between them. They seem sick of each other, and of her too, so she reclines into her seat and settles in for the drive. Shannon cracks open the window, closes it after a minute. She presses open the glove box, rifles through its contents, scans the car manual. She opens the visor, examines her face in the mirror.

'Is something the matter?' Patrick asks.

'No,' Shannon says.

'You're fidgeting. It's distracting.'

Shannon snaps the visor closed, places her hands in her lap. 'Don't send me money anymore,' she says.

Neve perks up, but remains expressionless in case they realise she is listening.

Patrick drums his fingers on the steering wheel, takes his time before replying. 'I don't mind, Shannon.'

'Neve's an adult now,' Shannon says. 'She doesn't even live with me.'

'I'm happy to do it.'

'I don't need it.'

'I know you don't need it,' he says. 'I want to do it.' When Shannon doesn't reply, Patrick sighs. 'It's just money. You don't need to make things difficult.'

'What's difficult, Patrick?'

They fall silent. Patrick turns up the volume on the stereo. Neve closes her eyes and begins to doze, drifts in and out of half-dreams. In one, she has inhabited the body of an old woman. There is a hard lump on her collarbone and when she takes a pocket knife and makes an incision, out crawl a litter of mice; nude, rubbered things. A sewing needle and thread materialise and she stitches herself back up again, no blood, no pain. She scoops the mice into her palm and drops them one by one into a pot of cloudy water where they float, belly up. It's not a bad dream. It feels like a memory of a past life, as though she has drowned someone before.

Neve comes to as they near the airport. She assumed they would let Shannon out at the drop-off point outside international departures, but Patrick parks the car. He takes Shannon's suitcase from the boot and wheels it into the terminal. They hang back as Shannon checks through her luggage, follow her to security, where Shannon folds Neve into a quick hug. Neve expected Shannon to cry and embarrass her but her mother lets go quickly, turns to Patrick. She is stung by the brevity of their farewell, but mostly she is glad her mother is going home.

When Neve turns to head back to the car park, Patrick hands her the keys and tells her to go ahead, he'll just be a minute. In the car, Neve locks the doors, crosses her legs. In the rear-view mirror she can see the painting in the back seat. She considers running it in to Shannon but knows her mother left it behind on purpose.

The car interiors still have the scent of luxury and she turns her face to the clean smell of the leather. Her fingernails are dirty from the night before. She picks at them, feels sticky and feral and wishes she'd changed into something clean. But soon she will be home. She will have a long, hot shower, eat leftover birthday cake for lunch. She will begin researching the trip to Italy. Patrick said Florence, but she'd like to go to the Vatican too, with her father, who gave her a rosary of pearl beads for her confirmation, which she dismantled and dropped into the clear blue water at Gordons Bay, casting some sort of spell over each milky treasure for reasons she cannot remember.

Patrick returns. Neve holds out the keys, drops them into his hand after he slides into the driver's seat. 'What did you have to talk to Mum about?' she asks.

He seems frosty still, which gives her the impression they were talking about her, or talking about money. Patrick reaches into the glove box and takes out a box of Tic Tacs, offers it to her.

It's not until they have driven through the boom gates, are well on the highway, that Patrick comes out with it. 'I think you should go home, Neve.'

She had been looking out the window, at the rolling hills, damp puffs of miserable sheep. She keeps her eyes on the sky, the colour of weak tea and far away. 'We are going home.'

'It was an experiment,' he says. 'I don't think it's working.'

'What's not working?'

'Your mum needs you back home.'

'Needs me for what?'

He whips his head around, changes lanes. 'She's going through something.'

'No, she isn't,' Neve says. 'She's fine.'

'Neve.'

'Is she sick?'

'No,' he says, shaking his head. 'No, nothing like that.'

'Then what?'

Patrick sighs. 'It's complicated.'

'She would have told me if something was wrong,' Neve says. She tries to look at him with contempt, but he is facing forward and its impact doesn't reach. 'She tells me everything.'

They drive in silence for a few more kilometres. Neve is too stunned to press him further. She isn't going home and he can't exactly force her. She stares out the window and tries to keep her body still so it appears as if she is unaffected by what he has said, what he thinks he can decide about her life. Neve focuses on the woman addressing them through the GPS. She has a crisp British accent, chilly, detached. They place so much trust in her disembodied voice, which could be leading them anywhere.

As they drive along a ridge running parallel to a lake Neve has a sudden, intrusive image of Patrick swerving and plunging them into the ice water. She's had these types of thoughts before but not for a long time: Patrick shooting her and Shannon in their beds, or dousing them in petrol and setting the terrace on fire. She imagines how distraught Shannon would be if Patrick ran them off the road; perhaps she would follow soon after, and they'd be stuck with one another for eternity, the three of them, and the formless blob of Anya still suctioning the air from around them. Or maybe Shannon would be glad to start afresh; to be rid of the dead weights making things difficult, bringing her pain. She's still young, not yet forty. She could live another entire life if she wanted to.

The woman says: *In three hundred yards, take the second exit.* They don't even need the GPS, Neve thinks. Her father knows the way back. If he plunges them into the water it will be his own doing. The pressed-down version of himself rising, punishing.

Closer to home Patrick brakes abruptly. He was driving too fast along the narrow roads and Neve lurches forward when the car stops, the seatbelt sawing her collarbone. The force and suddenness of the brake makes her think they've hit something. Neve remains seated as Patrick opens the door and exits the car. She is scared to turn and look in case something mangled and bloody is lying lifeless on the road: a lamb or calf or worse. The key is in the ignition, the car lightly humming, a smell of burnt rubber, sheep shit. She adjusts the rear-view mirror to see Patrick walking around the back of the car, appearing at the back seat and opening the door. He takes the painting and carries it towards a gate, stalks out into the field. Neve watches from the window and then gets out of the car. She climbs onto the wooden fence railing. The grass is the dull colour of the sea when it's overcast, everything washed with blue, the sheep scared and bleating, and Patrick disappearing into it.

When a truck trundles past and beeps its horn Neve loses her footing and stumbles backwards off the post, lands in a squat, her heart hammering. She goes back to the car, climbs into the back seat and reaches forward to cut the engine. She waits, and she waits, until Patrick returns, empty-handed. His shoes are wet, the cuffs of his pants rimmed dark. He gets into the car, slams the door. He takes off his shoes and flings them into the back seat. They smell like peat, damp and dark, the leather swamped. Neve nestles back, pretends to be asleep as Patrick puts the car in reverse. Once they launch into motion Neve opens her eyes. She glances into the rear-view mirror to see Patrick watching her: his watery eyes, his puffy face, which is also her face. He shifts into gear and continues on, driving carefully now, slowing for the hairpin turns, the potholes, as though trying not to wake a sleeping baby, trying to protect something precious, which Neve knows she is not.

They drive like this all the way home, Neve trying to remain quiet in the hope he will forget he just asked her—told her—to leave. After the kind of parent he's been, it was the least he could do, let her come here to start anew, and now he wants to send her back, just like that.

When they pull into the driveway, he still hasn't returned to normal and Neve is starting to worry. Maybe he and Shannon had been conspiring all along and Patrick had never wanted her to live here in the first place. She can't stand not knowing, and before he has the chance to flee she asks, 'What did Mum say to you?'

He unbuckles his seatbelt. She expects him to be vague with her again, but he replies without hesitation. 'Your mother asked me for a divorce.'

It's not what she was expecting and she lets out an involuntary snort. 'About time.'

Patrick turns around to face her. She thought he might be smiling, trying to make her feel better. They'd joked before about her parents still being married, how lazy they both were to never get around to it. But he isn't smiling. There is no tenderness there when he asks, 'Has she spoken to you about it?'

Neve shakes her head. 'About what?'

She is confused now. His eyes are boring into hers impatiently. She tries to speak, stutters, and he interrupts. 'When we first met,' he says, 'your mother and me, I was a little older than her. You know this, don't you, Neve?'

She nods.

'And now she's decided that I did something wrong. That I took advantage. She thinks that everyone should know about it. What I supposedly did. I don't know. I don't know what she wants from me.'

Neve waits for him to continue, but he seems to be waiting on her for a response, for reassurance. She doesn't want to be here, to be listening to any of this. She tries to unbuckle her seatbelt, but her fingers are numb.

'You need to talk to her,' he says, 'and tell her this isn't what you want. Tell her how hard it will be. That it will fuck things up for you.'

She focuses on her hand, willing her fingers to work.

'Okay, Neve?' he urges.

When she starts to cry, he takes her hand. She lets him, because she is here alone, and they are the same, and he is all she has. Her whole existence is ugly because of him.

He squeezes her hand, wipes a tear from her cheek. If her mother does what Patrick wants, she realises, this will all blow over and maybe she'll be allowed to stay.

She nods, clears her throat. 'I'll talk to her.'

Neve has few clear memories of Patrick from when she was a child, but those she does have are of him sweeping in, centring himself. Even when Patrick was physically present, he was more like a nebulous benefactor whose whims dictated her life. It was his decision to enrol her in guitar lessons, gymnastics, send her to a Catholic school. She didn't hate it entirely. As soon as the other students realised who her father was, she immediately acquired social currency and was snapped up by an extraordinarily plain group of girls who only skirted on the cusp of popularity because their parents were illustrious in some way or another. One was the daughter of a boneheaded league player, another's father presented a morning talk show. Patrick never met either. He never met anyone Neve went to school with, except for Maggie, who appeared after the September holidays in year ten. A few days after settling in she turned her attention to Neve, claiming the seat beside her in the classes they shared, whispering inane commentary into her ear as the teacher lectured to them from the front of the room. She started asking Neve if she could come around after school, never seeming to have anywhere she needed to be. They'd pick up hot chips from the chicken shop on Victoria Street, lounge on Neve's bed scrolling on their phones, slicking grease on the screens, smudges of it on the sheets. Maggie had grown up on a sugarcane farm in the country and was expelled from her previous school for selling her mother's oxycodone out of her locker at recess. At least that's what Maggie told her. They had nothing in common, nothing to talk about, so Neve didn't understand Maggie's interest, her insistence on forging a friendship. But Neve went along with it, intrigued by the novelty. In a way it felt transactional, though she wasn't sure what she was getting in return.

Patrick called one afternoon after they had collapsed on the couch. The walk home had been hot and their ties hung loose around their necks, top buttons undone. They both were on their period, bloated and exhausted and close to falling asleep.

Her father was in Sydney for the night and wanted to see her. Neve took the call into another room. 'I have a friend over,' she said.

'Bring them.'

An hour later he was buzzing the intercom, a car waiting out front. Neve assumed they'd go eat at a restaurant nearby, just the three of them and maybe Nick, but he took them to a black, angular fortress on the North Shore belonging to a steely-eyed actor Neve had met a few times before. The actor's girlfriend greeted them at the door. She'd just founded a vitamin gummy company and handed pink jubes to the girls on arrival like they were party drugs. Dinner was sashimi, kingfish, wagyu tartare. They sat on the balcony: harbour views, lap pool glittering aquamarine beneath them. The actor was slick and delusional. He talked at length about his cryotherapy chamber, mostly ignoring the girls, while his girlfriend texted throughout the meal and fed sashimi to the toy Pomeranian perched on her lap. Neve ate slowly and tuned out of the conversation, tried to calculate the cumulative cost of the sashimi being fed to the dog, while Maggie picked at the food, clumsy with the chopsticks. When she put a whole edamame pod in her mouth, Neve watched with amusement as she attempted to gnaw through the tough, inedible flesh. It was the actor who pointed out her mistake, handed her a napkin, a look of paternalistic pity on his face.

Once full, Neve excused herself to go to the bathroom. She wandered around the house. The interior design was minimalist and bare, a cool, dark mausoleum. Abstract art hung from the walls, as angular as the house. She wanted to find the cryotherapy chamber but ended up in a nursery. Neve didn't even know they had a baby: neither had mentioned it or checked on it all night. The infant was asleep in its crib, a lullaby tinkling from an invisible speaker, a nightlight giving the room a somnolent glow. Neve stood over the crib and pressed her hand to the baby's chest, its immaculate, gender-neutral onesie. It woke as though startled and began to shriek.

When she went back to the balcony, only Maggie was at the table. At school, Maggie was cocky and loud, but from the moment Patrick picked them up, desperation seeped from her like rancid body odour. His presence had highlighted just how little Neve knew about Maggie, how little interest she had in her interiority. Every question Patrick asked revealed new information that made Neve like her less and less. On the drive over, when Patrick told her where they were going, who they'd be eating with, Neve saw a small current of ecstasy pass through Maggie's body and realised why Maggie wanted to be her friend, was embarrassed for not drawing the conclusion sooner.

'Where were you?' Maggie demanded.

Neve started to laugh, hysterically and uncontrollably. She has an awful laugh; wide-mouthed and silent. 'I just found a baby,' she said, once she caught her breath.

Maggie was unimpressed. 'I thought you'd left me here.'

Neve cocked an eyebrow. 'Where would I have gone?'

'Can we leave?' As Maggie stood, a flap of orange fish fell from her lap, slapping the tiles. 'I want to go home,' she said. 'Please?'

At first Neve assumed she meant home to school, to the boarding house, but her voice squeezed in her throat, the corners of her mouth quivering. She pictured Maggie among the sugarcane crops as tall as basketball players, her hair in braids, the tropical humidity. If she knew how, Neve would have said something soothing and gone to find Patrick with an excuse as to why they needed to leave. Instead, she went back into the house to look for more evidence of the infant's existence, whether it had a safe, happy life there.

The place was spotless, sharp and full of glass.

Back at school after the weekend, Neve knew the jewel of Maggie's friendship had shattered. A few weeks passed and they no longer acknowledged each other in the halls between classes. Neve wasn't bothered, did not consider it a loss, and she hardly thought of Maggie at all until a year later, when the rumours began to bloom. She'd heard and read all sorts of things about her father before and knew to take hearsay with a grain of salt. She also knew the accusations were not true. She replayed the evening over and over in her head, stretching it out and turning it over with care. Maggie had never even been alone with Patrick. If Neve were to mention Maggie to him now, he'd have no clue who she was. He would not be able to picture her unremarkable face.

The rumours lost steam eventually, but when she found a photograph of her mother in a box of Patrick's left-behind things something sharp tugged inside of her. Neve recognised the floral bedspread from her grandmother's house in Wantarra. Taken from above, Shannon is on her back, one arm stretched over her head. The tip of her braid looks freshly sucked, pointed into a wet tip, her tan lines creating crude geometry on her skin. She had always been beautiful, even at that awkward age; her dusting of freckles, the gap between her teeth.

Neve stole the photo. Over the following days she couldn't stop taking it out of her underwear drawer and staring at it, and before long the image was lodged in her brain. She undressed and stood in front of her mirror, tacked the photo to the frame and examined her own body. Shannon was slight and proportionate, but Neve's own reflection had a masculine quality, more of Patrick in her than Shannon. She could see him in her nose, her chin, her weird widow's peak. According to Patrick they had Romani ancestry. He told Neve his grandfather emigrated to Australia after World War II, got a job at a Christian supply store selling Bibles and Nativities, vestments to priests. He'd only been in the country a year when, one morning, he left his pregnant wife at home, set off on his usual route along the shore to work, but he never reached the shop. When Neve thought of her great-grandfather, of the body that swept up on the beach a week later, bruises to his waterlogged head, his eyes gouged out, tongue severed, she had the inexplicable feeling that he'd got exactly what he deserved. The ocean, and whoever put him in the ocean, was enacting a punishment, trying to amputate the bloodline at the knee.

Patrick had been gone a few years when she found the photograph. She knew she couldn't ask her mother about it, but the next time she was alone with Nick she asked him what Patrick was like in Wantarra, how her parents met. He told her the same story she'd heard before, about Patrick and Shannon having little to do with each other back then, reconnecting years later in Sydney, an accelerated, passionate love affair, the stars aligning. But there, taped to her mirror, was the evidence: her mother's body draped on the bed, the date and caption printed on the back of the photograph. Her father's elegant handwriting, all swoops and flourishes, the assertive cursive of a grown man.

When they get out of the car, Patrick heads for the studio, leaving Neve alone in the yard. She doesn't want to go inside, to her dingy, depressing room. The thought of eating cake, of eating anything, makes her queasy. She can't go see Elixir, who she knows she won't be seeing much of anymore. She doesn't feel like driving, doesn't want to take a walk through the woods. She can't go home but she doesn't want to stay here either.

The sun is now out, bright and warm, and she sits on the grass to take it in, closes her eyes, feels the rays on her skin. She does something she has not done in a long time, not since she was very small and panicked or lonely: she closes her eyes and pictures a rosary, rolls a bead between her fingers. She tries to remember a prayer from school. Though she was forced to learn them by rote, nothing comes to her. She keeps rolling. The bead is wax and melts into her skin. She takes another; again it melts. Her fingers are hot, they are scorching. When she holds her hands in front of her eyes, the prints are burnt smooth, blank as larvae. She opens her eyes and checks the time on her phone. Her mother's flight has just taken off, and she wonders if Shannon is trying not to cry as she settles in for the long haul, wonders what awful things Patrick said to her at the airport, or whether she feels free of him. More than anything, she wishes she was up in the air with her mother, never landing at a destination, never arriving here, never returning there, just hurtling through space and time forever.

# ALISON

ALISON WAKES TO PATRICK ALREADY dressed and perched on the mattress beside her. Her skin is slick and her head burns and she is afraid she is terribly ill, before she becomes aware of the heavy pad scrunching around her knickers and remembers that no, that's not it. She sits up in bed, the sheet around her middle, as Patrick says, 'We're leaving for the airport.'

When Patrick cups her breast and kisses her on the mouth it's an effort not to recoil from his touch. 'Let's talk about Belfast when I get back,' he says. 'Belfast and renovations, and a visit to Wantarra. It's time you met everyone, now you're up to travelling again.'

Alison nods.

'I was serious about what I said, about buying something there. Not Wantarra, obviously, but something on the coast maybe. Spending more time back home. You'll love it there. I promise.'

They both know that isn't true. When Alison was small, Frances would tell stories about her childhood in New South Wales: the oppressive heat; the blinding light, white and prickling as though radioactive; sun-seared eyeballs; the inescapable itchiness. Alison would rather rot slowly and wetly than burn.

'Okay?' he says.

'Yes, Patrick.'

As he stands, the painting resting against the cupboard enters Alison's eyeline. Something roils inside of her, the tail end of a cramp limping on. She knew there would never be a baby, but now that it is gone she can feel the lack of it, the loss, a swelling emptiness where this source of bliss had briefly lit her up from within. Alison pictures Shannon downstairs, her suitcase packed, ready to return to her beautiful life. The tidal pull she thought she felt towards her seems foolish now; she is embarrassed by how she let her mind make silly connections that were not there.

And yet, she still wants to see her. 'Fetch Shannon, please,' she says to Patrick.

'What for?'

'I want to speak to her.' He looks at her with suspicion, and so she adds, 'Just to say goodbye.'

Patrick looks at his wristwatch. 'We're running late.'

'Fine,' she says. 'I'll go to her.' When she moves to climb out of bed a sharpness twists in her abdomen; all the energy she had mustered fades. Defeated, she lies back down and covers herself with the sheet. In that moment of pain and exhaustion she wants nothing more than a day in bed, some of Patrick's painkillers. To drift.

'Can you get rid of that, please?' she asks, gesturing towards the painting.

'Back to the yellow room? I thought you were rather taken with it.'

'No,' she says. 'I don't want it in the house.'

'You want me to throw it out?'

'Give it to Shannon.'

'Shannon won't want it.'

'You don't know that.'

Patrick gives her another peculiar look, but he picks up the painting. Alison rolls over in bed so she doesn't have to look at it. She can feel Patrick hovering. After a moment, a sigh, footsteps. It's the sigh that does it: a burst of cruelty emboldens her.

'Did you talk to Shannon?' she calls out.

In the doorway he stops, turns. 'About what?'

Of course he's going to pretend the entire conversation last night in the library never happened. 'About her trying to ruin your life.'

'No,' he says firmly, avoiding eye contact. 'I was drunk last night; paranoid. Mine and Shannon's age difference hasn't been an issue for over twenty years; I don't know why she'd see it differently now.'

He takes the painting, leaves, and Alison is glad to be alone.

She falls asleep again, wakes up hazy, unsure of how much time has passed. When she looks out the window, the car is still gone. There is blood on the sheets, a few smears of it dried on the white linen. She is hungry for dry toast, but reaches for the laptop and props herself up. Alison wants to find out what she should do, if anything. How long she'll bleed for, when things will return to normal. Shannon would have known. She would have been kind and expected nothing in return.

She is reading an article on the risks of geriatric pregnancy when an email from Neil arrives in her inbox. He's made dinner reservations for Tuesday evening, arranged a meeting with one of the producers the following morning. Alison lets herself imagine how the day would unfold. Patrick driving her to the airport early, running lines under her breath while airborne. She would go to the hair salon before meeting with Neil, a manicure perhaps. Martine would organise it for her, if she asked. She'd even collect her from the airport. Alison decides to call her, later that afternoon. Maybe she can come stay for a few weeks soon, now that Frances's room is in order and ready for guests. She misses her. She never considered

Martine a friend before, but that is what she was, Alison supposes now.

Alison is googling the restaurant when another email arrives in her inbox. No subject line, only a video attachment, which she clicks without thinking. The video is of average quality, filmed on a phone by an unsteady hand, and Alison is confused by what she is seeing: feet ascending a set of stairs, a wobbly fumbling, the back of a door. Fingers enter the frame and open the bedroom door: her bedroom door. Alison has a bewildering sense she's been ravaged overnight, her brain atrophied and her cognitive function destroyed. She doesn't understand. There she is on the bed: the camera zooming in on her breasts pancaked over her rib cage, her legs kicked out at painful angles. It moves down to her thighs, the blood on the sheet at hip level, the white pad winging from her underwear. The camera pans out and moves closer to the bed, closes in on her face, sleeping and peaceful and blissfully unaware, and it is only then that clarity descends. There is shame—at her bloated body, spread brazenly—which quickly elevates to panic. She is watching a car crash, a snuff film, her own death.

She closes the video, snaps the lid shut. After dressing quickly she enters the hall, goes to the staircase. Her heart is loud in her chest and she tries to move without noise. Down in the kitchen she finds the knife she used to butcher the rabbit, grips the handle in her fist. They could be anywhere in the house still. They could be watching her at this very moment.

She waits for something shocking to happen, for someone to ambush her, and berates herself for being stupid and careless. Why didn't she call for help the moment she saw the video? Why don't they ever think to lock the doors? Patrick and Neve will come home and find her bludgeoned to death, her body hacked to pieces by some obsessive lunatic. He—she assumes it's a he; of course it's a he—will probably record the whole thing and post it online to one of those awful websites populated by celibate toads. Alison runs her free hand through her hair and checks her face in the window reflection. The weak look of fear on her face is pathetic. She should have put on trousers, something difficult to remove, if that's what it comes to.

Her back begins to ache and she lowers herself onto a chair to decide what to do. Maybe she should go outside to wait for Patrick, or walk down to Gareth's, call for help there. It's her own fault, really, for not taking it seriously. Sometimes, she even gets a thrill out of reading the emails, the vulgarity of them, the sick specificity. She's always felt very little fear for her life, a sense of invincibility she knows comes across as arrogant and glib. At first, Patrick was concerned that she wasn't disturbed enough by the threats and so she hammed it up a bit, agreed to the security cameras, made a show of finding the hunting rifles in the cellar. If anything does happen, at least she won't have to tell Neil she's letting him down again. She'll have a real excuse for pulling out of the film.

When a cough echoes through the house, Alison clasps the knife and, coming to stand, notices that Neve's door down the hall is open a crack. She's never been inside her room before; Neve always made sure the door was closed and Alison had no desire to pry. She slowly exits the kitchen, lingers in the hallway, building her nerve.

When she pushes on the door, she finds Elixir sitting at the edge of the bed. He looks up at her, his mouth open in surprise, before composing his face. It takes a moment for Alison's pulse to slow. She loosens her grip on the knife, presses it to the back of her thigh, out of his view. 'Does Neve know you're in here?' she asks. Her voice trembles. She swallows, tries to relax the tendons in her throat. For a second she is relieved it is only Elixir, that whoever filmed the video, whoever sent all those emails, must be gone already, before she thinks, *oh*, and feels small and foolish, like a girl.

'Thought you were still asleep.' He reaches down to tie a shoelace and Alison scans the room, which is as bare and beige as a hotel suite. Elixir's backpack and sleeping bag are packed up beside the made bed, blanket tightly tucked. He is dressed as he was last night and she can smell morning breath mixed with a boyish funk. She's only known him to be grossly upbeat, but now his shoulders are slumped, his face furrowed as he concentrates on his shoelaces, tongue tipping from the corner of his mouth. His fingers move slowly, fumbling over the loop. Alison tries to get a read on how concerned she should be. He's been in her bedroom; he's stood over her and filmed her while she was naked and vulnerable. He sent her the video. He sent her all those emails. He wanted her to see what he had done.

'It's okay,' he says calmly, as though reading her mind. 'I'm not going to do anything else. I'm not going to hurt you.'

She wants to laugh. That *he* thinks he could hurt *her*. But she remembers how scared she was while watching the video, being paralysed in the kitchen, unable to make a decision, not knowing what to do.

Alison remains in the doorway as he gathers his kit. She is taller and more muscular than he is and she's sure she could overpower him. Plus, she is the one holding a weapon. She presses the blade of the knife to her palm. It isn't even sharp, she realises, but when Elixir turns to her, he sees the knife, flinches and raises his hands defensively, not meeting her eye. 'Are you going to use that on me?'

There is a scene towards the end of the script where Alison's character disembowels the film's antagonist, uses the blood to fertilise her crops, which then flourish. She and her daughter thrive; the rest of the town slowly starves. Alison imagines doing this to Elixir, her hand tender on his shoulder, the spark in his eyes before the plunge.

'Of course not.'

He looks relieved, lowers his hands. 'You can, though, if you want to,' he says. 'I deserve it after what I did, after filming you like that. All those emails.'

She steps aside to let him pass but he remains in place, sleeping bag clutched to his chest. Alison waits. The seconds stretch on and for a moment she worries that he might be having some sort of minor stroke, until finally he looks her in the eye.

'I know I shouldn't have done it. I'm not a total freak or anything. I just wanted to frighten you—you know, after what you did to Franny.'

It's so awful, what she did, he can't even say it either.

'Just admit it,' he says. 'Just say what you did to her.'

Alison is finding it hard to breathe. She wants him gone, does not want to hear any more, but she cannot move while he is here.

'Didn't think so.'

She's never been looked at with such hate; all the disgust and anger he feels is entering her and turning her into slop.

Alison stands aside, holding her breath until he is out of sight. She closes and locks the door. Her legs weak, she goes to the bed. It is as hard as a prison cot, not fit for sleeping. There is a draught, despite the lack of windows, the room's stuffiness. She watches the goosebumps rise on her skin. The scent of rotten flowers wafts by, disappears. She has an urge to throw up but swallows it down.

When she hears the front door close she goes back into the kitchen, returns the knife to the drawer and goes upstairs to Frances's room. A window is open, the bed neatly made. She had hoped Shannon would have left something behind by accident but there is no trace of her. After stripping the bed, Alison presses the bundle of linen to her nose. When she lumps the sheets back down on the mattress, she is sure the flower rot has followed her, but it is gone in an instant and she knows it is a trick of the mind.

As she closes the window, she wonders if Elixir was up here earlier. Perhaps this is where he sent the email from, spread-eagled on her mother's bed, maybe under the sheets, watching the video over and over before deciding to press send. She wouldn't be surprised. When Frances was alive, she'd often find him up here. He'd slip through an open door or find a window to climb through. Most times she'd order him home and he'd skip off happily down the hill, or Patrick would call Gareth to come pick him up if the weather was bad. But the last time was different. She'd woken that morning strangely elated, bursting with goodwill. She picked flowers from the garden and decided to freshen up Frances's room in the hope that it would undo how absent, how neglectful she had been. Breakfast tray balanced in one hand, she entered the room expecting her mother to be asleep, but instead her stomach turned. There he was, cradled under Frances's shoulder, her hand stroking the utilitarian buzzcut of all lice-ridden schoolboys. At the sound of the door opening, Elixir looked up at Alison before closing his eyes, nuzzling back into Frances, who ignored her daughter completely, did not even seem to recognise her or notice she was there, which Alison had grown used to by that point: her mother forgetting her, having no memory of her birth.

There was a half-eaten cake on the bedside table, brown residue on Frances's cracked lips. It wasn't the first time Elixir had snuck food to Frances. Sometimes Alison would find chocolate biscuits melted into the bedding, a sweaty plastic bag full of ham-and-cheese sandwiches, loose raspberries mashed to juice. But that day, at the sight of the chocolate, something snapped in Alison. Something vile surged from her, something ugly and foul. They must have been so frightened, the pair of them, when she slammed down the breakfast tray, grabbed Elixir by the arm and untangled him from Frances's grasp. Though on the verge of puberty, he would have weighed no more than Frances by that point. As she pulled him off the bed, she was surprised by how weightless his body was, how pliable his limbs, but once she started dragging him towards the door, he resisted with ferocity. When he went for her arm with his teeth bared, it was by impulse that Alison bent him over and slapped him hard across the bottom with an open palm. He didn't cry; not at first. He went silent with shock and stared up at her wide-eyed with the disbelieving look of someone who had never been hit before, who'd never been mistreated by an adult, until the tears tipped over and he started to wail. And of course his wailing set off Frances, so Alison locked the door behind her and pulled him towards the staircase, crying and carrying on all the way. If she could have pushed him down the stairs with no consequence, she knows she would have.

When they got downstairs he was hysterical still, the sounds coming out of him primal. She shouted at him to calm down, held onto his wrist tightly, but his screams were so piercing, she knew if he didn't shut his mouth she'd hit him again, and again, and again. Knowing she couldn't return him to Gareth in this state, she pulled him over to the room beside the kitchen, shoved him in and closed and locked the door. She could hear his bangs against the door, the wailing. She'd planned on waiting outside the door until he calmed down and she could take him home, but his momentum was extraordinary and he did not relent, not even for a second. She could still hear it from the kitchen. In the library it was even worse. Up in her room, she put on a record to try to muffle the sound and give her a chance to clear her head. At some point his crying must have become breathy, before it trailed off and the house was silent again, but by that time Alison was fast asleep.

It wasn't until much later, when she was down in the kitchen making tea, that she felt a nagging within her. She knew she'd forgotten something but could not put her finger on what. Her head was foggy. She felt hungover and sluggish. Patrick wouldn't be home for a few more days and the night stretched ahead of her. When it came back to her, she didn't rush to release him. She drank her tea slowly, tidied up the kitchen.

Outside, she picked more flowers and arranged them in a vase, started chopping vegetables for her dinner. She had a shower, answered some emails, and when she finally mustered the will to unlock the door, she found him curled into a ball in the corner of the room. Not asleep, just lying there waiting: his pants wet from where he'd pissed himself, his face red and puffy from crying. She told him to go outside and was surprised that he deferred to her. She expected rebellion, but he accepted his fate willingly and climbed into the car, buckled his seatbelt, sat quietly with his hands in his lap and remained that way until she pulled up in front of the cottage down the hill. Once she'd put the car in neutral, he turned to watch her dumbly, awaiting instruction from the only adult available to him. 'Go on then,' Alison said. He unbuckled the belt, climbed out of the car and walked to the door with an affected limp, his hand clutching his bottom. Alison was already through the gate by the time she could see, in the rear-view mirror, Gareth come out of the house and crouch down, the boy heaving in his arms. The car reeked of his piss the whole way home.

She gave herself an hour to calm down, then she would call Patrick. The hour turned into two and then six, and then it was the following morning, and another day drifted past waiting for Gareth to show up on the doorstep. She waited for her punishment but it never did come. She couldn't stop sleeping. She couldn't stop eating. She couldn't make herself go up the stairs to her mother, who, by the end of the weekend would be dead.

⁂

A car horn bleats. Alison puts on a cardigan, smooths her hair with her hands and goes outside to where Gareth has pulled up in front of the house. He hasn't seen her and beeps the horn again as Alison appears at the driver's window. He is typing on his phone when she raps her knuckles on the glass. After rolling down his window he says, 'I'm after James. He called me to come and get him. Is he alright?'

Her first instinct, for once, is to tell the truth, to tell him about the video. 'He was here,' she says instead.

Relief illuminates Gareth's face, which is craggy, his eyes bloodshot. She can smell last night's liquor on him.

Gareth sets his phone on the dashboard, places his hands on the steering wheel. 'Good party, then? Did Neve have a good time?'

'It was lovely.'

His phone screen lights up. He glances over to read the screen but is unimpressed, flips it over. 'What's taking him?' he murmurs, more to himself than to Alison. He beeps the horn again, two quick gasps.

'He left already,' she says.

'Well, why didn't you say?' He looks up at her, baffled, and Alison sees herself as he must see her, how she looked in the video: her awful, lumpen body, the coldness that spreads right to her bones. She knows the sight of herself on the bed is a loop that will play in her consciousness for years to come until, like her mother, her mind is emaciated and everything falls away. Only then will she be free of it. She turns back to Gareth, rests both hands on the windowsill, thinks of Patrick, how much he wishes she were kinder.

'Would you like to come in? For a cup of tea?'

He rubs his brow. 'Patrick here?'

'He'll be back soon.'

He turns off the engine. Alison steps back as he opens the car door. She feels something lift. She is about to ask Gareth to text Patrick, tell him to pick up fresh milk on his way home, something sweet for afternoon tea. She'll put a few bottles of leftover champagne in the fridge, just in case. But before she has the chance, he reaches for the doorhandle. 'No,' he says, closing himself in again. 'No, I don't think I will, Alison.'

❧

Alison pulls a suitcase from the wardrobe, begins to pack enough for a few nights away. As she sifts through the coathangers, she finds herself gathering more and more things. A knitted dress, a pair of heeled boots. Trousers, silk shirts, an ankle-length coat. All of her very best things. She finds a second suitcase, fills it with underwear, leather gloves, a belt. Her credit card and passport, the script. She texts Neil and tells him she'll be arriving that evening. She tells him she'll be staying for a week, maybe longer.

There are tyres on the gravel and Alison moves to the window. She is filled with a rush of love when she sees Patrick emerge from the car barefoot, the cuffs of his trousers rolled to his shins. He was barefoot when they met, and it is as though she is seeing him again for the first time, as he truly is: unbuckling his belt, removing his pants and hanging them over the back of the patio chair. He passes Neve, who is out of the car and standing on the grass. They do not speak as he strides over to the studio, his flamingo legs sun-starved, the tense hunch of his back, the sharpness of him slicing through the afternoon. He unlocks the studio. He does not look back. Yes, she thinks, after what they've both done, they deserve each other.

And then there is Neve, turning her face to the close, grey sky, before lowering herself onto the grass, cross-legged, hands cupping her knees. *Look up*, Alison thinks. *Look up*. And she does! Something passes between them; something as imperceptible and precious as light.

# ACKNOWLEDGEMENTS

THANK YOU TO ANNETTE BARLOW, Christa Munns, Ali Lavau, Tessa Feggans, and the wonderful team at Allen & Unwin. For their invaluable feedback and support, thank you to Evie Wyld, Alex Philp, Emma Doolan and Lucy Nelson. This book was written with the generous support of the Australia Council for the Arts, a Varuna Residential Fellowship and a Queensland Writers Fellowship.